Cover Design and Interior Format

THE WEDDING VOW

BOOK
TWO

Never Court a Count

REGINA SCOTT

To those who feel invisible.
May you know yourself seen and loved.
And to the Lord, who sees and loves all His children.

CHAPTER ONE

London, England, June 1825

LADY CALANTHA DRYDEN, daughter of the Duke of Wey, had a unique talent: she could turn invisible.

She'd noticed it as a child, when the servants would pass by her without so much as a smile. The governesses would laud her older sister, Larissa, and her younger sister, Belle, while never mentioning her own accomplishments. And if she was very, very careful, she could avoid her grandmother's censorious comments about her looks and intelligence by sitting very still and silent. The trait had only become more apparent as she'd reached the age to come out in Society three years ago.

She wasn't entirely sure how she did it. Perhaps her pale blond hair or light blue eyes, like a faint reflection in window glass, made it easy to disappear. Perhaps her slight frame and preference for colors like pink and white allowed her to blend into the background. Perhaps her nature was too quiet and self-effacing. Whatever the reason, people tended to overlook her, look past her, or look through her while in her company.

And they said the most outrageous things as a result.

This ball being given in Belle's honor was no exception. Callie had been retreating to the safety of the paneled wall when a group of young ladies on their first Season had stopped directly in her path. Huddled near a bank of potted palms that disguised the door to the terrace, fans plying in front of their satin ballgowns, they hadn't paid her the least mind.

"He's ever so handsome," one of the young ladies was saying, head bent toward the others and curls thick about her face. "And so charming."

Hadn't that been said of most of the young men on the *ton* this year? Callie sailed past, determined not to eavesdrop, until the next young lady spoke.

"And now he's a count in the Batavarian court, not to mention the brother of a prince and the son of a king."

Oh. *That* handsome, charming gentleman. Her cheeks heated at the very thought of Frederick Archambault, Count Montalban—Fritz as he preferred—recently arrived in London with the Batavarian court. He had been a frequent caller at her family's London address, mostly because he was accompanying his twin brother, Crown Prince Otto Leopold, who had fallen in love with Larissa. He wasn't the sort of man Callie should admire as much as she did. Her hope for the future was a quiet life, book in hand, cat in her lap, pup at her side. He preferred action and intrigue.

"I hear he decided to pursue Lady Calantha," another of the young women said, voice disdainful. "He'll learn soon enough he ought to stay away."

"She's so odd," the fourth agreed.

Callie couldn't breathe. She turned from her goal and slipped behind the palms. The cool shadows couldn't stop the heat spreading through her.

Shy.

Quiet.

Invisible.

She shuddered. Why had she bothered coming?

Well, she had had a reason. Belle had wrung a vow from her, Larissa, and their best friend, Petunia Bateman, that they would all work to see each other happily wed by harvest. This was Belle's first Season, and she was determined to make it the best. This was the third long, painful Season for Callie, but she'd thought her sister might just be able to accomplish the impossible. Belle was like that. Few were proof against her charms.

Now, two months later, the brief hope she'd felt from her sister's optimistic encouragement had faded. Larissa was engaged, and Belle was admired. Even Tuny seemed to be making progress in finding a love, for she hinted of a man she found fascinating. Callie alone had no prospects. And when she thought about Fritz, any hope she had of changing that positively plummeted.

It was difficult seeking a plain, quiet gentleman when perfection came calling on a regular basis.

Beyond her sanctuary, the four young ladies moved on. Others secured partners, and the next set began. Her sisters and Tuny were all dancing. Her father was with their mother. Ivy, the Marchioness of Kendall—Tuny's sister and their hostess for the evening—was on her husband's arm. Callie could have named every couple in line, in fact. Many had known her since she was a girl. A few of the others probably didn't know she existed.

The Duke of Wey has three *daughters? Who else besides the elegant Lady Larissa and the adorable Lady Abelona?*

She puffed out a sigh.

Two men stopped just beyond the palms, their backs to her. Dressed in the requisite black of evening, they both had slim physiques and straight blond hair just touching their collars. Callie pressed herself against the glass-paned doors behind her and tried not to intrude on their conversation. But it proved impossible not to overhear them.

"Your plan came to naught," one said, voice low and deep. "Still they pursue their aims."

"For a time only," the other said. His voice hinted of an accent. Not the lyrical lift that rang in Fritz's often sarcastic drawl. She could not place it.

"Then you have decided your next steps?" The first man sounded decidedly eager about the matter.

"I have. Direct action failed us, but I am confident we can ruin them legally and socially." The cool calculation in his voice chilled her.

"Only tell me my part," the other begged. "With my power in the Commons, I could be of use to you. You know I long to be of service to Württemberg."

Württemberg? Nothing could have stopped her from listening now. Württemberg was a kingdom on the Continent. Ten years ago, after a decision at the Congress of Vienna, it had subsumed the tiny mountain country of Batavaria, leaving King Frederick and his two sons without a home. Since the Batavarian court had arrived in England, men representing Württemberg had been determined to stop them from approaching King George to request aid in returning their kingdom to them. Crown Prince Otto Leopold, Count Montalban, and Callie's Uncle Julian, legal representation to the court, had an audience with the king the week after next.

Were these men trying to prevent it?

"My superior is most appreciative of all you have done for us thus far," the fellow with the accent assured the other. "I will pass along instructions once the plan is in place. Quickly now. We should not be seen talking overly long together."

They parted and moved off. Callie squeezed closer to the last palm in the row in hopes of catching sight of at least one face. Instead, she spotted someone else bearing down on her. She shoved herself back into the very corner of the space and held her breath, heart stuttering.

If ever there was a moment to be invisible, it was now.

The palm branches rustled as another body pushed its way through. The man hunkered low as if trying to prevent anyone from noticing.

Callie found her voice. "This spot is taken, sir. Move along."

He stiffened, and the light filtering through the leaves caught on the curly blond hair of Fritz, Count Montalban.

"Callie?" he asked, voice colored with confusion.

She wanted to dive into one of the pots and burrow her way into the dirt. "It doesn't matter. Leave. Now."

His body deflated, and she heard a sigh that sounded positively relieved. "It *is* you. Be a friend and help me. I need to be invisible for a while."

His first luck of the evening. Despite her sharp tone at the moment, Lady Calantha—Callie as she allowed him and his brother to call her—was a surprisingly sweet, shy young lady who would in no way hinder his plans for the evening. If only he could say that about the other unmarried ladies at the ball.

He couldn't remember a time when he had had to actively hide at events. Since he'd reached his full height and been praised by his trainers in the military arts, he'd always stood in protection of the king, his father, and the crown prince, his brother. Leo, in the scarlet and gold of the House of Archambault, would take center stage, as was his birthright. Fritz would watch from the wings: Captain Archambault, head of the Imperial Guard. Only the most senior member of that guard knew the day he had let them all down, and he had done everything he could to prevent his lapse from ever happening again.

But since his father had seen fit to hand him a title of his own, he felt as if someone had painted an archery target on his chest, and every unmarried lady in London was taking aim. His father had joked that all young ladies wanted to be princesses. Apparently being a countess was just as coveted, especially now that his brother had announced his engagement to Lady Larissa, Callie's older sister. How was Fritz to do his duty when he had to keep dodging attempts to ensnare him?

"You cannot be invisible," Callie hissed beside him. "That black coat with all the gold braid is entirely too noticeable."

At least he was back in his dress uniform tonight. There was comfort in the familiar coat, the loose-fitting trousers that allowed for quick movement. For the last few weeks, he'd had to pretend he was the crown prince to give his twin brother the ability to determine who was trying to stop them from approaching King George. Leo believed the miscreants had been captured, but Fritz remained on guard.

As two young ladies promenaded past, he bent to keep his head below the tops of the palms.

"I don't see him anywhere," one complained, pausing directly in front of him. "He looks perfectly fit. Why won't he dance?"

"We must be persistent," the other said, gaze darting about. "He was trained to be a gentleman. If we make it appear he asked us to dance, Count Montalban will be honor-bound to take our arms."

He looked to Callie, and she nodded as if realizing why he might need to hide.

She was clever that way.

"Well, at least he hasn't asked Lady Calantha yet," the first said. "We still have a chance to turn his head."

Callie let out the tiniest of squeaks and pressed herself so far back against the door it was a wonder she didn't break the glass.

The door.

Fritz's gloved hand was on the latch a moment later. He jerked his head at Callie to indicate she should accompany him, then slipped out onto a terrace that ran along the back of the Marquess of Kendall's town home. She followed.

He closed the door behind them, shutting off all conversation. Only faint music from the ball hovered in the air as they stepped out onto the flagstones.

She drew in a deep breath. "You might have noticed that rumor has it you are courting me. Rubbish."

"Decided rubbish," he agreed.

She raised her chin. "Well, you needn't sound so sure of the matter."

Fritz gave her his most disarming smile. "It is rubbish because I am not courting any young lady, even one so winsome as yourself."

The moonlight showed her pink lips tightening. That was one thing he'd noticed about Callie. She had a preference for pink. Tonight, her ballgown was of a fine matte satin in a rosy color, with flowers decorating the hem.

"And you can cease the flattery as well," she said. "We both know you don't mean it."

"Of course I mean it," Fritz said. "Unlike my brother, who must veil his opinions in diplomatic platitudes, I have the luxury of saying what I like. You are pretty, intelligent, and delightfully original. I like you."

Her mouth dropped open before she recovered herself. "You do?"

He went to lean a hip on the stone railing edging the terrace, drawing a breath of the cool night air and savoring his few moments of freedom before he must return to the ball. "I do. I see no reason why we cannot be friends. After all, your sister is marrying my brother. It would be unseemly if we took each other in dislike."

"I suppose there's that," she allowed. One arm stole around her waist.

Fritz straightened. "Are you cold?" He started unbuttoning his coat.

She held up her other hand. "No. I'm fine." She purposely dropped her arm.

"So fine you had to hide behind potted palms?" he asked.

She lowered her gaze. "It seemed expedient. I'm sure you don't mind the number of people, but sometimes I find it a bit overwhelming."

"Focus on your goal," he advised. "Ever since I was fifteen and joined the guard, I have had to attend events with more than six hundred people, most of whom thought themselves better than me. But I know my purpose for being there—to keep my father, the king, and Leo safe."

"Oh!" She hurried closer, face turned up to his and eyes bright. "You will need to be on your guard. I overheard the most horrid conversation just before you joined me. Two men were plotting with Württemberg to harm your family."

"What?" Fritz put his hands on her shoulders to peer into her face, pale in the moonlight. "When? What did they say?"

Behind her, the door opened, and a tall, slender man stepped out onto the terrace. His bearing was noble, his movement confident. As his gaze narrowed in on Fritz and Callie, his nose looked like a dagger aimed in their direction.

"Calantha," he said, striding toward them. "Your mother is looking for you."

Fritz dropped his hold.

Callie turned to face the door. "Father. I'm so sorry. I just needed a moment alone."

The Duke of Wey's gaze fell on Fritz like an anvil. "Apparently not alone. I expect to receive a call from you tomorrow, Count Montalban."

"Father, no!" she cried.

It was one of the few times Fritz had heard her assert

herself in company. Every part of her lithe form vibrated with the same anguish that rang in her voice. He wanted to put her behind him, challenge her father to a duel, anything to keep her from harm.

What was he thinking? She wasn't his to protect. He wasn't looking for a bride. Courting would only slow him from doing his duty. And a wife would want to know too many things about a past he tried so hard to forget.

Her father's look softened as she ran to him, and he put his arm about her shoulders. "You must leave this to me, Callie. It is my duty to keep you safe." As he glanced at Fritz, his face hardened once more. "I will see you tomorrow after church services, my lord."

The king, his father, would not thank him for alienating one of their only allies, especially a man as powerful as the Duke of Wey. Fritz inclined his head. "Of course, Your Grace."

Callie sent him one last look before her father took her inside.

And Fritz knew he was well and truly trapped.

CHAPTER TWO

"YOU KNOW, YOU'RE not the one I usually worry about," Callie's mother said as they settled themselves in the coach. Her father was staying behind with Larissa, Belle, and Petunia. Only Callie was being sent home early. Not the most graceful way to end an evening.

"I'm sorry," she said.

Her mother cocked her head, lamplight making a halo on her dark brown hair, coiled simply around her face. "Are you? Why?"

Callie swallowed. Her mother was renowned for two things: her irrepressible nature and her ability to squeeze secrets even out of rocks. Then there was the fact that she had been their governess before their father had married her when Callie was eight. She knew Callie, inside and out. No sense trying to dissemble.

"I disappointed you and Father," Callie acknowledged, shifting on the leather of the seat as the carriage swayed in a turn. "I disgraced myself."

"Never the former and I'm not entirely sure of the latter," her mother disagreed. She leaned back against the squabs, sturdy figure only partially hidden by her black velvet evening cloak. "You were found alone with Fritz in the dark. Did anything untoward happen?"

"No! He was every bit the gentleman. He even tried to give me his coat when he thought I might be chilly."

"Quite the gentleman," her mother allowed, folding her gloved hands in her lap. "But you know the expectations of being a lady out in Society. Why go with him in the first place?"

Callie grimaced. "I wanted to escape the ball, and so did he."

Her mother raised a dark brow. "And you couldn't go one way while he went the other?"

"I didn't think of it at the time," she admitted.

"All that gold braid goes to a lady's head, doesn't it," her mother said with a smile.

Callie smiled back. "It does." She sobered and licked her lips. "Father asked him to call tomorrow. I think he expects Fritz to make me an offer."

Her mother shrugged. "He can make you an offer. Doesn't mean you have to take it."

Callie drew in a deep breath. "Thank you, Mother."

"Just be very sure of what you want, my love," her mother said. "Hiding away may seem comfortable now, but there's a price to be paid later, in loneliness, if nothing else."

Callie nodded. She was just glad her mother said no more on the matter as they rode home.

Her sisters and Petunia were another matter.

Because Callie was home earlier than they were, she had Anna, the maid she shared with her sisters, all to herself in the bedchamber she and Belle used in town. Belle had insisted on roses for the décor. They were printed on the bed hangings and embroidered on the quilts. They were carved on the walnut headboard and four wardrobes. They twined around the oval of the pier glass mirror in one corner and the edge of the dressing table next to it. Callie hadn't minded. She liked pink. It was soft, cheerful, and undemanding.

She was in her nightgown and dressing gown, sitting in a chair by the warmth of the fire with *Redgauntlet*, one of the more recent Waverly adventure novels, when Belle all but skipped in after midnight.

"Anna's seeing to Larissa," she said, tugging at the fingers on one of her long white evening gloves. "I called a meeting. As soon as everyone's changed, we'll all see what can be done about tonight. Will you help me with my pins?"

Callie set her book aside and rose. "Of course, but a meeting isn't necessary."

The look in Belle's jade-colored eyes said she doubted that, but she turned with a flip of her golden curls to allow Callie access to the back of her blue ballgown. There were reasons her sister was everyone's favorite in the family. Belle was bright, warm, and endlessly optimistic.

"I won't ask you what happened yet," her sister said as Callie began unfastening her gown. "It's better if we all hear at once. Just know that, whatever happened, I am on your side."

Callie smiled as she stepped back to allow Belle to slip the gown off her shoulders and down her curves. "I know. You are ever the optimist. The believer in dreams and unicorns."

Belle grinned as she bent to bundle the gown into her arms. "Well, they are on our family crest, so I can't be the only Dryden to favor them."

They were spared further conversation as Anna bustled in. The dark-haired young maid finished helping Belle then hurried off to perform the same services for Petunia. Only when the maid had been dismissed for the night did Larissa and Petunia—Tuny to those who knew her best—pad into the room in their nightgowns.

"So?" Belle asked from her bed across the room. "What happened?"

"If someone was rude, we can take them down a peg," Tuny offered, perching on Callie's bed. Her straight blond hair hung in two plaits onto the blue flannel of her gown, and her brown eyes were warm. That was Tuny—a complex combination of wonder and practicality.

"At the very least, commiserate," Larissa said, joining Belle, the curls of her own dark blond hair brushed flat so the tresses could be braided down her back. The simple look was at odds with her queenly demeanor. Of course she'd fallen in love with a prince.

"Does everyone at the ball know I left early?" Callie asked, glancing among them.

"No," Belle assured her, leaning back against the headboard. "I didn't hear a single rumor. We noticed you and Mother had gone, but I doubt anyone else did."

Perhaps invisibility had its benefits after all.

"So what happened?" Tuny echoed Belle's question.

How many times had they sat like this to debate decisions and share secrets? Callie, Larissa, and Belle had been gathering since they were children, either at the family castle in Surrey or here at Weyfarer House, their town home. Tuny was staying with them this Season with the hope she would have more opportunities to find a presentable gentleman.

Now Belle's eyes were turned down at the corners, and she was clearly ready to offer sympathy. Larissa's hazel eyes were soft; her sister always stood available to help shoulder any burden. Tuny's wide brown eyes were narrowed; she'd be more likely to fight for Callie's rights.

Callie sighed. "I'm sorry, Belle. I know the ball was in your honor. And Tuny, your sister took such pains to make the event beautiful. I simply couldn't endure another moment of company. I ducked behind a screen of potted palms."

Belle wrinkled her nose. "That's it? The way Father was frowning on the way home, I thought you'd poured punch on some duchess."

Callie's fingers tightened around each other in the lap of her pink nightgown. "Fritz joined me."

"Behind the potted palms?" Belle all but gasped.

Callie nodded. "And he showed me a way out onto the terrace. We just talked."

"In the dark, alone," Tuny surmised. She tsked.

"Not unforgiveable," Larissa insisted. "Leo can tell Fritz to say nothing. There is some good in being the crown prince."

Callie shot her a grateful smile. "Thank you, but Fritz isn't my concern. Father is. He ordered Fritz to call on him tomorrow. I guess that's today, now."

They all groaned.

"I won't marry him," Callie hurried to assure them. "Mother said I didn't have to. Besides, he doesn't love me."

Tuny eyed her. "I don't have your gift for hearing things, but I noticed you didn't say you don't love him."

Belle clasped her hands together. "Oh, Callie, do you love him? That would be perfect! You and Larissa would both be engaged. Then we need only find suitable husbands for me and Tuny to fulfill our vow."

Tuny and Larissa exchanged glances. Callie had never heard them say as much, but she suspected her friend and older sister didn't entirely believe in the vow Belle had elicited either. Still, her younger sister was right. Larissa was well on her way to fulfilling her portion of the agreement.

"I don't love him, Belle," Callie said, cringing inside as some of the light faded from her sister's countenance. "But I will not deny I find him admirable."

"And handsome?" Tuny suggested with a smile.

"Yes, and handsome," Callie agreed with a laugh. "Still, as Larissa has pointed out in the past, he's very full of himself, and he expects instant obedience to any order."

"Likely because he's the Captain of the Imperial Guard," Tuny said. "Still, no one wants to feel like saluting every few moments."

Callie certainly didn't. And she already had too many people trying to tell her how to live her life.

"So, you'll refuse him?" Belle asked, voice turning plaintive.

"Yes," Callie said. A shame the word didn't sound the least bit confident.

Though Fritz noticed the Duchess of Wey spiriting Callie out of the ballroom, he didn't have the option of leaving early. He'd come in the royal carriage with his brother, Leo, and his twin showed no signs of wishing to decamp. So, Fritz did what he generally did at diplomatic events.

He held up a wall.

At least it was a good vantage point. The duke's untimely interruption had prevented him from asking questions about Callie's statement that two men were plotting with Württemberg to harm the royal family. He didn't doubt that she had heard something of the sort. The first time he'd met her, he'd overlooked her entirely, something he rarely did with anyone approaching his father or brother. He'd since learned his mistake. Of the three sisters, she was clearly the most insightful. Whatever she had heard was reason for concern.

And then again, the leaders of Württemberg had been plotting against his family since the day they'd devoured his beloved Batavaria.

But, try as he might, he could spot no lurking danger among the happy attendees. Ladies smiled as they chatted. Gentlemen shook hands and clapped each other on the back. It was all terribly congenial.

And not terribly useful to his purposes.

Still, it gave him something to focus on until he and

Leo could make their bows to their hostess and go.

"There's something you should know," he told his brother as the carriage started away from the Marquess of Kendall's home. "There may be a plot afoot to hinder our efforts to enlist King George's support."

Leo, who had been looking out the window into the darkness, smile playing about his face as if he remembered the evening fondly, turned to Fritz with upraised brow. "Again?"

"Rather say still," Fritz said. "A friend overheard a conversation. I will look into the matter."

Leo nodded. He didn't question Fritz's rights or intentions. They both knew this was his role in the family.

"Tell me what you need, and I'll see it done," he said.

Fritz returned his nod in thanks, and conversation dwindled until they returned to the palace in Chelsea.

Their father had leased the massive house from a family that had too many properties to care. Shaped like an H, it featured opulent public rooms on one side and more cozy private rooms on the other. A wide corridor connected the two wings. Their Lord Chamberlain, Lawrence, had placed all the statues and artwork they had brought with them along the corridor so that it looked more like a gallery in some museum. His company of seven guards was a woefully small number to protect the place, but Fritz was proud of their attention to duty.

He sent Leo off to bed and made the rounds now, checking with each of the Imperial Guardsmen stationed at the various entrances as well as the one that was roaming the corridors. No one had seen anything unusual. He warned them that something more might be coming and encouraged vigilance.

He was passing the salon on the private side of the palace, heading for his own bed, when a voice heralded him.

"Count Montalban, a word."

Fritz gritted his teeth but stepped into the room. "Lord Chamberlain. How might I be of assistance?"

Lawrence was seated at the desk in the corner of the room. As the person in charge of the day-to-day activities of the court—from housing to entertainments—he had his own offices at the front of the palace. But ever since the king had left to travel to Württemberg himself, taking three of the Imperial Guardsmen and the Royal Steward, their chamberlain had appropriated the salon as well. He held up a hand a moment as he sprinkled sand with the other on the letter he had been writing.

Fritz was about ready to turn on his heel and leave the fellow to his mutterings when the chamberlain glanced up. Tall and gaunt, with white hair that barely covered his pate, he had a way of looking down his nose at Fritz, even when seated.

"Did the ball afford any opportunities to advance our cause?" he asked.

"I cannot recall the king requesting that I report to you," Fritz pointed out.

The chamberlain had the good grace to color as he rose. "Certainly not. But as his representative in his absence, it is my duty to see to the furtherance of his agenda and the wellbeing of his sons."

Fritz hadn't needed anyone to see to his wellbeing since he'd turned fifteen and joined the Imperial Guards. But at least the fellow was willing to remember that Fritz was one of the king's sons. Until his recent elevation to the position of Count and King's Advisor, the chamberlain had tended to treat him no differently than one of the servants. It had never been easy being the second son in a country that recognized only the firstborn as prince.

"I appreciate your zeal," Fritz told him. "Be assured I will let you know anything that might be of concern to you."

Lawrence inclined his head. "Thank you. Good night."

Fritz clapped his fist to his chest in salute and left him.

His valet, Pardue, was waiting for him in his bedchamber. The room wasn't small, but he felt as if the walls were pushing closer as the dapper older man helped him out of his dress uniform.

"Uniform or casual dress tomorrow, my lord?" he asked as he picked up the coat and trousers from the wide poster bed.

If he was going to have to face the duke, he might as well go with authority. "The dress uniform again, Pardue. And see that my boots are polished enough to see your face in them."

Pardue stopped, dark brown eyes glinting. "An important meeting tomorrow, my lord?"

Fritz cocked a smile. "You might say the meeting will determine the course of my life."

Pardue's eyes widened. He waited a moment, as if hoping Fritz would enlighten him further, then slumped a bit and bowed himself out.

He wasn't sure why the man thought he would offer confidences. Pardue had joined them when they had been living in Italy. He didn't know what it meant to be driven from the only home he had ever known, to be confined to the shadows as his father and brother struggled to come to terms with their new reality. And he certainly didn't know everything about what Fritz had been through.

Once more the walls moved closer. He strode to the double doors that let out into the garden. Danger might be waiting in the shadows, but meeting it face on was preferable to sitting in this cell.

No, not a cell. Never a cell again.

He threw open the doors and took a deep breath. In Batavaria, the air had been scented with pine and the warmth of growing things, living things. In Italy, where they had spent the first five years in exile, the air had been spicier, colored by the heat of the climate and the breeze from the Mediterranean. The palace in Germany had always smelled like baking bread to him. He wasn't entirely sure why.

Though he'd been told to expect rain and cool in England, this summer had been unusually hot, so that the brine from the Thames, which flowed past the foot of the garden, was all the more noticeable.

Perhaps it was his encounter with Pardue. Perhaps it was the damp air and the dark night, but he was too easily transported to a rank cell under a fortress in France. He rubbed his wrists, but he couldn't escape the weight of the shackles.

"Where are the rest of your troops positioned?" the interrogator had demanded in French. "How does Batavaria plan to protect itself?"

Fritz had spat blood from a split lip. "I know nothing. I am only a soldier."

"Liar!" the interrogator shouted before cuffing him again. "You are the crown prince. We have your likeness. Tell us what we want to know, and we will see you delivered to the diplomatic corps."

Fritz smiled, though his battered mouth and cheeks protested. "I know nothing. I am only a soldier."

The interrogator nodded to the other guard to bring the whip.

He stepped out onto the terrace now, drew in another deep breath. On occasion, his brother still liked to play the game of trading places. Leo had been masquerading as the Captain of the Imperial Guard when he'd met Lady Larissa. If Fritz understood his brother's story correctly, it had been Callie who had noticed the difference between them. Though Fritz was a little more muscular, and Leo a little taller, only close friends and family could generally tell them apart.

But even Leo didn't know about the one time being

taken for his brother had saved Fritz's life. The memories of that dark day came less often now, but Fritz still didn't like being confined. Not physically, and certainly not in his choice of bride.

And so he would tell the duke tomorrow.

CHAPTER THREE

CALLIE HAD THE hardest time sitting still on Sunday. She barely listened to the banter between her sisters and Tuny around the breakfast table. She couldn't attend to services at St. George's Hanover Square. Even the thought of curling up with a good book in the library did not calm her. Every moment she was home, she waited for the sound of the knocker.

When it came, she bolted from the withdrawing room, where she'd been playing charades with little success with most of the family, including her twelve-year-old brother Thal and eight-year-old brother Peter. She skidded to a stop in the entry hall just as Fritz was handing his tall, black-fur dress helmet to their butler, Underhill.

"His Grace is expecting you, my lord," the dark-haired butler was saying, nose decidedly out of joint. "This way."

Head high, chest up in his dress uniform, Fritz marched after him. As Fritz passed Callie, he favored her with a wink.

A wink! As if she'd been the only one up half the night worrying and wondering.

"Don't do it," Callie whispered.

He nodded, sandy curls glinting in the lamplight, but he kept walking.

"He's not off to the guillotine," her mother said, slipping an arm about her shoulders as she came to join her.

"It feels like it," Callie murmured.

Her mother squeezed her shoulder. "Come on. Thal's hoping you'll guess his riddle."

She very much doubted she was capable of guessing anything at the moment, including her own future, but she suffered herself to be led back to her family and Tuny, most of whom were smiling in commiseration. Only Peter, dark haired like his mother and green eyed like their father, looked confused, glancing from one to the other until Belle's enthusiasm pulled him back into the game.

Callie had never known the moments to pass so slowly. Every quarter hour felt like a year. What could Father be saying to him? How was Fritz answering? Was it really so difficult to just say no?

Or did he intend to offer for her after all?

Underhill appeared in the doorway and cleared his throat, head high and lean posture erect. Everyone turned his way.

"His Grace would like to see Lady Calantha in the library," he announced.

Callie rose to her feet from the sofa. Larissa patted her hand. Belle's lower lip trembled. Tuny gave her two thumbs up. Her two younger brothers exchanged glances as if they weren't sure what was happening.

"Remember what you want," her mother called.

Callie nodded and followed the butler from the room.

In another house, she might have felt all alone as she walked down the corridor, but Underhill, for all his haughty attitude toward visitors, had long ago let her and her brothers and sisters know he was forever on their side.

"Thinks very highly of himself, does Count Montalban," he murmured to her now, gaze straight ahead as befitted the butler to a duke. "But I have been impressed with his desire to protect his family."

"So have I," Callie admitted.

Underhill stopped before the library door. "I have never been blessed with children. But if my daughter was facing a potential suitor for her hand, I would tell her to do as her heart commanded." He leaned closer. "After making sure the fellow had the blunt to support her, of course."

Callie smiled at him. "Thank you, Underhill."

He nodded before schooling his face. Then he threw open the door. "Lady Calantha, Your Grace."

Callie stepped through the door. Libraries had always been a retreat for her. The one at the castle was vast and deep, with shelves that stood at right angles. She had happily lost herself there many a time. Here, the room was smaller, but bookshelves still rose to the ceiling along most of the walls, and comfortable upholstered chairs stood here and there to welcome readers.

Neither her father nor Fritz was sitting in them. They stood stiffly on either side of the wood-wrapped hearth, faces polite masks.

"Callie," her father said. "Count Montalban would like to speak to you. I rely on you to do what you believe to be right."

Right? What did that mean? Did he think she should marry Fritz? Did he think she should refuse?

"Thank you, Father," she managed, and he inclined his head and strode from the room. With a brief look of sympathy, Underhill shut the door behind them.

Callie stared at Fritz.

Fritz stared at the far bookcase.

She drew a breath. "I'll save you the trouble. The answer is no."

His gaze dropped to hers, brows up. "No? Will you give me no opportunity to explain?"

Callie threw up her hands. "Explain what? We both know how we reached that terrace, and we both know nothing happened that would require a proposal. You have done your duty. Move on."

He pressed one fist to his chest in what she had come to know was the Batavarian salute and bowed to her. "Thank you, Lady Calantha. I appreciate your intelligence even more."

What rot. He appreciated being let off from an onerous duty. "You can save the flattery as well."

He straightened, hand falling. "Why do you complain when I speak the truth?"

"Because it isn't the truth," Callie said. "You use words merely to attempt to change my opinion or my attitude."

He stuck out his lower lip. "At times, perhaps. But I leave the diplomacy to my brother. If I tell you I admire you, rest assured I admire you."

"*If* you tell me," Callie muttered.

He moved closer. "I had another reason for calling, regardless. Last night, you said you'd overheard someone threatening my family."

"Yes, of course," Callie said, tucking away her conflicted feelings. "I should have thought that would still concern you. Two men. My father's age or younger. Both blond and slender."

"Slender?" he asked, mouth quirking, as if he thought her description amusing.

"Well, I'm certainly not going to advise them they should ask their tailors for padding," Callie informed him. "Suffice it to say, they had their backs to me, and there were palm leaves between us, so I cannot be certain of their description. But I can tell you what they said."

She closed her eyes, remembering.

"The one with the deepest voice said, 'Your plan came to naught. Still they pursue their aims.' The other assured him it was only for a time. He had an accent, but I couldn't determine from which language. The first man asked whether he had decided his next steps. He was very eager about the whole thing. The other said he had. 'Direct action failed us, but I am confident we can ruin them legally and socially.' The first man begged to know his part, claimed he had power in the House of Commons, and said he longed to be of service to Württemberg. The other man assured him that his superior was most appreciative of all he had done for them thus far. He promised to pass along instructions once the plan was in place. He also said they should not be seen talking overly long together."

She opened her eyes to find him staring at her.

"You remember all that?" he challenged.

Her cheeks were heating. "Yes. I tend to remember everything I hear. In great detail. It is a burden."

"It is a gift," he countered. "Thanks to you, we know someone from Württemberg is here in London and working with the English to ruin us, both socially and legally." He paced away from her and back. "If you heard them talking again, would you recognize them?"

"Of course. I don't forget a voice."

He rubbed his hands together. "Excellent. We will attend every social event together until you can identify them for me."

He was so pleased with his plan she hated to point out the obvious. "I sincerely doubt you and I will be allowed to spend any time alone together after today."

He stilled, then slowly nodded. "I fear you are right. It seems we must become engaged after all."

Callie blinked. "What? No!"

"I see no other way," he reasoned, as if he wasn't commandeering her entire life. "If we pretend to be engaged, we can attend events and tour around town with no one asking questions."

Pretend to be engaged? Her shoulders came down the slightest. "But that would be a lie," she warned him.

"A temporary one," he assured her. "It is the simplest approach to the problem."

"Simple!" Callie sputtered. "You have no conception of what an engagement means, sir. Haven't you noticed all the events your brother and Larissa are having to attend?"

He waved a hand. "He is the crown prince. Of course everyone wants to make much of him."

"And you are a count," she reminded him. "They will want to make much of you too." The very idea made her stomach lurch.

"We will decline the honors, then," he said. "You are a delicate blossom, and I will not have anyone wearying you."

A delicate blossom. Very likely some would agree with him. Her lips curled. "I am made of stronger stuff than that, my lord."

"I believe it," he promised her. "But no one else needs to know. This will give you an excuse to avoid any event unless I am at your side. You need never hide behind a potted palm again."

He was right. Pretending to be engaged could take a lot of the pressure off her. Her mother, her sisters and Tuny, even her father would all breathe a sigh of relief. Belle and Tuny could focus on looking for suitors for themselves and stop trying to find her a fellow who understood her. That hadn't been likely to happen in any event. She'd let Belle convince her otherwise. Most people did.

"And how would we end this temporary engagement?" she asked.

He paced to the shelves and back again as if his energy could not be contained. "Your social Season ends in August, I believe?"

"Whenever Parliament adjourns," she explained. "But Father said that it may be earlier this year."

"We should have identified those plotting against us before then," he said with a confidence she could only find inspiring. "You can refuse my advances then."

It was only a month or two. A month or two of not

having anyone sneer at her because she had failed to find a suitor. A month or two of not having to hide at events.

A month or two with Fritz at her side.

"Very well," she said. "I accept your temporary proposal. We are engaged, for now."

Engaged. Temporarily, to be sure, but shackled to another just the same. He waited for the panic, the gnawing at his gut that any kind of confinement usually caused. Instead, there was a feeling bubbling up inside him, threatening to lift him off his feet.

If he hadn't known better, he would have thought it joy.

She did not look nearly so pleased. Already her hands were worrying in front of her frilly pink gown. "We can't tell them the truth. Father would never agree to the plan. He's a bit protective. But we must let them know that we are betrothed."

"Of course," he said, forcing his face into something more solemn. "Would you like to do the honors, or shall I?"

She visibly swallowed. "Perhaps you should do it. Sometimes, when I speak, the wrong words come out."

He wasn't sure what she meant by that, but he recognized the usual indications of fear. Her skirts were swaying, as if her legs were trembling, and she was biting her lower lip.

He linked his arm through hers. "I will explain to their satisfaction. I promise."

She nodded, and he led her toward the door.

As he started to open it, he heard a faint thump and a yelp. With a frown, he yanked wide the door.

Lord Thalston, her oldest brother, and Belle were

standing in the corridor. It all would have seemed perfectly natural, if the young man hadn't been on his rump, and Belle hadn't had both hands fisted in her skirts as if prepared to run.

"Very sound floor," Thal maintained, rising with the agility of a twelve-year-old. "I will report as much to Father."

"Yes, we should," Belle said, taking his arm and dragging him down the corridor.

Fritz looked to Callie and grinned. Her smile was as soft as the touch of her fingers on his arm.

They found the rest of her family and Miss Bateman gathered in the withdrawing room. They seemed to be holding their breaths.

"I am pleased to announce," he said, voice ringing against the spring green walls, "that Lady Calantha has graciously agreed to be my bride."

They all stared at him, as if he had declared there was to be a riot on their roof.

Callie found her voice. "Yes. Fritz and I are betrothed."

The duchess gathered her wits first. "Well, how fine." She popped to her feet and came to give Callie a hug. "Congratulations, my love!"

The others rose and followed, each taking a turn to hug Callie and offer their support. Larissa and Belle still looked shocked, and Miss Bateman kept eyeing him as if he'd done something to coerce her friend.

"I'm so delighted," Belle said, glancing between the two of them. "But I must know. What did he say to convince you?"

Callie glanced at Fritz, and, for a moment, he thought she would give away the game. "He pointed out the advantages of an engagement. It was all very logical."

Her sisters laughed at that.

The duke stepped closer to him. Those jade eyes seemed to see more than Fritz had intended. He had to stop himself from tugging on the collar of his uniform.

"Your Lord Chamberlain is currently working with our solicitor, Lord Belfort, on agreements for Larissa and Otto Leopold. I expect they will do the same for you two."

Fritz nodded. "I will be meeting with Lord Belfort tomorrow and can explain then."

The duke inclined his head. "It is not too much to say that I am entrusting you with one of my greatest treasures, Count Montalban. I will expect to hear nothing that would give me pause."

A *bit* protective? Callie had clearly understated. Fritz swallowed. "You can be certain of that, Your Grace."

The duke made way for his wife.

"Another Batavarian in the family," she said with a good-natured grin. "Do you have more brothers I should be watching for? I still have two more young ladies to marry off."

Fritz laughed. "I am the last of our line, Your Grace. Though, if I had a brother, he would likely fall prey to Lady Abelona's charms, to say nothing of Miss Bateman's."

Belle, standing nearby, beamed at him. Miss Bateman rolled her eyes.

"We really shouldn't keep Fritz," Callie put in. "He has a duty to his father this afternoon."

Fritz pasted on a smile. "Yes. My duty. I should go."

"Not before I have a promise from you," the duchess said, and he tensed.

So did Callie.

The duchess glanced at her husband. "A small family party, I think, to celebrate. Wednesday evening?"

The duke smiled. It was the first time Fritz had seen him do so, and the change was remarkable. The ice thawed into a spring meadow, and Fritz almost expected to hear birds start to sing.

"Perfect," His Grace said.

She nodded. "Good. Tell your brother, Fritz. I know your father is traveling. Is there anyone else you'd like to bring?"

Likely Lawrence would expect to be invited, but Fritz had a sudden desire for a moment of peace.

"No, Your Grace," he said. "Thank you for the invitation. I will see you all on Wednesday." That would give him two days to run these rumors to ground himself. With any luck, he and Callie would not have to remain engaged for longer than that.

And he refused to think about why that fact seemed to darken his day.

CHAPTER FOUR

JUST AS CALLIE had had to inform her family, so Fritz could not avoid alerting his brother to the betrothal. He thought about telling Leo the truth, but it didn't seem fair to Callie. After all, she had had to hide their plans from her family. Besides, Fritz had been instructed his entire life to put Leo's needs first. Surely giving his brother no reason for concern was the right approach. Fritz could tell him the whole of it once the two conspirators had been dealt with.

So, over a dinner of Westphalia ham in the family dining room on the private side of the palace that night, with his brother and Lawrence as company, he broached the subject.

"I have asked Lady Calantha to marry me."

Leo blinked, forkful of macaroni frozen partway to his mouth.

Lawrence frowned. "Lady Calantha. Do I know her?"

"Lady Larissa's sister," Leo managed.

Lawrence's frown grew. "No. I was certain Lady Larissa's sister was named Abelona. Engaging creature with golden curls and great green eyes."

Fritz skewered him with a glare. "Lady Calantha is the middle sister. She is lovely, cultured, and intelligent. I greatly enjoy her conversation and her company. We are engaged."

Leo set down his fork. "This is no joke? You really did

offer for her?"

He began to take umbrage on Callie's behalf. "Yes. Why is that so hard to believe? She is a lady in all ways. She is quiet and unobtrusive, yet there is a fire in her, a determination that draws me. I am a fortunate fellow."

"Certainly," Leo said, though he was frowning now too. "I've always liked Callie. I was simply under the impression that the two of you were not overly fond of each other."

Lawrence was glancing between them as if he couldn't make up his mind whose side to take.

"We disagree on occasion," Fritz allowed, "but I am convinced her insights will make me a better man. The Duchess of Wey invited us to dinner on Wednesday to celebrate."

Lawrence returned his gaze to his plate and proceeded to cut the succulent ham into precise squares. "Wednesday is inconvenient. You were offered vouchers to Almack's. I have already secured the tickets."

Now it was Fritz's turn to frown. "Almack's? The rooms where Mrs. Netherbough held her ball to honor the crown prince a few weeks ago?"

"Almack's, the club managed by the finest ladies in Society," Lawrence corrected him, little smile playing about his thin lips. "I am told it is considered an honor to be included. You will accompany the crown prince, as is your right."

As was his duty. Why did something inside him push in protest?

"Do you wish to visit this club, Leo?" he asked his brother.

Leo shook his head, picking up his fork again. "Larissa told me her family has been excluded. I have no wish to support something that disdains them."

"I told you it was an honor," Lawrence insisted.

"An honor I intend to forego," Leo said. "Nothing

would make me happier than to accompany you to dinner at Weyfarer House, Fritz."

Fritz nodded his thanks.

"Your Highness, if I may," Lawrence whined. "You cannot be seen to slight the patronesses of Almack's. Already there are those who whisper about the king and his sons."

Fritz stilled. "Who whispers?"

Lawrence toyed with his cucumbers. "I have not, of course, been approached directly. But the reporter who was here yesterday assured me we would be wise to issue a statement if we are to keep public sentiment on our side."

Leo shook his head. "Reporters will say anything to snare a story. Ignore them."

"If you want to see the inside of Almack's so badly, Lawrence," Fritz said, "go yourself."

The Lord Chamberlain drew himself up. "I would never usurp the prince's place. Besides, the tickets are not transferrable."

"A shame," Fritz drawled, applying himself to his meal. "But we will be at Weyfarer House on Wednesday evening."

Fritz had hoped to start his own inquiry into the men Callie had overheard as soon as possible on Monday, but first he had to accompany Leo to an appointment with Julian Mayes, now Lord Belfort. The solicitor had endeared himself to Leo and their father after helping them discover what had happened when the Crown Jewels had gone missing, to the point where King Frederick had awarded him a title in thanks. Fritz still wasn't entirely sure of the fellow.

Oh, Lord Belfort was always stylishly dressed, and his reddish-blond hair, mustache, and beard were always neatly trimmed. But there was something about those cool blue eyes, as if he had seen more than his forty-some years attested. He also had a wife with a cat that was far too canny. Fortune hadn't taken to Fritz right away, but he liked to think he had won her approval eventually.

That morning, the solicitor ushered them toward his office behind his bevy of clerks, black tailcoat and white cravat spotless. "Thank you for joining me, Your Highness, Count Montalban. I took the liberty of inviting another gentleman as well. I believe you know Lord Wellmanton."

Leo nodded. "The viscount who arranged for us to tour Kew Gardens." He looked to Fritz as if to jog his memory.

He needn't have bothered. The recent events at the Royal Botanical Gardens at Kew were firmly engraved in Fritz's mind. He'd become complacent, certain the real danger was to Leo. He had been right, of course, but he hadn't taken into consideration that he had been playing Leo's part. As far as most of England had known at that point, *he* was the crown prince.

And he'd been attacked and kidnapped coming out of an event. The exchange had been made at Kew Gardens, where, thanks to Leo and Larissa, they had managed to capture their attackers.

Or so he had hoped before Callie had overheard that plot.

Nothing had connected the well-meaning Lord Wellmanton with the kidnapping, but Fritz couldn't help watching him as the men shook hands in the solicitor's bookshelf-lined office. The light grey of the viscount's hair indicated he might have been blond once, and he had a deep voice, but no one would ever call him slender, much less in need of the tailor's art in padding his figure. He had padding to spare if the bulge in his paisley waistcoat was any indication. And he seemed genuinely pleased to see them.

"Delighted, delighted, Your Highness," he told Leo. "And I understand congratulations are in order for your brother. Count Montalban, eh?" He beamed as if welcoming Fritz to the club.

"Lord Wellmanton," Leo greeted.

Fritz merely inclined his head. Little more was ever expected of him. He moved to stand with his back to the wall as Leo and Lord Wellmanton deigned to sit on the chairs the solicitor had drawn up before his desk.

"I'm glad you had time for us today, my lord," Lord Belfort said, taking his seat behind the desk. "I was informed yesterday that you had intervened in the case of Alonzo Mercutio, one of the men implicated in the kidnapping of the crown prince, and I thought perhaps His Highness and Count Montalban might be interested to hear your reasoning."

Leo stiffened at the mention of one of the key spies for their enemy, Württemberg, and Fritz lowered his gaze to the viscount. Wellmanton's happy smile looked the slightest bit strained.

"It was a diplomatic matter," he assured them all. "Britain is on the best of footing with various countries on the Continent. We thought it best to release Signore Mercutio on his own recognizance."

"And I have been informed that he has since left the country," the solicitor said, as if attempting to fend off a protest from Leo. Lord Belfort seemed to know a great many things to which he should not have been privy as a mere solicitor, and Fritz and Leo had concluded he was connected with Britain's spymaster.

"And are you aware, my lord," Fritz said to Wellmanton, "that Signore Mercutio was involved in the attempted kidnapping of the crown prince?"

"I am convinced it was a misunderstanding," Wellmanton said soothingly. "The fellow does not appear to be well versed in English. He acted without understanding the intent of the British perpetrator."

Fritz had heard Mercutio speak fluently in English,

French, German, and Italian. Doubtful he'd stumbled onto the plot by accident. Besides, Mercutio had been the one standing next to the king, demanding payment for Fritz's release.

"And the British perpetrator, as you call him?" Fritz asked.

Wellmanton's look darkened. "Potterby has been tried and found guilty. I'm sorry to report that the magistrate sentenced him to transportation rather than hanging."

"A terrible oversight," Lord Belfort drawled.

"Indeed," the viscount said, missing the sarcasm. "I have already explained matters to Mr. von Grub, the secretary to the Envoy for Württemberg. I'm certain the envoy will be most displeased to hear of it when he returns to England, as will his Royal Majesty, King William of Württemberg."

The viscount was insufferable. "Do you generally support the efforts of Württemberg?" Fritz demanded.

Wellmanton spread his hands. "I do my best to further diplomatic relations among all our allies. I'm certain Lord Belfort can tell you I was an ardent supporter of your request to speak to the king."

"You did not protest overly much," the solicitor allowed.

"Unlike some," Wellmanton maintained. Once again, he glanced among them. "And were you successful? Did our Gracious Majesty King George grant you an audience?"

He could not be well informed if he had to ask.

"We are working toward that end," Lord Belfort told him. He rose. "Thank you for your time, my lord. I will not impinge on it further." He motioned toward the door.

Wellmanton heaved himself to his feet and bowed to the room in general. "Your Highness, my lords."

Leo waited only until the door had shut behind him before rounding on the solicitor. "What is this? I thought we had an audience with your king on Tuesday next."

"We do," Lord Belfort assured him, returning to his seat. "But I saw no need to tell Lord Wellmanton that."

"Then you suspect him of plotting against us," Fritz guessed.

"I am unsure of his lordship's ability to plot," the solicitor said, and Leo's smile twitched as if he appreciated the diplomatic phrasing. "But he has been mentioned as one of those who might benefit from keeping Batavaria part of Württemberg."

"He invested in the silver mines," Leo confirmed. "Larissa learned of it."

Then perhaps they had found one of Callie's conspirators, though how he fit the description, Fritz could not guess. Could the palm branches have obscured his size, the dim light made him look more blond than grey? She had mentioned the greenery had prevented her from seeing well.

Yet, according to Callie, the Englishman had spoken of the House of Commons. From what Fritz knew of English governance, viscounts like Lord Wellmanton sat in the House of Lords. And even if Wellmanton was one of the plotters, who was his confederate?

Callie had said he had an accent, so he was likely from Württemberg. The viscount thought the Envoy from Württemberg was still out of the country, though Fritz wasn't certain. But if the envoy had been in attendance at the Kendall ball, surely someone would have thought to introduce him to Leo and Fritz.

His brother and Lord Belfort went on to discuss their strategy in meeting with King George. Fritz only half listened, mind sorting through possibilities, potentials. How could he arrange for Callie to stand close enough to Wellmanton to confirm his identity? Where should they venture to find the other conspirator?

"My brother also wanted a moment of your time,"

Leo said, bringing Fritz's attention back to the moment. "We will need your help in negotiating another set of marriage settlements." He looked to Fritz again.

Fritz straightened. "Yes. I will be marrying Lady Calantha."

Lord Belfort's usually noncommittal face broke into a grin. "Congratulations! Callie is a wonderful young lady. Many fail to appreciate her because she's so quiet, so I'm glad to hear you saw the gem that she is. The Observer, I've always called her."

Interesting. "The Observer? Because she listens?" Fritz pressed.

"Listens, formulates opinions, tests them, and comes to logical conclusions," the solicitor explained. "Having such a young lady beside him could be a true asset to a gentleman."

Indeed. Fritz roused himself. "In any regard, you needn't hurry. I know what you and Leo have planned is more important. I'm used to biding my time."

They both looked at him oddly, as if they thought an impassioned suitor or Captain of the Imperial Guard would want to demand action, but he merely smiled politely. He had no intention of answering the questions in his brother's eyes, or the solicitor's.

As Monday rolled into Tuesday, Callie could not quite quell her nerves. She knew why. Her family loved her, and she was lying to them.

The fact dug into her, like a squirrel hunting for a nut it had buried. Larissa had been at her side, helping, guiding, since her earliest conscious moments. Belle had been her dearest friend since the first time her little sister had given her a toothless smile. Tuny had felt like part of the family since they'd met at her sister's home in Surrey when Callie was eight. She herself had helped Thal climb into the saddle on his first pony and held Peter's hands as he took his first steps.

And how could she keep anything from her mother and father?

She knew something she was not supposed to tell. It was the story of her life. And like so many other times she had had a secret, she found she simply had to share.

"Our room tonight," she murmured to Belle as they were leaving family dinner on Tuesday. "Tell the others."

Belle nodded.

Callie barely made it through the soiree they were attending that night. At least her mother put her silence down to her usual anxiety at such events. Callie took her first deep breath of the day when Anna left and the others filed in.

"Is this something to do with Fritz?" Belle asked as she stretched out on her bed in her lace-topped white nightgown, Tuny beside her.

"Yes," Callie admitted from her place beside Larissa on her own bed. She tucked the covers closer to her pink nightgown and launched into her confession. "We aren't really engaged. We're pretending."

They all gaped at her.

Tuny found her voice first. "Good. Never was too fond of the fellow."

"He can be quite charming," Callie protested.

Larissa raised a brow. "So charming he apparently convinced you to lie. I will speak to Leo about this."

Callie put a hand on her arm. "No, please don't. There's a reason for the pretense."

Belle wiggled on her bed, smile eager. "I knew it. He kissed you."

"No," Callie repeated, more firmly this time. "We did nothing untoward. But I heard something that night.

Two men were plotting against the Batavarian court. Fritz needs me to identify them. We thought it would be easier if we had an excuse to spend time together."

"Oh," Belle said, deflating. "Well, I suppose that's good."

"No, it isn't," Larissa said. "Callie should be looking for a suitable match. What gentleman is going to come near when he thinks she's betrothed?"

"Not the ones you want to marry," Tuny predicted.

The thought was enough to set Callie squirming. "It's only for a time. We can search for a suitor afterward."

Larissa did not look convinced.

"This might be a good plan," Belle said, head cocked. "Callie and Fritz will attract attention. Gentlemen will notice that she is lovely and cultured. When she cries off, others may be interested in taking his place at her side."

Oh, but she hoped her sister was wrong. Still, Callie pasted on a smile. "There is that."

"Very well," Larissa allowed, making the decision for them all, as she usually did. "We'll see how this goes. Let's not inform Mother or Father as yet. I wouldn't want to worry them."

Neither would Callie.

"But I expect Fritz to behave as a gentleman," her oldest sister continued, "and I expect to be able to put this behind us by the end of July. Agreed?"

"I'm sure he'll be a gentleman," Callie said, though she made no promises about a date. She truly had no idea how long it might take to locate those opposed to Batavaria's restoration.

And she felt a little selfish hoping it might last all the way to harvest in September.

CHAPTER FIVE

WHEN IT CAME to dinner parties, Larissa or their mother usually planned and Callie attended, if she couldn't find an excuse to avoid it. But, for some reason, she found herself keenly interested in the arrangements for the dinner for her and Fritz.

"Don't we generally use the good silver for company?" she asked Underhill when she located him polishing an urn in the butler's pantry.

"We do," he agreed, pausing as if to admire his reflection in the gleaming surface. "But Her Grace thought we should adopt a more familiar tone." He glanced at Callie, eyes crinkling at the corners, and lowered his voice. "But you can be sure I'll do it up right, milady. And may I offer my congratulations?"

"Thank you, Underhill," she managed. She fled before she said something she shouldn't.

She wandered into the dining room only to come upon Maeve, their housemaid, ironing a tablecloth.

"Oh," Callie said, pausing just inside the doorway to the paneled room. "I was hoping for the one with the scallops."

The heavyset Maeve stopped and began folding the cloth. "Just as you say, Lady Calantha. And many happy returns on your upcoming wedding."

Callie clamped her lips tight and smiled her thanks.

"Nice to see you taking such an active part," her mother

told her when Callie asked about flowers as the duchess was arranging a group of hothouse flowers to her liking. "And pardon me for not asking sooner. I wanted to do this for you."

"I know," Callie told her. She needed to occupy her hands, so she took the other pair of sheers and began snipping off leaves. "And I'm grateful."

Her mother smiled. "Anything for you, my love. You know that."

A confession pressed against her lips so hard that tears came to her eyes. She swallowed before laying down the scissors and enfolding her mother in a hug. She barely made it out of the room without spilling her secret.

She kept to herself the rest of the day, but the thoughts were never far from her mind. So much so that her younger sister had to bring her back to the present.

"They're all pink, you know," Belle said that afternoon in their room.

Callie tore her gaze away from the wardrobe that held her evening gowns and blinked until her sister's smiling face came into focus.

"All your evening dresses are pink," Belle repeated, "and they all look fetching on you. Pick one so Anna can help you into it."

Callie glanced to where their lady's maid stood by the dressing table, dark brows up in question.

As if she knew Callie was incapable of making a decision at the moment, Belle reached around her and pulled out a gown. "What about this one?"

She'd always thought the dress so clever, with rosebuds embroidered on the pink satin. The pink capped sleeves were covered with white netting that ran down to her wrists and was tied there with satin ribbons. Now she could only wonder whether she'd end up dipping the ribbons in her soup. And the way the pink satin was gathered over her bosom. Did it call too much attention to that portion of her anatomy, which had never been particularly noteworthy?

Callie sighed. "I suppose it will have to do."

Belle hugged the gown closer. "*Have* to do? Wear another if that pleases you more."

But none of the remaining dresses seemed good enough. One had too many stripes. She would look like part of the chair upholstery. And another was too puffed at the hem; she'd feel the pressure against her shins all night. And why had she thought they should all be pink?

Her sister lowered the gown to peer at her. "You can't be nervous, not tonight. It's just family and Fritz and Leo, who will shortly be family."

Callie drew in a breath. "You're right. Let's get this over with."

Belle nodded to Anna, who came to take the gown from her. Then her sister put both hands on Callie's shoulders. Those jade eyes were knowing. "A young lady might be expected to show some enthusiasm for her betrothal party."

She was right. If Callie could not convince her mother and father she was happy, how could she fool the rest of the *ton*? And Fritz deserved the opportunity to find those who wanted to harm his family, before they acted.

She put on a smile. "Thanks, Belle."

Belle released her. "What are sisters for?"

She remained at Callie's side as they finished dressing and had Anna arrange their hair, suggesting a different placement of a curl, a change in the choice of necklace. When they came out of their bedchamber, they found Larissa and Tuny waiting in the corridor.

"We'll be with you every step," Tuny promised, reaching out to squeeze Callie's hand.

Her heart swelled.

Their parents, Thal, and Peter were already in the withdrawing room when the four entered. Although her brothers were generally considered too young to be included in entertainments like this, everyone had agreed they should be allowed to join in the celebration. Their unruly dark-brown hair had been pomaded in place, and they each wore evening dress with long trousers and jade-colored waistcoats that matched their eyes. Thal was chatting with their father as if he dined at table every night, but Peter was already fussing with his white cravat. It seemed Callie wasn't the only one nervous.

She went to stand beside him near the hearth. "The more you touch it, the more it will wilt," she murmured. She gave the cloth a gentle tug, then looked into his pale face. "Better?"

She could see him swallow. Then he smiled. "Yes, much. Thank you."

Underhill cleared his throat from the doorway, and everyone looked to him. Callie might not have been wearing a cravat, but her throat felt unaccountably tight as well.

"His Royal Highness, Prince Otto Leopold of Batavaria," Underhill announced, "and Frederick, Count Montalban, Captain of the Imperial Guards." He stepped aside to allow Leo and Fritz to enter.

Callie was used to seeing them both in the scarlet and gold of the crown prince, but tonight there was something different about Fritz. His shoulders looked broader in the tailored coat, medals crossing his chest, and his smile deepened as he looked her way. With a nod to all in the room, he came to stand by her side, slipping an arm about her waist.

The touch sent arcs of warmth through every inch of her body.

"Thank you all for this dinner," he said, all congeniality when she could scarcely breathe. "You honor us with your kindness."

Once more, Callie clamped her lips shut and nodded,

but words trembled on her tongue, and she wasn't sure she'd survive the night before they tumbled out. The only question was which secret would spew first.

Ever since he was a child, Fritz had pretended. He'd take Leo's place at some event his brother abhorred. It hadn't mattered if Fritz loathed it too. Or he'd pretend to be Leo to ensure his brother's safety. And though he knew tonight's charade had ultimately the same purpose, for the first time it felt wrong.

And oh-so-right.

He and Leo had always been close. Being twins saw to that. So did their duties. But he had always known Leo came first. The English had a saying that a peer who had two sons had an heir and a spare. Their father had an heir and a sacrificial lamb. Most days, it did not trouble him.

But there was no such thing in the duke's household. Lady Larissa might be the oldest and now betrothed to a prince, but she was given no pride of place. Thal might be the heir and his brother the spare, but both were accorded equal courtesies.

And Fritz was treated as if he were one of the most important people in the room.

"Any word from your father, the king?" the duke asked after the footmen had served the creamy mushroom soup and asparagus that made up the first course. His Grace was seated at the head of the table, with his wife at the foot. Callie had been placed at his right hand and Fritz at his left, another first.

"He reached France safely and is enroute to Württemberg," Fritz told him.

"And what chance of success do you give him in convincing King William there to take your side?" he asked.

"That is not my place," Fritz said, stabbing an asparagus spear. "I leave all strategy and diplomacy to the crown prince and king."

"Interesting." The duke selected a spear of his own. "As head of the Imperial Guard, have you no role in strategy?"

"Only as it pertains to the kingdom and its rulers," Fritz allowed. "And that strategy is not shared."

Across the table, Callie's eyes had widened. Very likely no one denied the duke, even in the provision of information, but Fritz wasn't about to trust the fellow with state secrets. He had defied the French who had captured him, despite torture and starvation. A few questions over dinner were nothing.

"Understandable," her father said, nodding to the footman to replenish his crystal goblet. "We each have a responsibility to our nations and our families. Your position has a broader overlap than most." He turned to Callie. "I have not heard a date for the wedding."

She hastily swallowed her mouthful of soup. "We thought after the harvest, when we are back in Surrey."

"Late September, then," he mused. "Liverpool has been making noises about bringing us back sooner next session, but that likely won't be until November at the earliest. I imagine you'll want to use the castle."

She nodded, but she appeared to be sinking in her seat. Fritz felt as if he'd heard the bugle of the French army sound in the distance.

Her father apparently noticed nothing wrong, for his smile lit the room. "Unfortunately, I'm not sure we can fit the wedding party in the library." He looked to Fritz. "It's her favorite room."

Callie paled. "Father, I…" Her look veered to Fritz, and he recognized desperation. What had she said, that her words sometimes came out wrong? More likely they came out unintentionally. She was having second thoughts about this engagement.

"And what is it about the library you find so fascinating, Callie?" he put in smoothly. Perhaps if he gave her something else to talk about, their secret would survive the dinner intact.

She shifted, as if attempting to rally, but her youngest brother down the table must have had the same gift of listening as she did, because he answered for her.

"It's huge!" He spread his arms and bumped into Leo beside him in the process. "Like a fortress!"

"I always thought it resembled a maze," Belle put in with equal enthusiasm. "Bookcases line every wall, and some of them jut out at angles from each other."

"It was the perfect place to hide in a game of hunter and hunted," Miss Bateman agreed with a fond smile.

Callie had grown in her seat, and a smile played about her lips as well. He could imagine her in the cavernous library, surrounded by books, safe in the quiet.

"You'll have to come out to Surrey and see," Her Grace said. "You and Leo both."

Belle clapped her hands. "What a wonderful idea, Mother! We should hold a house party, right after the Season ends."

Her mother met her father's gaze down the table.

"We can consider the matter," he said.

Belle wiggled her shoulders in eager anticipation.

"In the meantime," Her Grace said. "Callie and Tuny have their society to consider."

He was used to Londoners calling the social activities Society, and he could hear the capital S on the word. This seemed something different.

"Society?" he asked.

"The Society for the Prevention of Cruelty to Animals," Miss Bateman said. "Callie and I support it. We're sponsoring a benefit dinner and auction later this month."

"To raise funds for a campaign to stop the use of ponies in mines," Callie put in, and Fritz was relieved to see her color coming back. "They are treated most abominably and put into dangerous situations. New machines are becoming available to take their places. We'd like to help mine owners who wish to convert as well as find homes for the ponies who are retired from service."

It was the most he'd ever heard her say in one sitting, except when she'd recited what she'd heard. Her eyes were shining with fervor, and her head was up.

"Bravo," Fritz said. "A worthy cause."

Pink climbed in her cheeks. "An important cause."

"Perhaps you'd care to contribute," Miss Bateman fired down the table at him.

"Delighted," Fritz said. "The Royal House of Archambault would be glad to support the society's goals. How much would you say, Brother?"

Leo gulped down his mouthful of soup and sat taller. "I will need to speak with the Lord Chamberlain, who is managing the Treasury while the Lord Steward is traveling with the king."

"But you'll both come to the benefit," Larissa said. It was not a question.

Fritz had a great deal to do, and charity events fell squarely under his brother's purview. But gazing across the table into Callie's hopeful blue eyes, he could not find it in him to refuse.

"Of course," he said.

She beamed.

And everything tasted even better after that.

After dinner, instead of the ladies leaving the gentlemen to their port, they all adjourned to the withdrawing room. Fritz expected polite conversation. He hadn't noticed an instrument in the room, and he doubted the duke would suggest cards in such a mixed group. To his surprise, the duchess stood in front of the hearth, the picture of her and her children above her, and rubbed her hands together. "Right. What shall we play?"

Peter bounced on his chair. "Buffy Gruffy!"

His brother made a face. "No, Callie always wins."

Fritz had been seated on the sofa next to Callie, so he leaned closer while the others debated the merits of various parlor games. "Buffy Gruffy?" he murmured in her ear.

The silk of her platinum hair teased his cheek as she turned to look at him. "It's a blindfold game. Everyone changes places, and the gruffy must guess their identities by their voices."

Fritz smiled. "No wonder you always win."

She shrugged, but her smile was pleased.

In the end, the duchess led them through a series of games that involved changing places, guessing riddles, and making up rhymes. He hadn't enjoyed himself so much in years.

"We will see you both tomorrow, then," Her Grace said as she, Callie, and Larissa walked them to the door.

Fritz frowned at Leo, but his brother was nodding.

"For the king's birthday celebration," he agreed.

The duchess looked to Fritz expectantly. It was his cue to offer his escort to Callie, but he wasn't even sure he had been invited. Still, if Leo was going, it behooved him to be on hand to protect his brother.

"Did you care to attend, Callie?" he asked.

Her shoulders were climbing. "I would prefer not to."

"Nonsense," her mother said. "You won't have to do anything. The king likely won't get around to even greeting us, that's how many people will be there."

The fact did not seem to comfort her. Still, if so many would be attending, it might be the perfect time to catch their enemies.

"I promise you can be as anonymous as you please," he

told her. "I would simply enjoy your company."

She met his gaze, and he had the odd notion that she could see inside him to the dark places he kept hidden. He willed himself not to flinch.

"Very well," she said. "I'll come."

"Good," Her Grace said. "That's settled. Say your goodnights, now." With a smile to them all, she returned to the withdrawing room.

Leo bent and pressed his lips to Larissa's. She melted against him. Callie's gaze darted to Fritz, and once more he could see panic building. In other circumstances, he would be expected to follow his brother's lead and kiss the woman to whom he was betrothed.

Instead, he took Callie's hand and bowed over it. "Good night, my dearest Callie."

As he straightened, his gaze tangled with hers, and something flashed through him, like a shooting star against the Batavarian peaks in summer.

And he knew he would have to be very careful, before this pretend engagement felt any more real.

CHAPTER SIX

CALLIE HAD FOUND excuses to avoid attending the King's Drawing Rooms ever since she and Larissa had been formally presented three years ago. But she'd promised Fritz, so no excuse would work this time.

She remembered the routine. First, spend the morning donning required court costume with hooped skirts and train and arrange her hair in complicated curls surmounted with ostrich plumes. Then, travel in the carriage to Carlton House on Pall Mall with her mother, father, Larissa, and Belle without disturbing said hoop, train, and ostrich plumes. Tuny seemed resigned to staying behind. As the sister of a baronet, she didn't generally receive invitations to see the king. Callie only wished she could trade places with her friend.

Once she and her family reached Carlton House, she had to clamber out of the carriage, then lift her hoop and train to climb the steps. Mincing through the tall columns on the portico allowed her to reach the entrance hall with all its marble and arched coffered ceilings. There, voices echoed, and the air was too perfumed for easy breath.

Or maybe that was just her.

They made their way with the crowds through the vast octagonal vestibule into the Ante Room, where she gave her cards, one to the King's Page on duty and another to be delivered to the Lord in Waiting.

Both of whom looked right through her.

In this case, she didn't mind her invisibility. The page and the Lord in Waiting were far more deferential to her father and mother, and bemused by her Uncle Julian and Aunt Meredith, who joined them a short while later. Uncle Julian had been friends with her father since they were boys together in Surrey, and Aunt Meredith had been involved in the match between her mother and father, with the approval of her cat, Fortune. Callie couldn't help smiling, remembering the moment when Fortune had first met Fritz and stalked out of the room in high dudgeon. What would the cat think to find Callie masquerading as his betrothed?

Her smile slipped.

As if she was as prescient as her pet, Aunt Meredith moved closer to Callie. Though she and Uncle Julian were making their first appearance at court as members of the diplomatic corps representing Batavaria, her aunt did not look the least out of place. Her raven hair boasted no less than seven plumes, waving elegantly over her head, and her lavender court dress, the exact shade of her eyes, had enough lace, embroidery, and metal sequins to look impressive.

"I understand congratulations are in order," she murmured as others in court dress began filtering in, all maneuvering for positions to enter the throne room beyond.

Callie inclined her head, not trusting herself to speak. Somehow, lying to Aunt Meredith was worst of all. She followed the others as the Lord in Waiting announced them by ones and twos, then entered the throne room. She only had a moment to glance around at all the gilding and crimson before Uncle Julian nodded toward the entrance. "Ah, here comes His Highness and the Count."

"His Royal Highness Prince Otto Leopold Augustus of Batavaria and Frederick, Count Montalban," the Lord in Waiting announced.

For a moment, it was as if every voice stilled. Callie shook herself, and sound returned, voices murmuring in an uneven drone, as Leo and Fritz approached them. As usual, Leo was in the scarlet, but Fritz was once more in his black dress uniform. The gold braid crossing his chest rivaled that on King George's opulent upholstery. He moved in beside Callie with an appreciative smile that made the trouble of dressing for court worth every moment.

"Isn't it a marvelous crush?" Belle asked with a bright smile after everyone had greeted each other.

"It is that," their mother agreed, glancing around. "His Majesty has ever known how to throw a party."

As someone laughed overly loud nearby, Fritz moved closer to Callie as if to protect her. It seemed she felt the touch through all the layers of her court costume.

"I believe His Majesty is expecting a formal greeting from us," Uncle Julian said with a nod toward the top of the throne room, where the great, gilded throne sat, draped by a canopy of crimson velvet. With an apologetic look to Callie, Fritz joined Leo and her uncle as they moved away.

"Will you be all right if I speak with Liverpool a moment?" her father asked her mother.

Her mother smiled. "Oh, I'd like to join you for that. Meredith?"

"I'll stay with the girls," their aunt offered quickly, and, for the first time, Callie wondered whether she might be nervous too.

"You can go if you like," she murmured as her mother and father moved away through the crowd. "We'll be fine."

Aunt Meredith patted her shoulder. "I never doubted that. But I have no interest in discussing politics with the prime minister, especially when I have a moment to spend with my girls."

Uncle Julian and Aunt Meredith had never had children of their own, but they treated Callie and her sisters and Petunia and her sisters as if they were their own. So it was little wonder that her aunt was soon in conversation with Larissa and Belle.

Callie allowed her mind to wander. Under gilded cornices and yards of crimson and gold draperies, the tall windows looked out on a lush garden. She could imagine the cool breeze, the soft rustle of the foliage and the song of the robin, so much quieter than the rumble of discussion around her.

"So of course I told him he must go."

That voice. The deep eager note sent a chill through her. She looked right, left, tilted her head to one side to see around her sisters. Oh, why were there so many blond, slender Englishmen!

"Excuse me," she murmured, moving around her family. If her sisters or Aunt Meredith called out to stop her, she didn't hear them. All of her was focused on picking out that one voice, that one man. The one who wanted so badly to help Württemberg.

She detoured around this group, skirted that one, but she simply could not detect him. She was about to give up when she caught her own name from a group of women near the windows.

"Lady Calantha has every reason to cry off," a well-endowed older woman with white hair was maintaining, and Callie recognized Lady Wellmanton, whose family lived not far from hers in London. "His behavior is nothing short of shocking."

"Normally I would say we should overlook the peccadillos of young men," her companion, an equally buxom brunette, said. "But his seductions are simply too much to ignore. The daughter of a merchant captain in Portsmouth? The wife of his steward in Chelsea? He is a cad of the first order."

They could not be talking about Fritz. Yet what other engagement would Callie cry off from? Surely news of their so-called betrothal hadn't spread so far. They hadn't even appeared in polite Society as a couple until today.

"I heard he even attempted liberties with her sister," a third woman put in, pointed nose in the air. "I knew that Lady Abelona was too forward for her own good."

Fire flushed up her. Callie hefted her train and marched into their midst. For once, her invisibility must have failed her, for they all stared at her, mouths open in mid-gossip.

"That," she said, "is a lie and an unkind thing to say about my sister. Count Montalban is a gentleman, and I will have neither of them slandered. You do not want me to repeat the stories I've heard about you, your daughters, or your husbands."

Lady Wellmanton drew herself up. "I'm sure I never."

Callie affixed her with a look. "Sally Nockville."

Lady Wellmanton blanched, and both chins quivered.

Her two friends turned to her. "Sally Nockville? Who is Sally Nockville?"

Callie left Lady Wellmanton stammering an explanation about the maid who had been found with child in her household and turned out without penny or reference. Servants had a way of talking when their own were wronged. And, like so many others, they didn't appear to notice Callie nearby.

She took a few steps away from the trio, and the righteous indignation she'd harnessed galloped off like one of Belle's unicorns set free. Her legs wobbled, and tears burned her eyes. She made her way out of the throne room into the rotunda next door. Only a few of His Majesty's friends had escaped into it, but she went to the nearest window and steadfastly gazed out, back to the others. If a few tears fell, the embroidery on the bodice of her court gown obscured them.

"What happened?"

She drew in a breath as Fritz moved up beside her. His brow was furrowed, but the tone of his voice sounded more like concern than censure.

"I heard things I shouldn't," she explained.

"Ah," he said. "And not about my father, the king, this time."

"No," she said, turning to face him. "I heard them about you."

Fritz shook his head. He'd noticed the cool reception the moment he'd entered Carlton House. The King's Page had looked at him longer than he had at Leo. The Lord in Waiting's nose had turned up just the slightest. Fritz was used to that treatment from those who considered themselves better than a mere Captain of the Imperial Guard. But after his elevation?

It had been worse when he, Leo, and Lord Belfort had had their moment with King George. Finally, to see the monarch face-to-face. His birthday celebration was no time to make their case, but Leo had been hoping to show their family in a good light.

Unlike Fritz's father, who still looked like the Lion of the Alps he'd been named as a young king, time had not been kind to King George. Despite a tight-fitting coat and, if the gossip sheets that found their way into the Chelsea Palace were any indication, a corset, his gut bulged over the top of his white satin breeches, and the jowls of his face sagged.

"Your Majesty," Leo had said with a bow after the British Lord Chamberlain had introduced him, Fritz, and Lord Belfort. "Thank you for including us on this auspicious occasion. May you enjoy many more such birthdays to come."

King George had inclined his head. "Prince Otto Leopold. Your fame precedes you. Quite the hero in the Napoleonic wars, I hear. I don't remember seeing you at Waterloo."

Fritz didn't recall seeing King George, who would have been England's crown prince ten years ago. He was fairly sure if the fellow had been at the battle, everyone would have known it.

"I did not have the pleasure of leading my troops to our shared victory," Leo had said. "I leave such matters to my brother, Count Montalban."

King George's eyes had flickered over Fritz, cold as a mountain stream. "Ah, yes. I have heard of you too."

He turned to Lord Belfort as if dismissing both brothers. "I believe we will be meeting soon. I will have more to say at that time."

Lord Belfort had inclined his head. "Of course, Your Majesty." He, Leo, and Fritz had backed away to give room to the next group desiring to speak to the king.

"We appear to have offended him," Leo had murmured when they were safely out of hearing. "Do you know why?"

The solicitor had shaken his head. They had separated to find their ladies, but now it seemed as if Callie knew the answer they all had sought.

"About me?" Fritz asked her. "What could I have done? Failed to bow low enough to suit some lord? Spoken too harshly in my family's defense?"

Her blue eyes met his, puckered and concerned. "No. You seduced and abandoned women from one end of England to the other."

Fritz stared at her a moment. He'd been called many things in his life—lazy, unskilled, obtuse—but never predator. "And this troubles you," he surmised. "Which means you give it credence."

She looked absolutely miserable as she twisted her fingers together over the wide circle of her skirts. "I don't want to."

He should not have to defend himself at every turn. He bent closer and pitched his voice for her sharp ears alone. "Then ask yourself this question: when would I have had the time?"

She blinked, and then she grinned as he straightened. "Well, that's a very good question. You are far too busy protecting your brother and father to have a moment to yourself some days, from what I've seen. I imagine it would be quite challenging to pull off a seduction." Color climbed in her cheeks, and she dropped her gaze once more. "Not that I have any experience with such things."

It was on the tip of his tongue to offer to correct that lack of experience, but he swallowed the urge to tease her. For one thing, it would only have made her uncomfortable. And it hardly proved his innocence to these charges.

Instead, he took her hand and tucked it into his arm. "Put the matter behind you. People are always looking for reasons to find fault."

She sighed. "Don't I know it. Oh!" She pulled away. "Fritz, I nearly forgot. I found him!"

Steel straightened his spine. "Where?"

She made a face. "That's just it. I'm not sure. I heard his voice among the dozens in the throne room, but when I tried to narrow in on it, I lost it. I'm sorry."

"No need to apologize," he assured her, turning toward the throne room. "Perhaps if we strolled around a bit, you might locate it again."

She nodded, accepting his arm. They moved back into the room.

But there they must go carefully, and not just because danger might be hiding among the powdered coiffures and velvet coats. No one was to turn their back on the king. It was the same in Batavaria. When he and Leo were alone with their father, the king allowed more familiarity, but here, where Fritz appeared to be on low standing with King George, he must be on his best behavior.

Accordingly, he navigated through the other courtiers with care, keeping Callie at his side. But though they nodded and smiled and made polite conversation where necessary, her face remained slightly puckered.

"It's no good," she said after a half hour of traversing the space. "He must have left."

Frustration simmered inside him as they came to a stop beside a massive painting that showed King George in his younger years. "At least we know he is close enough to the king to be granted entrance to this event. Doesn't that mean he is an English lord?" Lord Wellmanton sprang to mind.

"More likely a member of the House of Commons or the diplomatic corps," Callie said.

The last was even more concerning. "Could the Envoy from Württemberg have returned?"

She glanced up at him, sunlight from the window glittering on her pale lashes. "Perhaps, but would he speak perfect English? The other man had an accent. He may be from Württemberg. I believe Mr. Eager to be thoroughly English."

He smiled at her name for the fellow she had overheard. "An Englishman who started this gossip about me? It seems rather cowardly."

"Gentlemen are not immune to spreading gossip," she informed him, hands resting on the curve of her hooped skirt. "Though they are more likely to make it appear that they are bragging. You would not believe some of the things I've heard." She shuddered, setting her skirts to swinging. "I told you. It's a curse."

"Or a blessing." He glanced around the room, noting

the number of gentlemen, all in tailcoats and breeches. "You are convinced this Mr. Eager is a member of your Society. Where else will those members be congregating in the next few days?"

"Almack's," she said. "But that's no good. I haven't received vouchers. And many of them will be attending Parliament, though some are poor at doing their duty, according to Father."

"Parliament," he mused. "Excellent suggestion. Is there a way to view the proceedings at the House of Commons? The king's court in Batavaria had galleries running along three of the walls for those interested in watching."

"There's a gallery in the House," she said, "but it's only for men. There's a women's gallery as well, screened off from the chamber. Mother went once with Father to hear a member speak."

"Perfect," he said. "Be ready tomorrow afternoon, and we will see if we can catch Mr. Eager."

CHAPTER SEVEN

MEREDITH THORN PULLED off the ostrich plumes her maid had worked so hard to affix in her hair and grimaced as a few dark strands came along with them.

"You didn't enjoy your presentation nearly as much as I'd hoped," her husband Julian said across from her as the carriage started back toward their home on Clarendon Square.

She offered him a smile. "It was never my dream to be presented to the prince."

"No," he agreed, mouth turning down. "It was mine. Did you mind very much?"

"Seeing you get your due at last? No. That was splendid." She shoved the hoops as low off her chest as she could given the construction of the court costume. "But this, this is ridiculous."

"I've heard any number of ladies say the same," he assured her. "You needn't come to another drawing room if you prefer."

"If you want me there, I will be there," she promised. "It isn't the event that has me down. Something's wrong with Callie."

He frowned. "She seemed no different to me."

"Precisely," Meredith said as the carriage pulled into traffic on Piccadilly. "She is betrothed to a personable gentleman about to make his mark. Why not look happier?"

"Even such delightful circumstances might not make her any less shy," Julian pointed out. "And the drawing room was abominably crowded."

Meredith cast her gaze out the window to where the green of Hyde Park was beginning to appear in the distance. "It was more than the crowd. I'm sure of it. Perhaps Fortune and I should visit tomorrow morning, see what we can learn."

Julian smiled. "If anyone can ferret out the truth, it's Fortune. Now, why don't you swing those hoops in this direction and allow me to express my appreciation for your willingness to don them."

Sharing his smile, Meredith slipped across the carriage and into his arms.

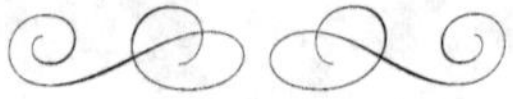

Parliament did not start until a quarter to four in the afternoon on Mondays, Tuesdays, Thursdays, and Fridays, so Callie had time Friday morning to work with Tuny on the preparations for the benefit dinner and auction they were managing to support the Society for the Prevention of Cruelty to Animals. Callie's father had agreed to fund the rental of the hall, an upstairs room off St. James's. He was also funding the cost of the catering staff. Sir Matthew, Tuny's brother, was donating the rental of the silver and plate, and her oldest sister, Lady Kendall, was sponsoring the flowers.

Callie frowned at the menu their caterer had recommended.

"Too much?" Tuny asked from her spot on a chair near the hearth in the library, blue skirts angled toward the glow of the fire. "Not enough? I wondered whether they'll pay twenty pounds per plate, even for pheasant."

Callie set down the menu on her father's desk and picked up the list of attendees from among the many notes they'd made. "Of the eighty we invited, forty have already sent their acceptances."

Tuny raised her brows. "Perhaps we aren't the only ones interested in supporting the society."

She could hope. Besides the cost to attend, they had thought to gain additional funds from an auction of art that had been featured in recent years at the Royal Academy Summer Exhibition as well as paintings and sketches by local artists of note. Battlefield artist Lady Emily Cropper, daughter of the Duke of Emerson; allegorical painter the Countess of Brentfield; and landscape artist Mrs. Abigail Bennett of Grace-by-the-Sea had all contributed.

"Let's go over the schedule again," Callie said, selecting the next piece of paper. "You and I will meet with the caterers three hours before dinner to allow them to dress the tables."

Tuny grinned at her. "Will the tables be wearing silk or wool? I wouldn't want to match."

Callie giggled. "I have it on good authority they will be dressed in damask. So you may wear silk or wool." She perused the schedule. "We told the guests to arrive at half past seven. I imagine a number will come a bit early."

"And others will come late," Tuny said. "Making an entrance and all that."

Callie leveled her with a look. "We must ask Larissa and Mother to keep an eye on Belle."

Tuny shook her head. "She'll outshine us all no matter what we do. You know that."

Callie smiled. "I know. I only wish some of that vivaciousness would rub off on me."

"Why?" Thal asked, wandering into the library. "You're already engaged."

Callie exchanged looks with Tuny, then aimed her smile at her brother. "There is that. But sometimes, engagements don't turn out as we expect. Besides, I know any number of young ladies who wish they had half of Belle's charm. Then they wouldn't have to fear spinsterhood."

"You don't have to be afraid of being a spinster," Thal said, striding for the bookshelf that held the titles on military battles. "You don't have to marry anyone, if you like. I'll take care of you."

Her heart melted. "Oh, Thal. That is so kind of you."

He selected a book and turned to face her. "It isn't kind. It's what one does for family."

She nodded. "That's what Mother always says."

"Besides," he said, heading for the door, "I expect I'll need someone to manage my household. You're clever. And you won't fuss over me like some do."

Her brother had been ill a good part of his childhood. Their parents still worried over him at times. Still, the thought of spending her life managing his household did not bring the comfort it once might have.

Neither did the newspaper Belle brought in a few moments later.

"You must see this," she announced with a crackle of paper. She spread *The Times* out over Callie's notes. "There, that column. Positively scurrilous."

Callie peered at the headline, then reared back. Tuny rose to come look as well.

"Batavarian More Cruel Than Count," she read aloud. She glanced up. "What's this?"

Belle waved a hand, setting the lace at her sleeves to fluttering. "Lies, if you ask me. The reporter claims to have talked with *sources* within the Batavarian court who confided that Fritz is a cruel master. It seems none of the staff has the strength to escape because his brutal guardsmen watch their every move. He even sneered at an invitation to Almack's!"

"What nonsense!" Callie cried, pushing the paper away

as she would have liked to push away these rumors. "He should not have to dance to the patronesses' whims like the rest of us. And I have never seen the least indication that any of the staff or servants at the Batavarian court are unhappy."

"Well, they wouldn't show it, would they?" Tuny put in, straightening. "Not if they want to keep their positions."

"I won't believe it," Callie said, hands on the hips of her pink day dress. "Fritz may appear gruff at times, but he would never be intentionally cruel. Look how loyal he is to his family, even when they put him in difficult positions."

"Like when Leo asked him to impersonate him last month," Tuny agreed. "I'm willing to give the fellow the benefit of the doubt."

"Father isn't," Belle informed them. "I took this paper away from the breakfast room, but it seems he'd already read it, because Underhill said Father had sent word to the Batavarian court to have Fritz attend him immediately."

Callie's stomach lurched. "Oh, poor Fritz! Perhaps I should speak to Father."

Belle stepped aside. "If you intend to, now is the time. Fritz could be here any moment, if he heeds Father's call."

Callie excused herself and hurried out into the corridor, only to find Underhill opening the front door. Aunt Meredith stood waiting, Fortune up in her arms. Callie kept her head down and started for the stairs.

"Calantha," her aunt called, "please don't go. I'd like to speak with you." Her voice was as polished and proper as ever, but the tone brooked no disobedience.

Callie glanced in the withdrawing room and then up the stairs but spotted no sign of her father. Perhaps he was with Thal and Peter at the moment. And her mother and Larissa were out shopping, worse luck.

She turned fully to her aunt. "Of course. But I'm sure

Belle or Tuny could address your needs better."

"Perhaps not," her elegant aunt all but purred. She nodded to Underhill, who shut the door before she lowered Fortune to the floor.

The grey-coated cat held herself still a moment, as if knowing she had the attention of every person in the entry hall. Then she deigned to stroll up to Callie and twist herself about her skirts.

Callie bent and picked her up. "And a very good morning to you too, Fortune."

The cat rubbed the top of her head against Callie's chin.

"I see the withdrawing room is empty at the moment," Aunt Meredith said. "That will do."

Callie followed her into the room. Fortune arched her neck as if giving her permission to stroke the white fur at her throat, so much like a cravat.

Her aunt perched on the sofa and nodded Callie down beside her. "You seemed unhappy yesterday," she said without roundaboutation. "Is everything all right between you and Count Montalban?"

No, no, no. She could not face this temptation now. Aunt Meredith had always encouraged and supported her. It would be all too easy to blurt out the truth, pour any concerns into her capable hands. Callie closed her eyes and willed herself to hear only the rumble of Fortune's purr and not the voices clamoring for attention in her head.

Once more the knocker sounded, sharp and hard, as if the person on the other side of the door was completely out of patience.

Her heart lifted, and she rose, bending to hand the cat to her aunt, whose brows were up in obvious surprise.

"We're expecting Fritz," she explained. "If you'll excuse me."

She darted out of the withdrawing room as Underhill

once more opened the door.

Fritz stood on the step, dressed in his uniform, head high and frown on his handsome face. She had never been happier to see him. Her relief must have shown, for he too raised his brows as she hurried to meet him.

"There was a story in the papers," she told him, taking his hand and pulling him into the house. "Father saw it before I did. I'll speak to him."

He gently removed his hand from hers. "No, Callie. I have never run from a fight."

"Precisely why I'd like to talk to you," her father said, starting down the stairs toward them.

Leo had first spotted the wretched piece in *The Times* that morning. Fritz had actually found it amusing until his brother had pointed out how King George or the duke might take it. That only made him wonder how Callie might take it. She'd already been subjected to gossip at the king's birthday celebration. Neither those stories nor this one was true, but she couldn't know that. And he needed her support if he was to uncover Mr. Eager and his confederate from Württemberg.

So, he'd left saber practice with his guards to come at once at the summons from His Grace.

He inclined his head to Callie's father as the duke stepped down into the entry hall, his green eyes wary. "Your Grace. Thank you for the opportunity to explain."

"In the library, if you please," he said, turning in that direction.

"Father, wait!" Callie darted forward, and Fritz shook his head at her. As her father paused and looked back over his shoulder, she put on a smile. "Tuny and I have been working there on the benefit. Please give her a moment to gather her things."

"Of course," His Grace said. "I am not a monster, Calantha."

She cringed as his look settled on Fritz.

As the duke continued toward the library, Fritz took Callie's hand and gave it a squeeze. "All will be well. Trust me."

Her smile said she intended to try.

He followed her father to the library.

Miss Bateman and Belle started gathering up the papers as the duke entered.

"Leave *The Times*," His Grace directed, and the two exchanged glances before hurrying out, papers thrusting from their grips in all directions.

Callie's father nodded him into one of the upholstered chairs near the tall bookcases. "You've seen the article, then."

"Yes," Fritz said, waiting until the duke was seated before taking the chair he'd indicated. "I have no idea who gave the reporter such a story, but it is untrue."

"I'm glad to hear that," the duke said, leaning back. "I have seen no indications of the vices described in that article. But you must realize why the matter would give me pause. To whom, exactly, am I entrusting my daughter?"

"To a man who will honor and cherish her all the days of his life," Fritz said. Odd how easily the words flowed, as if they stemmed from a truth deep inside him. Time later to worry about how the duke would take it when Callie's father learned the truth.

"Honoring and cherishing her," the duke said, "is a start."

Fritz swallowed at the commanding tone. "What would you have of me, Your Grace?"

"First, understanding," he said. "Callie is special. Of all my children, she is most like her mother, my first wife, in coloring. But she resembles none of my children or her forebears in character. The House of Dryden is a strong one. We have fought floods and famine. If the stories are true, we were here fighting off Romans. We give no quarter and ask no mercy."

Fritz nodded. "A noble history."

"So I have been told," he said. "But Callie, Callie has always seemed to me like the wildflowers that grow near the Thames: pretty to look upon, but easily bruised. An unkind word, a distressing bit of gossip, oversets her."

"Because she hears everything," he surmised.

The duke inclined his head. "Then you know my daughter better than I thought."

"Perhaps I do," Fritz said. He caught himself edging forward in his seat and made himself sit taller. "And because I am coming to know her, I can tell you that you are wrong about her. There is a strength inside her, a determination that will not be denied. Like her ancestors, she will fight when she must."

"I hope you are right," her father said. "And I hope I can trust you not to put Calantha in a position where she must fight. It could well break her spirit, once and for all."

CHAPTER EIGHT

CALLIE PROWLED THE corridor outside the library, Fortune stalking along beside her. Tuny and Belle were with Aunt Meredith in the withdrawing room. Underhill watched Callie from the entry hall with a marked frown on his face, and Thal and Peter peered over the balustrade of the stairs. If Larissa had returned by now, she likely would have been pacing too. This was worse than when Fritz had been about to propose! Then Callie hadn't cared what her father had said, so long as she wasn't forced into an engagement.

Now she didn't want her pretend engagement to end.

She skidded to a stop and dropped her gaze to keep from staring at the butler. Fortune looked up at her, copper eyes knowing. Of course the engagement would end. That was the agreement. She would help Fritz catch the men who wished to harm his family. He would keep her family from forcing her into the Society she abhorred. As soon as the Season ended, so did their association.

Even if the thought was sharp enough to poke a hole in her heart.

The door opened down the corridor, and her head jerked up. Her father glanced from her to Fortune. Underhill began rearranging items on the hall table. A thud upstairs told her Thal and Peter were scrambling out of sight.

Her father stepped into the corridor and bent to run a

hand along Fortune's back. The cat dutifully gave him a purr before strolling past Callie as if looking for someone more challenging to bring up to scratch.

"Callie," her father said, straightening to step aside and allow Fritz out of the library. "Count Montalban tells me you would like to view a session of the House of Commons. I don't expect the speeches this afternoon to be very interesting, but I would be willing to take you."

Meaning she would not be going with Fritz. Her shoulders sagged of their own accord, but she would not give up their mission. "Thank you, Father."

He turned to Fritz. "Will you join us as well?"

"Delighted," Fritz said with a look to Callie.

The sun must have come out from behind a cloud, for the corridor appeared brighter. It seemed she was still engaged after all.

She managed to make her excuses to Aunt Meredith without sharing any secrets. Belle and Tuny accompanied her upstairs to change for the trip.

"Anna can help me," Callie said, even as their maid bustled into the room.

"Of course she can," Belle said. She turned to the maid. "Anna, Callie must look particularly fetching this afternoon. Her green walking dress, I think, and my hat with the peacock feathers."

"I really shouldn't…" Callie began, but Belle pushed on her shoulders to make her sit at the dressing table.

"I'd lend you my red walking dress, but the color wouldn't suit you," her sister confided. "Tuny, would you be willing to allow Callie the use of the shawl your sister gave you for Christmas?"

Tuny put up her thumb. "Perfect. Back in a moment." She hurried out.

Callie met Belle's gaze in the mirror. "You know this isn't necessary."

"Because you're engaged," Belle said, tipping her head

to indicate Anna approaching with the dress in question. At least it was one of the few she owned that wasn't pink.

"But I saw your face in the corridor," her sister continued. "You were very glad Father didn't turn Count Montalban away. So loyal to the man you love."

Belle was wrong. She didn't love Fritz. She enjoyed his company. Some moments, awe would steal over her that he would want to spend time with her, until she remembered he needed her help. No, she couldn't love Fritz. That wasn't smart or safe. And it certainly didn't align with the plans she'd made for her life.

Belle leaned closer. "It never hurts to look your best."

She couldn't argue there.

The process took longer than she would have liked, but she eventually came down the stairs to join her father and Fritz. The serpentine green walking dress had a white lace collar over a broad, Van Dyke set of scallops across her bosom. It paired rather well with Belle's high-crowned green, fabric-covered hat with its trio of peacock feathers waving from the satin band. Tuny's shawl, mostly white with vines woven along the fringe, draped her shoulders.

"And it sways when you do," Belle had pointed out. "That's always good."

By the way Fritz was smiling, it was very good indeed. She felt unaccountably warm as she took his arm for his escort to the carriage.

Her father had called for the town coach, a narrower affair that seated two abreast facing front and back. Fritz gallantly took the rear-facing seat, leaving Callie to sit beside her father. Fritz kept smiling at her, and her father kept glancing between the two of them as if he could not understand what they saw in each other.

Callie tried to think of something insightful or endearing to say to Fritz. Belle would have had no trouble coming up with a clever phrase and a winning smile to cap it off. But what if Callie's attempt drew her father's attention to that hateful piece in *The Times*? Perhaps a soulful glance would be sufficient to further their ruse. Her face must have looked more panicked than longing, for Fritz began to ask her father's advice about everything from approaching King George to searching for a proper mount.

"Thank you," she murmured when he handed her down in front of the Houses of Parliament.

He tucked her arm in his. "It was my pleasure."

That smile said as much. He'd always been good at carrying conversations, a skill she lacked, but this time she thought he meant that doing her a kindness pleased him, and she could only marvel anew.

She glanced up at the building as they approached. The pale stone façade with its narrow windows and crenelated roofline always made the building look like a medieval castle to her. She stayed at Fritz's side as he and her father walked her through the gate in the wall surrounding the building and then the stout oak doors into the marble-tiled entry hall. There, gentlemen in tailored coats hurried past, clerks and secretaries to the more powerful members of Parliament. Those worthies ambled along, chatting with colleagues, secure in their positions. A few actually glanced her way. Who knew all it would take was a few peacock feathers in her hat to make her visible?

Of course, it might have been the man at her side. Fritz too moved with an air of confidence, certainty, as if he had every right to stand beside men of power and purpose. Still, he bent his head to answer her questions and kept one hand protectively on her elbow. Anyone else watching would see a doting fiancé.

They accompanied her father up a series of stairs, until she thought they might be approaching the roof. Finally, he opened a door to a dimly lit room where a dozen pairs of eyes peered at her from the darkness.

One must have known her father, for she nodded at him. "We have room for only two more in the Women's Gallery, Your Grace."

"Then please allow my daughter, Lady Calantha, to join you, Mrs. Tridon," her father said.

As if she were in charge of the room, the lady in question inclined her head in agreement, setting the flowers on her hat to bobbing.

"I will return for you soon," Fritz promised Callie.

She had only a moment to give him a smile before her father took him away.

Left to her own devices, Callie ventured into the room. It appeared to be an attic, for the roof beams crossed far too close overhead, and the walls on three sides had no plaster. A single lantern with a sputtering candle in a tin candlestick hung from the wall near the door. She counted a dozen women on rickety chairs clustered around what looked like a watchman's box, though no one was inside it.

"Sit here," Mrs. Tridon said. She had dark hair pulled back from her round face and a sturdy figure in her black gown. In fact, she reminded Callie enough of her mother that it was no trouble doing as she ordered and taking one of the last two chairs.

The woman nodded her approval. "You're tall enough. You may not have to stand to see."

Callie glanced around. "See what?"

"There," another of the women said, nodding toward a floor screen that resembled a stained-glass window with the colored glass removed. "That's our view."

It was a wretched one. All that was visible was a large chandelier, candles far brighter than the one left for them. Half rising from her seat, Callie peered through the grating to find a table directly below.

Another woman had been standing by the grating. Now she stiffened. "Here they come."

Indeed, Callie heard the murmur of voices over the thud of feet and the rustle of clothing. Two men in powdered wigs appeared, seating themselves at the table and taking up quills as if ready to record the proceedings. With a bang, a mace was lowered onto the table.

"Order!"

"That's the speaker," Mrs. Tridon explained. "Things should grow interesting soon. Will a friend of your family be speaking today, dear?"

"No," Callie admitted. "I simply wanted to know more about how the House of Commons operates."

"My son intends to speak," one of the other women said. Pride glowed on her narrow face.

The voices below them quieted, and the speaker of the house read a bill about how rents were to be collected.

"It's the third reading," Mrs. Tridon murmured. "If they finish their deliberations today, they may vote." She sounded almost eager for the moment.

Following the reading of the bill, various voices spoke up for and against, some of them impassioned. One fellow was particularly concerned about the plight of widows.

"This bill," he declared in ringing tones, "would disenfranchise those already without voice or recourse in our empire."

The provisions hadn't sounded all that dire to Callie, but she supposed she could see his point. Widows might have no more than a small jointure from their husbands. Raising their rents could impose a hardship.

Another could not seem to understand what all the fuss was about. "We should not be interfering in what until now has been a matter of honor between landlord and tenant."

"Some landlords have no honor," one of the women muttered, and a few of the others echoed agreement.

Meanwhile, the room grew warmer and warmer. Soon, sweat trickled down from where Belle's hat sat on Callie's forehead, and she pulled off the shawl and placed it in her lap. Other women were fanning themselves, but they only succeeded in wafting hot air about the closed space. Two fell asleep, their chins on their chests. One began to snore, and another nudged her. She jerked upright and glanced around as if to make sure no one else had noticed.

"Form your divisions, then," the speaker ordered. Once more, voices grew louder and feet shuffled.

Callie craned her neck to see more of the chamber. "What are they doing?"

"The vote must have been close," Mrs. Tridon told her. "They must walk out into their respective lobbies to be counted. This will take some time."

Callie stood and moved closer to the grate, ears attuned. There—the murmur of her father's voice as he explained something to Fritz. And there, a hint of Fritz's lovely accent as he responded.

"Bit of nonsense," Mr. Eager said, passing directly below her. "A chorus of ayes should have been sufficient. The crown has no true support for this issue."

She pressed herself as close as she dared to the grate, but it was no good. All she could see were the tops of the members' heads as they exited the chamber. There was simply no way to determine which belonged to their quarry.

How did Leo manage it? Fritz shook his head as he exited the Strangers' Gallery, as the Duke of Wey had told him this balcony overlooking the chamber was called. Some of the arguments had been interesting, some of the speakers earnest, but a great deal of the debate had been posturing. Others, it seemed, simply liked the sound of their own voices, for they droned on far longer than necessary to make their point. He was thankful for the division, for it gave him an excuse to leave and find Callie.

And why did the British squeeze their women into a dark attic room when the men were allowed to sit on three sides of the chamber in the balcony? They should be glad to have anyone show interest in how laws were made and issues settled. The gallery around the throne room in Batavaria had welcomed any citizen, male or female, young or old.

It had been stuffy in the chamber, but the farther he climbed the stairs, the warmer it grew. He wasn't surprised to find perspiration outlining the face of the woman who answered his knock on the door to the Women's Gallery.

"If I may speak to Lady Calantha," he said.

She turned, and Callie hurried toward him. Her face was flushed, and tendrils curled damply around her cheeks. "Thank you, my lord. Will you escort me down to the lobbies?"

"Of course." He stepped aside to allow her to exit.

She drew a deep breath as if even the humid air of the corridor was preferrable to that of the gallery. "Hurry. I heard him, but I couldn't see him. That so-called gallery is atrocious!"

He felt as if she'd lit a candle in the darkness. As she lifted her skirts, he took her elbow and escorted her down the long staircase.

But clerks stood at each doorway leading to the lobbies, blocking any entrance. Fritz was prepared to shoulder his way past, if necessary, but Callie seemed to know her purpose. Indeed, he had seldom seen her so animated.

"I'd like to find my father," she explained to the black-coated clerk, "the Duke of Wey, but I'm not sure his location at the moment. If I could just look…"

"Sorry, your ladyship," the young man said. "Only members of the House allowed."

"Then if you'd just be silent a moment," she said.

Fritz raised his brows, but the clerk frowned at her. "But…"

She held up a hand. "Shush!" She leaned forward and gazed into the room with a frown, as if she would gather every word spoken into her head. Then she straightened and looked to Fritz. "Nothing. Let's try the other."

The clerk was still staring at them as they hurried away.

"You amaze me," Fritz said as they approached the second doorway.

She was more interested in interrogating the clerk there. Unfortunately, it was the same story at the other room. She puffed out a sigh. "I cannot find him. I'm so sorry, Fritz."

"Can you see a message delivered to the Duke of Wey in the Stranger's Gallery?" Fritz asked the clerk.

"Yes, my lord," he answered warily, gaze veering from him to Callie and back.

"Tell him that Count Montalban and his daughter will await him at Gunter's."

"Of course," the clerk promised.

Fritz led Callie out of the building. The air there was still warm, but not nearly as close as it had been inside.

"I had no idea women were supposed to hear but not see," Callie complained as they reached the street. "It's barbaric."

"Perhaps that is the next cause you should take up," Fritz said, raising a hand to hail a hack. "Englishwomen should be able to take part in your government."

"I will speak to Father at my first opportunity," she promised. She drew in another breath as if she could not get enough. "And Gunter's is inspired, by the way."

"Someone in the gallery mentioned it," he said as the hack pulled in beside them. He gave the driver the destination, then handed Callie inside before hopping up after her.

She leaned her head back against the squabs. "The benefits of a supposed engagement. Father cannot say too much about me being in a closed carriage with you for a short time. Otherwise, we might cause a scandal."

Fritz chuckled. "Particularly with me being such a seducer of innocents."

She shook her head, nearly dislodging her fetching hat. "I wish I knew who was starting those rumors. I'd give them a piece of my mind."

"Or the flat of my sword," he suggested.

She grimaced. "That would only fuel the other rumors, about you being cruel to your staff and servants."

"I dislike having to watch every action," he confessed. "I am generally the one watching the actions of others."

"Me too," she said.

"And why?" he couldn't help asking. "You are not called to guard your family's safety. Your father's position guarantees your standing. You have no need to watch from the wall."

Her fingers were pleating the fringed shawl in her lap. "You're so confident, Fritz. I can see things seldom rattle you. I don't feel nearly as brave sometimes."

If she had seen him in that French dungeon, she would not be so sure of his confidence. "Bravery is acting even when we fear."

Her smile was tremulous. "Then perhaps I am braver than I think. But I suppose that might come from being invisible."

"Invisible?" Fritz chuckled. "You could never be invisible."

Her brows shot up. "How do you think Mr. Eager and his colleague failed to notice me?"

"You were hiding behind a row of potted palms," he reminded her.

"It doesn't matter," she insisted. "I've stood right next to people, in the middle of a well-lit ballroom, in broad daylight for that matter, and they don't notice me in the slightest. In fact, some in Society are shocked to this day to learn the Duke of Wey has three daughters."

He could only remember Lawrence's comment when Fritz had told him he intended to marry Callie. "They are fools. You are well off without them."

"Perhaps," she said, but he could tell he had not convinced her.

And he wasn't sure why everything in him demanded that he try.

CHAPTER NINE

THE FAMOUS CONFECTIONARY of Gunter's was crowded. The sheer number of people might have deterred Callie, but for two things. One was the heat. A lovely cup of pineapple ice sounded divine at the moment. The other was Fritz.

Perhaps it was the glint of his curls in the sunlight, perhaps the implied authority of his uniform, but women stopped to watch him pass, and gentlemen stepped aside as if in deference. In moments, he and Callie were at the counter, and he was giving their order to the clerk. Shortly after, they were seated on a bench under the trees in the park at the center of Berkeley Square, breeze brushing away the last of her perspiration.

"They're staring," Callie said, gaze on the group of people waiting to enter Gunter's across the street.

He nodded, silver spoon digging into the raspberry ice he'd ordered. "Most men pause to look at a pretty woman."

And here she thought she would feel cooler. Callie downed another scoop of the pineapple ice in hopes it might put out the fire of her blush. "I don't think they're looking at me. They're looking at you."

He shrugged. "They look at Leo too, even when I play his part."

She eyed him. He and Leo were supposed to be identical twins, but she saw the differences. Leo had a lightness about him, both in physique and manner. Fritz seemed more solid, as if his feet were securely planted in the earth. "You are not *that* alike."

He snorted. "You are one of the few to notice."

"That's because you play his part so well," she told him.

His smile lifted. "Leo likes to say I play his part better than he does. You would not believe how many places he must be. Once, when we were living in the German states, he was asked to speak at a dinner for those who collect snuffboxes."

Callie raised her brows. "Snuffboxes? Does your brother take snuff?"

His nose wrinkled, making him look younger, less formidable. If his enemies had seen him now, eating ices and speaking fondly, they would likely not have worried he could defeat them.

"Neither of us touch the stuff," he assured her. "But Leo had intended to dine with two members of the aristocracy who might be willing to support our cause. So, he sent me to speak to the snuffbox collectors in his place."

"What did you say to them?" she asked, trying to picture it.

He shrugged. "I told them the truth: that taking snuff was a disgusting habit long-since abandoned by civilized nations. They did not ask Leo back."

She laughed. "Well, at least I've never been asked to impersonate Larissa or Belle. I doubt I could have pulled it off half so well."

His spoon clanked against the bottom of the crystal cup as he scraped out the last of the ice. "Ah, but you have another talent. You hear things. What is the most interesting thing you have heard, besides the conversation with Mr. Eager?"

Callie thought for a moment, gaze going up into the branches of the trees, the leaves forming patterns like lace. "Most of what I hear isn't so much interesting as troubling. I often heard servants talking about my sisters and me when we were younger. After our first mother died, we were a bit of a handful. We went through three governesses before Aunt Meredith and Fortune sent us Mother."

She dropped her gaze to find him eyeing her. "Lady Belfort's cat sent you your mother?"

Even if she hadn't had her gift, she would have caught his skepticism. "Fortune has a gift too. She knows when a person is worthwhile."

"Ah." He seemed to be contemplating the bottom of his cup, as if the ice had run out far too soon, and she remembered belatedly how Fortune had first reacted to him.

Callie put a hand over his. "Fortune allowed you to pick her up at your elevation," she reminded him. "And she hasn't shown the least concern since."

"True," he acknowledged.

Callie pulled away, trying to think of something amusing to relate that would return a smile to his face. "There are very few surprises in my house, at least, to me. I generally hear about every present, every journey, and every plan well in advance. The worst part is having to pretend I don't know. When I was little, I tended to repeat everything I heard. Now, I'm better at being selective."

His gaze returned to her face. "What else have you heard about me?"

Oh, but that was dangerous. People didn't always like what others thought of them. She busied herself setting her empty cup on the bench. "The usual sorts of things."

"You can tell me."

His smile had returned, making his silvery-blue eyes sparkle like stars. She licked her lips. "Well, most of the ladies in London find you quite attractive. Some are impressed by the number of honors on the chest of your uniform. You know some are setting their caps at you."

"Setting their caps?"

"It means they hope to attract your attention and marry you. That's one of the reasons you wanted to pretend we were engaged."

"Ah, yes," he said as if he'd needed reminding. He leaned back. "And what do they say of you?"

The bench seemed harder. "I'd rather not say."

"Let me guess. They are jealous of your cool beauty. They complain about your intellect."

Her fingers were twisting in her lap again. She forced them to stop. "If you must know, they consider me odd because I don't adore all the soirees and balls and such. And they don't complain about my intellect. They question I have any."

"I told you. They are fools."

The simple words, said with such conviction, drew her gaze to his. Heat simmered in the blue, anger at those who would slight her. It seemed she had a champion. The very idea left her mute.

He set aside his cup as well and took both her hands in his.

"People see what they want to see," he said. "Otherwise, I would never be able to impersonate Leo. A young lady entering Society for the first time, under pressure from her family to perform well, would likely be only too happy to find excuses why others are inferior to her. That proves her own anxieties and takes nothing from the fact that you are to be praised."

No one had ever spoken to her that way, not in her hearing and not in her overhearing. "Praised?" she whispered.

"Praised," he insisted. "You are clever, you are kind. You seek to use your gift to help or protect others. Your hair is like spun silk, your eyes like sapphires. And I am very much afraid I will kiss you if you give me the least encouragement."

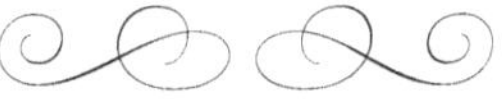

It was a ridiculous statement. They weren't really engaged, and they were in a public place. He had no right to kiss her. But with her gazing up at him, hope shining on her expressive face, the desire was nearly impossible to ignore.

Then her eyes fluttered closed, and her head bobbed. Was that a yes? She wanted him to kiss her?

He didn't question the command.

He bent his head and pressed his lips to hers. Her lips were cool from the pineapple ice and tasted as tart, but they quickly warmed beneath his, melding to his mouth as if made just for him. His hand rose to her cheek, cupping the softness. She stole his breath.

He swallowed as he pulled back. Where was his calm, his command of the situation? He only wanted to gather her to him, protect her from the idiots who questioned her abilities. She was his.

But she wasn't. The engagement was merely an act in a play designed to catch his enemies. He'd been good about knowing he was playing a part when he took his brother's role. He'd always known when to hand it back. Why was he getting caught up in the role of besotted bridegroom now? Why did he begin to envision a real future together?

She was watching him, waiting, and he could tell to the moment when the doubts set in. Her lower lip trembled, and her eyes dipped down at the corners.

"Stop," he said, taking her hands in his again. "I can see you fretting. What can I say? That your kiss humbled me?

That I am in awe of you?"

She giggled, but she did not pull out of his grip. "Don't be silly."

It hadn't been a joke, but if it put a smile back on her face, he would not argue. "Perhaps I like being silly around you. You are one of a few who allows it."

She sobered. "It must be difficult, being on guard at all times."

He pulled away. "I was trained for this." The fact reminded him of his duty. He glanced around, assessing their surroundings. The crowd still thronged the confectioners', and a number were ogling him and Callie. What she might have heard if they were closer.

One man separated himself from the group and headed in their direction.

"Your father is here," Fritz told her, and she swiveled to look.

Fritz rose as the duke approached. Those long strides could mask anger, but that set face was impossible to read. Had he seen Fritz kissing Callie? He could still hardly credit she had allowed it.

"Your Grace," he acknowledged with a nod.

"Count," Callie's father greeted, voice clipped. Then he turned to his daughter. "Ready to go home, Calantha?"

She hesitated, and for a moment Fritz thought she would insist on staying with him. But she stepped to her father's side instead. "Of course, Father." She looked to Fritz. "When will you call?"

Said so plaintively, he wanted to assure her it would be immediately, but he rather thought her father would be less tolerant, supposed betrothal notwithstanding. "Might you be available on Sunday afternoon for a drive through the park?"

"A ride would be more appropriate," the duke said. "I believe you were looking for a mount, my lord."

He shouldn't have used that excuse for conversation

earlier. "I regret we have not had the opportunity to purchase riding horses since arriving in England," Fritz admitted.

"I'll see one is made available to you," he said. "Three in the afternoon will be sufficient."

Riding instead of sitting together in a carriage, a strange horse Fritz would have to pay attention to guiding: the duke was giving Fritz and Callie no opportunity to repeat that kiss.

"You are too kind, Your Grace," Fritz said.

The duke inclined his head, and Fritz bowed. Callie's father led her off to their waiting carriage, leaving Fritz to find his own way back to the palace.

And giving him entirely too much time to brood over what had happened.

Yet how could he call himself a man and refuse that sweet look? She deserved to know he found her attractive, for it seemed she struggled to see herself that way. He could have happily pummeled the governesses and other ladies who had caused her to think less of herself when she was so much more.

Then there was their quest. They had confirmed Mr. Eager was a member of the House of Commons, but they still had no way to identify him. Worse, Fritz had allowed his feelings to come between him and his duty, and that was unacceptable.

He was glad Saturday was reserved for training with the rest of the Imperial Guard, for it gave his mind something else to focus on. He had hand-chosen all but the oldest guardsman, Johann Wyss, who had originally trained under his father. And Wyss was the only one who knew all of what had happened during the war with France.

But even in training, Fritz had trouble remembering his duty.

"You are slowing," his second in command told him as their swords clanged against each other that morning in the front courtyard between the two wings of the palace. "Your mind is elsewhere."

Several of the other guardsmen exchanged grins. Likely they expected him to be thinking about Callie. Word of his supposed betrothal had spread through the palace, and more than one of the staff had emboldened themselves to congratulate him.

Still, his guardsmen would not be in error that Callie was on his mind now. That kiss had stayed with him all night and into today. He pushed Wyss back.

"We are *all* slow today," he declared, lowering his blade. "What is it?"

Two of his newer guardsmen, Keller and Huber, looked to Wyss. A craggy fellow, with hair the color of his sword and eyes as sharp, his grizzled chin worked a moment before he spoke his mind.

"We saw that report in the British paper," he told Fritz. "They call us brutes, barbarians."

The others nodded.

Fritz glanced around. "And this troubles you?"

Keller stood taller, sunlight glinting on his blond hair. "*Nein.* They will fear us now."

"That could be to our advantage," Huber agreed with a nod of his dark head.

Fritz sheathed his sword. "We did not come here to invade. We came here to see our lands returned."

"So we can go home," Keller said.

The others frowned at him, and he dropped his gaze and fiddled with the hilt of his own sword.

"I know you long for home," Fritz told them all. "So do I. But home is where we are surrounded by those we love, those we protect. Home is here with us."

Other heads were nodding now.

"Home is also where our comrades are buried," Wyss said, deep voice a rumble. "We left many behind. We must do them proud."

He looked to Fritz, who nodded. Though sorely tried, he had never betrayed his country, but that did not mean a part of him hadn't been buried there.

A movement at the edge of the graveled courtyard caught his eye, and Fritz turned to face it, hand going to his sword. Lawrence trotted out of the shadows of the building and blinked in the sunlight.

"Excuse me, my lord, but I was hoping for a word."

Fritz tipped up his chin to Wyss. "Rifle drill next."

Wyss clapped his fist to his chest in salute.

Fritz loped to join the chamberlain. "Is there a problem?"

For the first time he could remember, Lawrence hesitated. He glanced right, left, as if thinking the enemy was hiding behind one of the alabaster pillars that edged the courtyard. "I fear I must apologize, my lord. I have failed Batavaria."

Fritz drew up short. "What? How?"

Lawrence was twisting his hands together in front of his tailored coat, and Fritz was reminded of Callie. He gentled his voice. "You have ever been a loyal supporter of the House of Archambault, Lord Chamberlain. I doubt anything you could do would change that."

By the depth of Lawrence's sigh, the chamberlain had his own doubts. "This report in the newspaper, it is my fault."

Fritz frowned at him. "How could that be?"

He cringed as if even the memory hurt. "A reporter came to see me, asking questions. I remembered what you and His Majesty said—that circumstances had conspired to make the English think we are weak. And if their king thought us weak, he would never support our request to regain our lands."

"So you assured the reporter we are strong," Fritz guessed.

Lawrence sighed, the skin of his skull turning a deeper

pink through his sparse hair. "Strong, yes, but never cruel. I cannot understand how I gave him the impression otherwise."

"It may not have been you," Fritz told him. "Some in England are working against us. They may have given the reporter the wrong impression, and he was looking for words that would reinforce it."

"And I provided them to him," Lawrence lamented.

"You did what you thought best," Fritz allowed. "Now we must do all we can to show England that we are a civilized nation, a people worthy of their support, and preferably before we meet with their king on Tuesday."

If only he knew how to go about it.

CHAPTER TEN

CALLIE WAS NO good to anyone on Saturday. She ended up hiding in the library for a good part of the day, until Thal came to demand she join a game of bouts-rhyme with the family. The game involved writing a poem using five words in certain positions. The one she created with the words her brother provided was far from her finest work.

"I suppose bits does rhyme with Fritz," Tuny allowed, though Larissa raised her brows and Belle smirked.

She was only thankful they did not question her. And when Belle called for a meeting that night in Larissa's room, Callie did not volunteer what had happened at Gunter's.

Fritz had kissed her.

Kissed her.

She could not convince herself she had dreamed it. The sensations still continued to haunt her—the firm pressure of his lips, tasting of raspberry ice; the warmth of his caress on her cheek; the joy of being wanted, cherished.

If that kiss had been a figment of her fevered imagination, why did these feelings persist?

If it had been real, what did it mean for her future with Fritz?

"Callie!"

She blinked, and Belle's face came into focus. Her younger sister was sitting next to Larissa against the pillows of Larissa's bed while Callie sat with Tuny on the blue and white coverlet at the foot.

"Sorry," Callie said. "What did you need of me?"

"We are here to talk about Tuny," her sister informed her. "Larissa is engaged, and everyone thinks you're engaged, so it's her turn."

Tuny shifted beside Callie. "Don't see why. You started this vow. You should get a turn."

"I will," Belle promised her. "But you've been out longer. Everyone will expect you to garner an offer first."

Tuny shook her head, her blond hair sticking to the flannel of her nightgown. "But you're the belle of the ball." She grinned. "Pun intended."

The others all smiled. Belle turned to Callie. "So, what have you heard? Has any particular gentleman expressed admiration for Petunia?"

Her sister was just trying to help, but she didn't seem to realize the harm the answer to that question could do. It was as bad as Fritz asking what others thought of him. However she answered, Tuny might not be pleased. Indeed, a frown was forming on her friend's face as the others waited for Callie to answer.

She cast her mind back, trying to find any snippet that might reflect well on Tuny.

"Alpheas Turner," she said. "He was standing just behind us a few weeks ago and commented that he had seldom met a more engaging lady than Miss Bateman."

Tuny's frown eased.

Belle shook her head. "It's no good. He's announced his engagement to a Jamaican heiress."

"Oh," Tuny said, slumping. "That's that, then."

"There must be other gentlemen," Belle insisted. "What about Lord Ashforde? I'm sure I saw him glancing your way more than once."

"Only to find fault, most likely," Tuny informed her. "If you must settle on someone, you might see what we can learn about Owen Canady. He stood up with me the other night, and I won't deny he has a certain charm."

Belle rubbed her hands together. "Perfect. I haven't had the pleasure of meeting Mr. Canady. Larissa?"

"Neither have I," Larissa admitted. "But he might not approach if he knows I'm betrothed."

"Callie?" Belle asked.

She had already been searching her memory. "Warm voice, just a hint of an Irish accent?" she asked Tuny.

"That's him," Tuny agreed eagerly.

"He's new to town," Callie said. "Staying with a friend, but he didn't say who."

"So no one prestigious enough to mention," Larissa mused.

"And he is very fond of his horse, Jasper," Callie continued. "I've heard him speak three times, and he always found a way to mention the horse."

Tuny blew out a breath. "Well, perhaps he's not the fellow for me, then. I barely ride."

Belle waved a hand. "You've been doing splendidly. Besides, Jasper may be a racehorse, not a riding horse. We will watch for Mr. Canady while we're out and see if we can convince him to call."

The plan agreed, they separated to their own rooms.

"I haven't given up on you, you know," Belle said as she and Callie climbed into their own beds. "I'm sure we can find a happy solution once this betrothal between you and Fritz is sorted out."

Callie made a noncommittal noise and pulled the covers up over her head.

She spent Sunday morning at services and part of the afternoon working on the preparations for the benefit dinner, which was now a little less than a week away. But she was downstairs, in her riding habit, shortly before three.

Their town house featured a mews behind it, where her father kept a quartet of riding horses. Callie had ridden each of them before, so she wasn't surprised to glance out the window and see a groom coming around the front of the house holding her father's favorite, a spirited roan gelding named Atticus, along with her favorite, a black mare Belle had dubbed Tandy.

"Very kind of you to allow Fritz to ride one of our horses," she told her father as he came down the stairs. She swallowed as another thought occurred to her. "Or were you planning to come too?"

"Not today," he said, and she smiled, until he added, "but Belle and Thal will be joining you."

Of course her reticent father would never mention having seen Fritz kiss her in public, but she could only wonder whether he was taking every precaution to prevent it from happening again. Either way, Belle was soon standing beside Callie in the entry hall, in her navy riding habit with its black braid crossing her chest and a flat black riding hat covering her curls.

"That looks very good on you," she said approvingly, nodding to Callie's cerulean blue habit with its double row of gold buttons down the front and the white lace jabot held in place with a cameo pin.

Callie tucked a few strands of hair back under the top hat. Anna did her best, but Callie's hair was so fine it frequently slipped from its pins. "Thank you. I hope you won't find me a slug."

Belle smiled. "Never fear. I intend to ride ahead with Thal and allow you and Fritz time to converse about things more important than the weather."

Before Callie could comment, her sister pasted on a smile as their father returned to the house after talking with the groom about the four horses that now stood waiting. "Hello, Father. It's a lovely day for a ride."

"It is indeed." His own smile appeared as their mother came to join them too. He slipped an arm about her waist, and she leaned into him.

Larissa had once told Callie to find a gentleman that fit well beside her. Suddenly, Callie knew her sister was right. Callie needed a gentleman that fit her like her mother and father fit, completing each other, helping each other fulfill their dreams. If Belle remained fixed on looking for a gentleman for Callie, that's the sort of man Callie should request.

She would not dwell on the fact that Fritz's face came first to mind.

Her mother tipped her chin to the open door. "He looks well on a horse. Tell me how he rides when you return."

Callie looked out and caught her breath. The royal carriage must have left Fritz at their door, for he was already astride Atticus, grip on the reins as if he had been born there.

"This should be fun," Belle said.

"No racing," their father warned as Callie followed her out the door.

"No promises," Belle whispered to Callie with a grin and a toss of her golden curls.

Thal ran down the steps to join them, and soon all four were riding into Hyde Park, a short distance from Clarendon Square. The surprising heat of the July day had deterred many who would otherwise have been strolling along the paths, and the shade from the tall trees was most welcome. The still air was like a cozy blanket around Callie. With a wink, Belle urged her horse ahead, taking Thal with her.

Fritz drew Atticus abreast of Tandy. "Did you arrange that?"

"No," Callie admitted. "That was Belle's idea."

"I must thank her," Fritz said with a smile.

"She's hoping we'll spend the time billing and cooing," Callie explained, face feeling warmer at the very idea. "She knows we aren't really engaged. I simply couldn't hide the fact from my sisters and Tuny, but she's trying to fulfill the vow Larissa, her, Tuny, and I made to each other, that all four of us will be wed by harvest."

His brows shot up. "So, you could not keep the secret entirely."

She swallowed. "No. Sorry. But they won't tell anyone."

"Apparently not," he allowed. "And I can understand why you might want to tell them, close as you are. I should have realized this pretend engagement would hinder your plans for the Season."

"Not mine," she assured him. "Belle's. I never really thought I'd find the perfect gentleman."

He was quiet a moment, and she wondered whether she'd given him a disgust of her. Then he asked, "And who is the perfect gentleman?"

After her realization in the entry hall, she knew the answer. The perfect gentleman for her was someone who valued her enough to truly see who she was. Someone for whom she would never be invisible.

Someone like him.

No, *not* someone like him! Someone quiet, calm, thoughtful. Someone who would never embroil himself, or her, in scandal. Someone who wouldn't expect her to stretch to the very limits of her abilities.

Someone it wouldn't hurt to love.

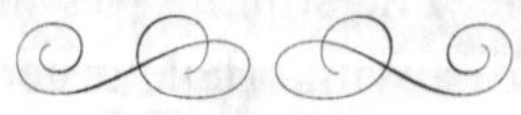

Callie was quiet so long Fritz began to think he'd blundered. But he couldn't call the question back. There had been a longing in her voice, along with a note of loss, as if she knew she would never find the man for her.

Even as he began to wonder whether he could be that man.

"There are no perfect gentlemen," she said at last, far more blithely than the haunted look in her eyes attested. "No perfect ladies, either. Now, we don't know when Thal will grow bored of our ride and want to go home. Let's talk of more important matters. How are we to find Mr. Eager and his colleague from Württemberg?"

Fritz wasn't sure whether to be relieved or disappointed she had not really answered him. "We now know for certain he is a member of the House of Commons."

"But we are no closer to picking him out of the dozens in the chamber," she protested as they rode out of the trees onto a wider sweep of green lawn.

"There's always the Monday session," he said, glancing her way. "Willing to give it another try?"

"Not in the Women's Gallery," she said with a shake of her head that threatened to unseat her hat from her platinum tresses. "It's impossible to see more than the top of a few men's heads. And we can't be assured he'll speak. We need to catch him in conversation."

"When they stroll the corridors, then," Fritz suggested, "before and after the session."

"Before the session," she said. "We are expected to take part in a musicale Monday evening."

He tried to imagine her standing up in front of a dozen or more of her father's peers. "Do you sing?"

She seemed to be studying the reins in her hand, as if she suddenly wasn't sure what to do with them when he'd admired how she rode since the moment the groom had boosted her into the saddle. "No. I play the pianoforte for Belle."

So, she hid behind her bubbly sister. Clever tactic. It took the focus off of her while still allowing her to take part in Society. "I'm sure your sister is appreciative."

"She is. She has a beautiful voice. It's a pleasure to accompany her." Her proud smile faded as her brother cantered back toward them, Belle just behind.

"It's dull as ditchwater this afternoon," he complained. "Belle refuses to race. What about you, Callie?"

She turned a pretty shade of pink. "Father asked us not to."

Her brother sighed as Belle pulled abreast of them.

"Your father didn't ask me," Fritz pointed out.

Thal grinned. "Rotten Row, then."

Callie reined in her horse, forcing Fritz and the others to do likewise. "No, Thal. Count Montalban has already attracted unwanted attention. Racing in Hyde Park will do his reputation no good. And you know Mother would worry for you."

Thal rolled his eyes. "Oh, very well. But you can be sure I'll find someone more amendable to manage my household." He pressed his heels to his mount and took off down the path.

"Manage his household?" Fritz asked as soon as Belle apologized and went pelting off after her brother, leaving a few indignant cries in her wake from passersby.

The pink in Callie's cheeks was only deepening as they urged their mounts to follow her brother and sister on the graveled path. "Thal offered to let me live with him and manage his household should I end up a spinster. Apparently, I must look for other lodgings."

Only if she ended up a spinster.

He didn't say the words aloud. He was in no position to offer for a bride. First, he had to get his own house in order.

They finished their ride, and Callie agreed to meet him at Parliament the next day. He wasn't sure why she didn't want him to bring the carriage to Weyfarer House to fetch her. Perhaps she feared her father would assign them chaperones again. As it was, Miss Bateman and a strapping fellow with dark hair and equally dark eyes were waiting for him near the entrance to the regal building. Fritz might have taken the man for a footman, but the cut of his coat was too fine, the swagger in his step too pronounced, for a servant.

"Count Montalban," Callie said when Fritz joined them, "allow me to present Sir Matthew Bateman, Petunia's brother."

The fellow eyed him a moment as if sizing him up, and Fritz met him look for look. Sir Matthew stuck out a meaty palm. "Pleased to meet you, my lord."

Fritz took his hand in a firm grip. "And you, Sir Matthew."

"My brother investigates mysteries," Petunia announced.

Sir Matthew shrugged his massive shoulders. "Hobby. But I have had some little luck. Tuny tells me you and Callie are looking for a member of the House she heard talking poorly about you and your family. I don't suppose you have more details to offer."

Fritz looked to Callie.

"A little taller than me," she said, "but not as tall as you and Fritz. Blond hair, fairly straight and pomaded in place. Slender."

Sir Matthew quirked a dark brow. "Could cover half the fellows in Parliament and a good portion of their clerks."

Callie sighed. "I know. If only I could hear him speak."

Sir Matthew nodded thoughtfully. "Tell you what. Come inside with me, and follow my lead. You too, my lord."

Fritz was used to giving orders, not receiving them except from his father and brother, but there was something about Tuny's brother that told him it would be wise to comply. He followed them into the building.

And Sir Matthew set about accosting every blond,

slender fellow they came upon.

"Ho, there, you," he said to the first who was striding past. "What's your opinion on this latest bill sent over from Liverpool?"

Tall and gaunt, he stopped long enough to look Tuny's brother up and down. "Who wants to know?"

Callie, standing close behind Sir Matthew, shook her head.

"Never you mind," Sir Matthew said and stalked off to find the next fellow.

"Ingenious," Fritz murmured to Callie. "I wish I'd thought of it."

"Your accent would give you away as a foreigner," she whispered back. "It's better this way. If Sir Matthew finds Mr. Eager, you'll be on hand to take him aside and question him."

And so they made their way up and down the corridors. Only a few fellows showed reluctance to answer Sir Matthew's questioning. Most took one look at his size and scowling face and stammered answers readily enough.

"He was a pugilist of some renown," his sister explained to Fritz as if she'd noticed him watching in admiration. "The Beast of Birmingham, they called him. He saved the king's life when he was still the prince. That's why Matthew was elevated to baronet. He wasn't born to it." She cast Fritz a look.

He hadn't been born to his title either, for all he was the second son of a king. In Batavaria, only the first born was accorded the honor and title of prince. Leo had beat him to it by less than a quarter hour, according to the stories.

Most days, he didn't mind. Leo could never have wandered about the House of Commons demanding answers. His sphere was strategy and diplomacy. Fritz preferred the physical.

Unfortunately, no matter how many slender, blond

members of the House of Commons Sir Matthew approached, Callie kept shaking her head.

"This is maddening," she said when they regrouped after most of the Parliamentarians had gone into the chamber. "Did he simply not attend today?"

"Or did we miss him entirely?" Fritz ventured, gaze swinging around the space.

"Happy to do this again tomorrow," Sir Matthew offered, cracking his knuckles.

Fritz sighed. "Unfortunately, my brother and I have an appointment tomorrow with your king."

Sir Matthew clapped him on the shoulder, nearly oversetting him. "Good for you. He's a bit mad, our king. Not like his father," he hurried to add. "Just has his own ideas about doing things. Otherwise, he would never have knighted a bodyguard like me."

"Sometimes I think my father, the king, is a bit mad too," Fritz confided. "Otherwise, he wouldn't have made the Captain of the Imperial Guards a count."

Sir Matthew nodded thoughtfully. "We both have had to deal with unexpected elevations. But, since they've seen fit to raise us to their stature, the least we can do is look them in the eyes and tell them the truth, even if they don't want to hear it."

Fritz could only agree, but somehow he didn't think Leo would share his views and neither would King George, especially if Mr. Eager and his cohort had been poisoning the monarch's mind.

CHAPTER ELEVEN

CALLIE PLAYED FOR Belle at the musicale that evening, but her mind was elsewhere. She barely heard the applause as her sister finished, but she rose and dutifully followed Belle back to their seats near her parents and Larissa on the spindle-backed gilt chairs that had been brought in for the event. She couldn't have said what else was played and sung.

She was sorting through options to locate Mr. Eager.

They could hardly enlist Sir Matthew every day on the chance the Parliamentarian would be in the right place at the right time to make his acquaintance. Neither could they be certain the fellow would attend any of the events they planned to attend. She knew every man in the room tonight, had heard each speak at one time or another. They were not the men Fritz sought.

What, did she and Fritz need to put an advertisement in *The Times*? Wanted: Information on the men plotting to discredit and destroy the Batavarian court. Even those accusations might make things difficult with King George.

She was still ruminating, safely ensconced in the library, on Monday when the door opened, and Aunt Meredith and Fortune came in. As her aunt set the cat onto the carpet, showing every intention of making herself at home, Callie surged to her feet from behind the desk.

Aunt Meredith straightened and held up a hand. "Do

not offer to find your mother, your father, your sisters, Petunia, or the cook. I came to speak to you."

As if to prove it, Fortune scampered to one of the upholstered chairs and sprang up onto the seat to regard Callie expectantly.

Saying a prayer for strength, Callie sank onto the chair behind the desk. "Of course, Aunt. What did you need of me?"

"The truth," she said, going to one of the other chairs and spreading her fashionable lavender skirts to sit. "Are you happy being engaged to Count Montalban?"

Callie nearly tipped back her head in relief. *That* question she was perfectly capable of answering without betraying her agreement with Fritz. "Yes. Very happy."

Aunt Meredith cocked her head, dark curl brushing her cheek. "Why do I sense there's more to that answer?"

She should have known it couldn't be that easy. "I'm not sure what you want me to say."

Fortune slipped off the chair and padded around the desk to eye Callie as if just as determined to learn her secret.

"Tell me you love him," Aunt Meredith said. "Tell me you can't wait to be his bride. Tell me you see a glorious future together."

Callie couldn't tell her any of those things. Tears burned her eyes, and she bent and gathered Fortune into her arms to hide the fact.

"That bad?" Aunt Meredith asked gently.

"Not bad," Callie hedged, one hand stroking the silky fur. "It's difficult for me to talk about my feelings for Fritz. But I will tell you this. I find him the most admirable of men. Just standing beside him emboldens me, as if I have absorbed some of his supreme confidence. I don't know what the future holds, but I am quite satisfied with the present."

She glanced up to find Aunt Meredith smiling at her.

"That is a very good beginning," her aunt allowed. "Perhaps Fortune and I can help."

The cat wiggled, and Callie set her down. Fortune sent her an arch look before going to patrol the corners of the room, as if intent on finding a mouse or claiming the space as her own.

"Everyone is trying to help," Callie told her aunt, leaning back in the chair. "Belle, Larissa, Tuny, Father, Mother. Is it possible that I might know my own mind?"

"Entirely possible," Aunt Meredith said, leaning back as well. "And equally possible that Count Montalban does not know his mind. I will look for opportunities. In the meantime, Julian and I are very looking forward to your benefit. How go the preparations?"

Callie blinked back the last of her tears and focused on the other subject nearly as dear to her heart. It was only later, after her aunt had taken Fortune and gone to speak to Callie's mother, that Callie realized Aunt Meredith had never explained what she meant by opportunities.

The confines of the royal carriage had never felt cramped until Fritz climbed in after Leo and Lord Belfort following their meeting with King George on Tuesday. The satin-padded walls were so tight around him he nearly braced both hands against them with the idea of holding them at bay. A shame it wasn't the walls but his circumstances that were closing him in.

"We will never gain his support after this," he told the other two men.

Leo and the solicitor exchanged glances. Fritz knew it was their role to placate and cajole, but neither response was palatable at the moment.

"He gave us leave to approach him again at a more

opportune time," Lord Belfort reminded him, one finger stroking his reddish-gold mustache. "That alone might be considered a victory."

Fritz snorted and turned his gaze out the window.

"Clarendon Square next," Leo said to no one in particular. "I promised to tell Larissa about the results of our meeting."

Dismal though they were.

Still, Fritz couldn't help the way his spirits lifted. It was the thought of seeing Callie again. When she looked at him with eyes full of trust and faith, he felt as if there were nothing he couldn't do. At the moment, even a little taste of hope would help. After all, she was the only one who could help him run these rumors to ground.

Lord Belfort made his excuses as they stepped down in front of Weyfarer House.

"Lady Belfort will be as eager to know the outcome as Lady Larissa. I will await your instructions as to our next move, Your Highness, Count Montalban." He inclined his head and started down the block toward his own town house.

The butler let them in immediately and ushered them into the withdrawing room. "The duke and duchess are out on calls, but the ladies and young gentlemen are busy with preparations for the upcoming benefit," he offered. "I'm sure they'll see you shortly." He bowed himself out of the room.

Leo waited beside the sofa, but Fritz paced to the hearth and back under the watchful eyes of the duchess in the portrait above. The painting showed her surrounded by her three daughters and two sons. There was no mistaking Callie. That pale hair, those luminous eyes. The look on her face was assessing, as if the painter alone had seen the depths in her.

He saw those depths, and he was humbled by them.

He was only glad she and Larissa appeared to have left

the others behind when they hurried in a few moments later. Callie took one look at him, and her smile of welcome evaporated.

Larissa glided to the sofa and spread her green plaid skirts to sit. "Leo, Fritz, how nice to see you."

Only her sister could be so poised. She and Leo were well-matched, for he went calmly to join her. Fritz dropped onto the chair closest to Callie's as she sat.

"How did the meeting go?" Larissa asked, gaze on his brother.

Leo was enough of a diplomat that his smile did not waver. "It was a beginning."

"It was a disaster," Fritz argued, unable to keep the anger from his voice. "He made us no promises."

Callie's fingers tightened around each other in the lap of her soft pink gown.

Leo spread his hands. "This is the way of kings. You ought to know that."

Fritz clamped his mouth shut to keep from making a harsh retort.

"I don't understand," Callie said, glancing between the two of them. "The king agreed to meet with you. What did he think you wanted by an audience if not to petition his help?"

"He knew," Leo answered, shoulders coming down as if he felt the weight of his responsibilities anew. "He was well informed about what we planned to request, more so than Lord Belfort and I had been led to believe."

"Someone has been filling his ears," Fritz agreed, hands pressed against the black trousers of his dress uniform.

"His Majesty expressed concern for his subjects," Leo said. "That is his duty."

"And our duty is to Batavaria," Fritz said. The anger, the frustration, pushed him from his seat. He was no fit company for Callie at the moment. "Excuse me." He stalked from the room before his emotions got the better of him and he did or said something he would regret.

Callie rose as well as Fritz disappeared through the door, taking some of the energy in the room with him. She had had all her sisters, brothers, and Tuny working on place cards for the upcoming benefit, the thick paper, list of names, bottles of ink, blotters, and quills scattered around the dining table, when Underhill had announced they had visitors. Even though the dinner was only days away now, she would never be too busy to see Fritz. Besides, like Larissa, she was dying to know how their fateful meeting had gone with the king. She could only conclude that things must have gone badly indeed if Fritz could not even bring himself to speak of them.

"Shouldn't we go after him?" she asked his brother and Larissa.

"Fritz will come around," Leo said with a sigh. He turned to her sister. "What were your plans for the evening?"

How could they sit there and talk of commonplaces when Fritz was obviously in pain? She frowned at Leo, but neither he nor Larissa appeared to notice. It seemed Callie was invisible again. She turned and went after Fritz.

Underhill was directing Davis on the cleaning of the chandelier in the entry hall. Callie stepped up to him. "Have you seen Count Montalban?"

Their butler tipped his head toward the door. "Count Montalban had to take his leave. But I believe you'll find it a lovely day for a walk in the park, your ladyship. Davis can accompany you."

Their footman eagerly began untying the strings on his long apron.

"Thank you," Callie told their butler before he opened

the door for her with an encouraging smile.

A moment later, and she and Davis were across the street in the park that lay in the center of Clarendon Square. The tall green trees, artfully trimmed shrubs, and banks of flowers usually allowed her to breathe a little more freely. They also made it easy to spot that black uniform.

"Fritz!"

He stopped at her call and waited for her to reach him. Davis stayed respectfully a few feet away.

"I'm so sorry the king wouldn't listen," she told him.

He shook his head, sunlight threading through his curly hair. "We barely broached the subject. He spent most of the time expounding on the duties of a monarch, as if Leo hadn't been trained in the art since he was born."

"King George probably doesn't have the opportunity to teach," Callie reasoned. "His only daughter died when I was twelve. The whole country went into mourning. His heir will likely be one of his brothers or their children."

His impressive chest relaxed just the slightest. "I could forgive him if I thought he only sought to pass along his knowledge. But it was clear he had heard stories, and he did not like them."

"Stories?" she asked. "But Leo and your father have done nothing wrong."

"Our father caused a few incidents over the years," he told her. "He does not suffer fools gladly. But that wasn't what concerned your king. He had heard stories about me."

Callie stiffened. "Not those rumors about the seductions!"

"He was careful not to specify," he allowed. "But it was clear by his mention of our duty to the fairer sex that he had heard the rumors. And there was the story in the newspaper. He spent a full quarter hour on the duty to one's servants and staff."

Callie shuddered. "Oh, Fritz, I'm so sorry! Couldn't you explain?"

"He gave us no opportunity." The anger was back in his voice. "You don't interrupt a king. I learned that at an early age."

"Not even your father?" Callie asked.

"Especially my father. The Lion of the Alps has quite a roar."

Callie put a hand on his arm. "Then we must show King George that you are above reproach."

He covered her hand with his. "Thank you. He did congratulate Leo and me on our recent betrothals. He made it sound as if being connected with the Duke of Wey was one of the only things in our favor."

Callie swallowed. If the king found Fritz acceptable because of his supposed engagement to her, how would he react when he learned that she had cried off? Would he take it to mean Fritz was a monster after all?

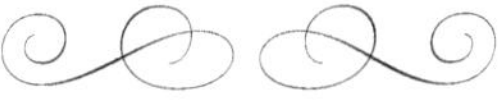

Amazing how the touch of her hand, the kindness in her voice, made the world seem brighter.

"There must be other ways to show you in a favorable light," she said now.

Fritz chuckled as he tucked her arm in his and turned to wander the flowered-bordered paths. "Your Saint George is famous for fighting off a dragon, I understand."

"We have no more dragons, alas," she told him. "And we don't want you to be known for fighting."

"No damsels in need of rescue?" he teased as they turned onto another path leading back toward Weyfarer House. "Wrongs needing made right?"

Her head came up, until he could have brushed his cheek against the silk. "Yes, of course! The benefit. You and Leo will be attending. The society numbers many Parliamentarians and other respected gentlemen among its members, including Mr. Wilberforce and Reverend Broome. If you're seen with them, surely others will notice."

He had heard of this Wilberforce, a man who had championed the abolition of slavery. Associating with him might indeed go far to promote their cause, while furthering Callie's cause at the same time. He owed her that at least.

"We will be there," he promised her. "It would be expected that I support your efforts, as your intended groom."

"It certainly would." She smiled at him. "And I know the Batavarian court will be generous."

She could not know that the Batavarian court had overextended its credit, but Leo had promised to see what could be done, and Fritz would make sure of it. If spending money protecting animals would impress King George, even Lawrence could be made to see reason.

"Is there anything I can do to help?" he asked.

She glanced up at him. "I should be asking you that question. I've been trying to think of another way to find Mr. Eager."

Fritz sighed as they approached the wrought-iron gate that led onto the pavement. "Given my reception by King George, my investigation will go nowhere until I can clear myself in the eyes of the British."

"And, in the meantime, we leave your enemies to continue plotting." She made a face as if the notion was unacceptable.

Fritz shrugged though something inside him protested. "Who knows? Perhaps Mr. Eager and his colleague from Württemberg are a member of your society."

She jerked to a stop, giving her footman time to edge around them and open the gate for her. But Callie didn't go through.

"They most certainly are not," she told Fritz, blue eyes snapping fire. "Everyone in the society is dedicated to the eradication of pain and suffering, even in our loyal companions, the animals. They would never plot to harm you!"

"Not with you looking at them that way," Fritz agreed, chastised.

She blushed, gaze falling. "I'm sure how I look has nothing to do with the matter. I will keep thinking, about how to find your enemies and about how you can help with the benefit. The latter will be far easier, I fear."

CHAPTER TWELVE

CALLIE AND PETUNIA spent Wednesday morning going over arrangements for the benefit with Mr. Broome, secretary for the society. Aunt Meredith accompanied them as chaperone. The rotund reverend could not have been more pleased with their plans, though his pudgy fingers trembled just the slightest as he pointed out a few things on their list yet to be accomplished.

"I consider myself something of an orator," he said, "but I fear I may not have the presence to command the prices you hope from the wonderful art that has been donated. Have we considered hiring an auctioneer?" He paused to take out a handkerchief and mop his brow. Once again, the day was warm, and Callie was glad she and Tuny had worn their lightest sprigged muslin walking dresses for the interview at the minister's vicarage.

Tuny made a note on the list with a pencil. "We'll see to it."

He leaned back in his chair as Tuny folded the note to put in her reticule. "I can hardly wait, ladies. We are so fortunate for your patronage. Please thank your esteemed father, Lady Calantha, and your excellent brother-in-law, Miss Bateman."

"You notice he didn't thank Matthew or Ivy," Tuny pointed out when she, Callie, and Meredith were seated in the duke's town carriage for the ride back to Clarendon

Square.

"Merely an oversight, I hope," Aunt Meredith said soothingly. "Everyone has done their utmost to make sure this benefit is a success."

"Now, if we can just resolve these last few issues," Callie said, mind going to the list.

They were still debating next steps as they climbed down in front of Weyfarer House. Aunt Meredith left them there to walk to her town house, and Callie and Tuny continued up to the door, which Underhill was holding open. In the quiet of the entry hall, the voices from the withdrawing room sounded all the more loudly. One had an unmistakable accent to it.

Callie clutched the butler's arm. "Who's with Mother?"

"Mr. von Mandelsloh," Underhill replied, slight frown attesting to his curiosity. "I take it he's from one of the embassies. He came seeking your father."

"What's wrong?" Tuny asked as Callie stood frozen, listening. "Do you know him?"

"I might," Callie allowed. "And he's the last person I'd expect to find here." She turned to the butler. "He may be a villain, Underhill. Be on your guard."

Tuny's eyes widened in obvious surprise, even as the butler stood taller.

"I will, your ladyship," Underhill vowed. "But if he is a villain, perhaps we should simply throw him out on his ear." He looked particularly eager to do so.

"No," Callie told him. "At least, not until I know for sure. Petunia, I'll meet you in the library."

"Of course," Tuny agreed, hurrying down the corridor.

Callie's pulse was pounding in her ears. Every time she and Fritz had discussed finding those who wished his family harm, it had been with the understanding that she'd point them out, and he'd pursue the matter in his usual style. But Fritz wasn't here now, and there was no way she could keep Mr. von Mandelsloh at Weyfarer

House long enough to send Fritz a note and have him travel back into town to confront the fellow.

If she wanted to make sure she was right, she would have to do it alone. She drew in a fortifying breath and straightened her spine. Surely, if Fritz could spend a good portion of his life pretending to be his brother, the crown prince, she could pretend for a few moments that she was brave enough to beard a lion.

She sailed into the withdrawing room as if she didn't know it was occupied, then paused. "Oh, Mother. I didn't realize you had plans to be at home this morning."

Her mother nodded from her place on the sofa, blue cambric day dress settled about her. "Come in, Callie. This is Herr von Mandelsloh, Envoy for Württemberg. He was just telling me how much he admires Prince Otto Leopold and Count Montalban."

Mr. von Mandelsloh, who had stood on Callie's entrance, offered her a congenial smile. In his tailored navy coat and fawn trousers, it was clear that he was of medium height, with a slender build. But his hair was more sandy than blond, trickling over a high forehead.

Say one word. One word, and I'll know.

"Admire might be too strong a word," he said, and Callie nearly sagged. The accent was right, but the voice was wrong.

She couldn't very well just turn and walk out, much as she wanted to, without embarrassing her family, so she made herself go and sit beside her mother, so he could return to his seat across from them.

"Herr von Mandelsloh," her mother said, "this is my daughter, Lady Calantha. She's betrothed to Count Montalban."

"Ah," he said with a thoughtful nod. "So the rumors are true."

Callie smiled politely back. "Yes, although you may have noticed a great number of rumors circulating about the count."

"So my secretary has informed me," he acknowledged. "It is, alas, the fate of all men determined to make their presence felt."

"And was it those rumors that prompted you to seek my husband?" her mother asked, head cocked.

"I have only recently returned to your fair isle," he said, "but my secretary tells me that His Grace is interested in the history of one of our provinces. I sought merely to be of service clearing up any misperceptions."

Meaning he wanted to make sure Callie's father knew Württemberg's side of the story about what was happening in Batavaria.

"I think you'll find that my husband rarely has misperceptions," her mother said. "But I will be sure he knows that you called." She rose, forcing the envoy to his feet once more as well. "Please send our regards to your king and assure him that we ever have the best interests of the Batavarian people at heart."

"You are too kind." He bowed to her and Callie, then made his way to the door. Callie craned her neck to make sure he had left. Then she stood and threw her arms about her mother.

"Oh, Mother! You handled him so well!"

Her mother returned her hug. "I'm glad you approve, but I feel as if I've come in on the third act. Why, exactly, did the Envoy from Württemberg need such careful handing?"

"Just as you surmised," Callie said, disengaging. "He came in an attempt to sway Father from involving himself further in the cause of Batavarian restitution. We must go out to the Chelsea Palace and tell Fritz."

Her mother's dark eyes narrowed. "Now?"

"Yes," Callie said. "It's terribly important."

Her mother raised a brow, waiting.

That was all it took for loyalties to rise inside Callie,

take up arms, and advance on each other. She couldn't betray Fritz, but how could she continue lying to her mother? Her mother might not realize it, but she'd filled a hole in Callie's heart that no one else ever had. Was there a way to be true to both Fritz and her mother?

Callie plunked down on the sofa. "The night Father found Fritz and me on the terrace at the Marquess of Kendall's home, I overheard two men planning to harm the Batavarian court. I didn't get a good look at them. Fritz and I have been trying to find them ever since."

Her mother sat beside her. "And Herr von Mandelsloh is one of them?"

Callie shook her head. "I thought he might be when I first heard his accent. But it wasn't him. Still, Fritz needs to know that the envoy has returned to England and that our conspirator may well be a member of his staff, perhaps this secretary he kept mentioning."

"Herr von Grub," her mother said. "Larissa and Leo met him last month. They were not impressed."

Neither was Callie, and she hadn't even been introduced to the fellow yet. "Whoever it was said something about his superior, so I'm not willing to absolve Herr von Mandelsloh just let. Please don't ask me to put all that in a letter. I must speak to Fritz."

Her mother patted her hand. "You love him a great deal, don't you?"

Callie swallowed. She'd denied it to her sisters, Tuny, and Aunt Meredith. What was it about her mother that squeezed the truth right out of people?

"I'm afraid I might," she confessed. "But it's not mutual."

"Then he's an idiot," her mother said. She cupped Callie's face with her hands and looked deep into her eyes. "And I don't see Fritz as an idiot. Still, if you want to make sure he knows how you feel, show him." She released her with a smile. "You know the story of how your father showed me."

Callie's heart felt lighter. "I remember. Our old butler had the temerity to sack you when you were our governess. Belle didn't understand the word then. She told Father she didn't want anyone to put you in a sack."

"Sweet of her," her mother said. "I'd already left on the mail coach, headed back to London and a dismal future. And your father came riding after me."

"On Belle's Unicorn," Callie remembered. "That horse is fast now and even faster then, I imagine."

"Fastest you ever saw," her mother confirmed. "Your father ran down and stopped the mail coach, which, I don't need to tell you, stops for no man."

"But Father is a duke," Callie said. "No one turns down a duke."

"No one turns down a Dryden," her mother corrected her. "There's a difference. Now, let's go talk to your fiancé."

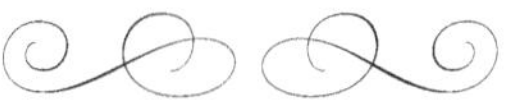

After the last few days, saber practice had never felt better. Silver flashed in the sunlight. The heat of the day and his exertions penetrated his black uniform, loosening muscles that had gone tight with frustration. Fritz took the first deep breath in hours.

"Faster," he barked to Huber as they disengaged with a ring of steel on steel. "Put your back into it when you thrust."

Huber was usually a quick study, but he froze now, staring past Fritz as if the Württemberg army was bearing down on them. Around them, Wyss and the others also jerked to a stop, as if just as stunned. Fritz whirled, sword up.

Callie was watching beside one of the pillars that edged the overhang along the sides of the courtyard. A breeze set her pink skirts to swaying and tugged at the ribbons on her broad-brimmed hat. Huber and Keller stood taller.

"Keep practicing," Fritz ordered. He sheathed his sword and strode to meet her.

She was positively vibrating again, ribbons bobbing and hands clasped tightly in front of her as if to still their trembling.

"What's wrong?" he asked. "Are you all right?"

Her head bobbed as well. "I had to come tell you, Fritz. The Envoy for Württemberg has returned to England. He came to see Father, but Mother and I talked with him instead."

He had to take her elbow. "Then he's the man you overheard, plotting our ruin."

She opened her mouth, then frowned, and he realized his men had moved closer, as if to drink in every word. Well, whatever she had to say concerned them too.

"It's all right," he said, gentling his voice. "Tell me."

"He wasn't," she said. "But he had the same accent. I think it may be a member of his staff, perhaps his secretary. The man I heard plotting mentioned something about a superior."

A growl rumbled behind him. It could well have come from his own throat. "And were you able to confirm this staff member's name?" he asked.

"No," she admitted. "But you should know that the envoy was concerned that Father might be supporting you. Mother sent him off with a flea in his ear." Her eyes dipped. "What will you do now, Fritz?"

"Attack," Wyss said behind him. "We have waited too long."

Fritz silenced him with a look.

"I don't think you can, much as you must want to," Callie said. As if she saw she was now the focus of all their attention, she paled, but she continued on doggedly. "I gave it some thought as Mother and I were riding out to the palace. Herr von Mandelsloh is a respected member of his country's diplomatic corps. Anything you do to him will come to the ears of King George."

Who already took a dim view of Fritz. He would only be making Leo and Lord Belfort's jobs more difficult if he did as his heart demanded and rode in to confront the fellow.

"I cannot like leaving him or his staff to plot," he told her.

She lay a hand on his arm. "Neither can I. But we have only my word on the matter that I heard someone from Württemberg plotting. Few will believe me."

"Why not?" Wyss asked. "You are clever. You are well connected. You are lovely to look upon. Who wouldn't listen?"

Fritz glanced around to find all his men nodding. He ought to reprimand Wyss for speaking out of turn again, but he was proud that the guardsmen recognized a diamond when they saw one.

As he returned his look to Callie, her color was climbing again, and she dropped her gaze to the gravel of the courtyard.

"You are very kind," she told them all, "but I fear I'm right. Even though I'm the daughter of a duke, too many find it easy to discredit the word of a woman. It would be better if we could put a hedge around you, something none of these rumors could penetrate."

"Like armor," Wyss said.

"We should also look for his colleague," Fritz said. "By cutting off his allies, we weaken him."

His men murmured their agreement.

"You and I can continue working on that," Callie said, raising her gaze to his, then tilting her head to look at his guardsmen. "In the meantime, I intend to show London that you are the gentlemen I know you must be to fight beside your captain."

To a man, they stood taller and smacked their fists to their chests to salute her. Fritz hid a smile.

"Allow me to introduce my men," he told Callie. "Wyss, my right hand."

Wyss inclined his head. "My lady."

"Keller and Hartmann, my best swordsmen."

The two blondes followed Wyss's suit, but Keller was turning red.

"Widmer, Huber, Roth, and Tanner, experts with pistols and knives."

Widmer, Huber, and Roth nodded, smiling.

"An honor, beautiful lady," Tanner said with an impressive bow.

Roth caught him in the ribs with an elbow as he straightened. The only indication Tanner had felt the blow was a slight *oomph*.

"A pleasure to meet you all," Callie said, smile hovering about those pretty pink lips that had warmed beneath his. It was all he could do to focus on her next words and not on how he might kiss her again.

"I shall endeavor to show you in the best possible light," she assured them all. "For the next few days, you must be visible in doing good deeds. And I know just how to achieve it."

Fritz wasn't sure what she had in mind, but he promised to put himself and his men at her disposal. So, the next day found Wyss interviewing and hiring an auctioneer for the benefit while the others took turns picking up art donations and delivering them to Weyfarer House while the remaining guards watched over Leo and the palace. His men collected monetary donations as well, and Fritz provided them to a foundling home known to be patronized by the royal family.

"A worthy cause," he told Callie and her mother, who had accompanied him. "But I cannot help but feel that we are using them for our purposes."

Her Grace winked at him. "You might reconsider that after you see the next item on Callie's list."

"The Causeway Kennels," Callie called up to the driver, who obligingly turned the carriage and headed north.

"You want me to purchase a dog?" Fritz asked as they stood beside a white-fronted farmhouse a short time later. Just outside of London, with heath surrounding it, the house was fairly small compared to the long, low building next to it. From that building came a series of barks and yips as the owner jogged around the end to meet them.

"Father purchases many of his hounds from Mr. Gernhaus," Callie explained. "They're very good for watching over sheep and cows."

"Which we have in abundance at the palace," Fritz quipped.

"Your Grace, my lady, my lord," the breeder said with a respectful bow. "I understand you may be looking for a companion for Count Montalban." A heavy-set fellow with silvery grey hair, he eyed Fritz as if he wasn't sure he deserved one of the prize pups.

Fritz hated to disappoint Callie, but he'd never owned a dog. Between his work and their persistent relocations, there hadn't been time or space. Besides, would having a dog really redeem him in King George's eyes?

"Yes, please," Callie answered for him. "An older dog, if you will. One already trained."

It was on the tip of his tongue to disagree with her when Gernhaus turned, put two fingers in his mouth, and gave a sharp whistle. A dog trotted out from behind the kennel.

And what a dog! His black back came nearly to Fritz's hips, and he carried his plumed tail straight out with an assurance that nothing he faced would be beyond him. The massive face had a stripe of white from forehead to chin and either side of his strong nose, with streaks of orange above each bright eye and around his generous mouth.

"A *Sennenhund*!" Fritz bent to rub the long, soft fur as the dog came to him. The wagging tail brushed him with force enough to knock a lighter man off his feet. "We have them in Batavaria. They help the farmers with the cattle."

"His father was from Batavaria," Gernhaus said. "He's larger than most, and he doesn't always take well to strangers, but I think he likes you."

He sounded as surprised by the fact as Fritz.

Callie put out a hand, and the dog trotted up to her, pink tongue lolling. "What's his name?"

"Augustus Adolphus," Mr. Gernhaus allowed. "We call him Dolph."

She stroked the massive shoulders. "Oh, but he's a dear. Won't you keep him, Fritz?"

With her gazing up at him that way, how could he refuse? And so he found himself the owner of a Batavarian *Sennenhund*. Mr. Gernhaus agreed to deliver the dog to the palace the next day.

"Which gives you time to determine where he's going to sleep and who's going to be in charge of him when you're unavailable," the duchess told him with a smile that said she knew exactly why he'd agreed to purchase the dog.

"You'll love having him about," Callie promised, eyes still shining. "I always thought the best place in the world would be a cozy chair in a library, with a pup at your side and a book on your lap."

He could see the picture she painted. He would come in from practicing with the guard or squiring Leo and his father about to find her curled up with a beloved book in the library of their home. He could imagine patting the dog, then picking her up and putting her on his lap while she told him all about what she'd been reading and the cause she next wanted them to support. The Count and Countess Montalban, friends to all.

Was it possible? Could he be that man?

CHAPTER THIRTEEN

CALLIE'S CAMPAIGN TO show Fritz and his guardsmen in a better light must have been working, for he saw no more evidence of rumors circulating about them. The newspapers found more worthy stories to cover. The people he and his men met when ferrying artwork around London and ultimately to the Athenian Rooms treated them with friendly interest rather than fear and indictment.

"And we have a dog," Leo said when Fritz told him what he'd observed. His twin glanced to the large black puddle of fur spread out before the fire in the salon. Dolph must have had no concerns, for he straightened his muscular legs and groaned in appreciation.

"The fact still shocks me as well," Fritz told his brother. "But he seems to have settled into palace life, thanks to the footman you assigned to him, and Wyss tells me he prowls the corridors at night on occasion, guarding us."

As if to prove as much, Dolph raised his head off the carpet a moment before Lawrence traipsed into the room. The hound didn't growl, but the sight of him stopped the Lord Chamberlain in his tracks.

"I thought we agreed to keep that beast outside," he said. "I distinctly remember ordering one of the boxes in the stables cleared out for it."

No one Fritz knew was getting put in a cage.

"He would only attempt to herd the horses," Fritz

said. He patted the side of his chair, and the *Sennenhund* rose to join him. A rub of the dog's ponderous head was enough to set Dolph to sighing happily.

"The kitchens, then," Lawrence persisted, though he made no further move into the room, as if prepared to flee at the least sign of aggression from the dog.

"Only if you want the roast and mutton to go missing on a regular basis," Fritz warned.

Leo took pity on the chamberlain. "Did you have need of us, Lawrence?"

"Nothing that cannot wait, Your Highness." With a sniff, Lawrence stalked out.

Fritz scratched behind Dolph's ear. "I knew I liked you."

Finally, Callie's big night arrived. Fritz and Leo were to meet the duke and his family at the Athenian Rooms.

"Quite a crowd," Leo mused as the royal carriage drew up in a long line of coaches letting off their passengers near the doors.

Too much of a crowd for Fritz's taste. Callie had seemed certain their enemies could not be members of the society, but how easy it would be for one of them to slip into this event unnoticed. He kept his wits about him as he and Leo climbed the stairs to the door, removed their evening cloaks and left them with an attendant, then entered the rooms.

He'd seen the preparations, but the final result was nothing short of outstanding. The room's wood paneling reflected the pristine white of the tablecloths, while silver and plate gleamed in the candlelight. Gentlemen in fine tailcoats and ladies in silks and satins strolled past the artwork, set on gilded easels around the room, to stop and exclaim over some piece. Voices wove through the air.

Callie, Miss Bateman, and the duke were standing near the entrance, greeting each arrival. Callie was gowned in her usual pink, the material gathered over her bosom and at her hem. With her hair done up in tight curls, she looked as fragile as one of the little shepherdess statues the English seemed to favor. He was likely the only one who realized there was a will of iron under the porcelain.

Fritz bowed over her hand. "Well done. You have reason to be proud."

"Perhaps not yet," she confessed with a smile as he straightened. "But I'm hopeful."

"My wife and daughters have seats waiting for you," the duke informed him and Leo with a look into the room. Fritz spotted the duchess at a table near the front.

"You will join us?" he asked Callie.

She nodded. "As soon as everyone is in."

He accompanied Leo to the damask-draped table.

Leo bowed to the duchess. "Your Grace."

"Good evening Leo, Fritz," she said. "And it's Jane, if you recall. We are going to be family, after all."

Guilt made Fritz's collar tight. He was only glad Larissa came up before he had to respond to her mother.

"Leo, you're at the next table with me," she explained. "But you'll want to go and look at the art before dinner. We expect bidding to be heated."

Leo took her arm. "Go ahead, Fritz. See what you think."

He'd already had a look at most of the art when he'd helped Callie arrange it, but Leo's directive gave him an excuse to patrol the perimeter of the room, so Fritz didn't argue.

Callie and her friend had solicited a number of fine works. Perched on gilded easels along three of the walls, the paintings included oils, watercolors, and charcoal sketches. There were landscapes showing hills and streams, seascapes depicting churning waves and tranquil coves. The bowls of fruit and vases of flowers held little interest, but he contemplated the scene of horses galloping through a pasture for a time. He could almost hear the thunder of their hooves.

He paused to glance around the room again. Could one of those distinguished faces mask a schemer? Was one of these men plotting behind his back? Why was he destined to look for darkness? Could he not, just once, appreciate the light?

He turned away to find the next painting one he hadn't seen before. The card tacked below it said the title was the Battle of Saxony and the artist was Lady Emily Cropper, but he could not credit it. What could a lady know of war?

Yet she'd captured it in all its glory and misery.

The hills were thick with action. Smoke drifted from the cannons to mask the sun, casting a pall over the soldiers charging with drawn swords and pikes. Faces showed determination, anger.

Fear.

Now it wasn't just his throat that felt tight. The polished paneling was pushing closer. He could hear the jeers of his jailors, smell the stale scent of his cell. His back burned as if the lash had fallen anew.

He closed his eyes, took a deep breath. Around him came the sound of voices, chatting, laughing, as if the whole world wasn't on fire.

It wasn't. He knew that. He was the one burning.

"Fritz?"

He seized Callie's voice and hung on. Opening his eyes, he turned to face her, smile firmly in place.

She took a step closer. "What's wrong? Did you find Mr. Eager?"

He took her arm, grounding himself in the feel of her,

the sound of her, the rosy scent of her platinum hair. "No. Leo asked me to look over the paintings."

She glanced around him. "Oh, Lady Emily's work. It always affects me."

It had affected him too, but he was not about to admit it.

"Let's get you to your seat," he said.

He could only be grateful when she agreed with no further questions.

Fritz, pale, shaken? He spoke haltingly, as if he had become lost and given up all hope of ever being found. She wanted to hold him close, promise him all would be well, whatever troubled him. But even being betrothed had some limitations, particularly in so public a place.

So she merely allowed him to lead her back to their table and sat beside him with an encouraging smile. Somehow, she didn't think he would voluntarily explain more later.

When she and Tuny had planned the dinner, they'd decided that their cause might be furthered if they divided their most ardent supporters among the tables, so as to encourage others. Accordingly, various members were salted around the room. Aunt Meredith and Uncle Julian were at one table. Larissa, being engaged to Leo, had been allowed to host her own table with him at her side, and Callie was to be at another with Fritz. Belle was to have been with their father and Tuny with their mother.

But when Callie and Fritz returned to the table, she discovered her youngest sister had made other arrangements.

"I'll have much more fun with you and Mother,"

Belle said from her place across from Callie at the table, dispensing her most charming smile. "So, I moved a few of the place names."

More than a few. Callie and Fritz were now seated with Belle, their mother, and Tuny; an older man with bristling grey eyebrows and a mustache to match, who introduced himself as Colonel Stanton; Lord Ashforde; and Owen Canady.

Callie knew Lord Ashforde. The dark-haired, quiet-spoken baron had been a follower of Larissa before her sister had announced her plans to marry Leo. Was Belle interested in him now?

And then there was Tuny's Mr. Canady. With ebony hair waved back from his sharp features, a neat mustache and beard, brilliant blue eyes, and a ready smile, he looked thoroughly pleased to focus on Tuny sitting on his left. Tuny did her best to leave Lord Ashforde, on *her* left, to Belle's good graces at the foot of the table. Since Belle loved to talk, and he seemed less inclined, they might get on well.

So, Callie couldn't find fault with the arrangement. Her mother, whose first husband had been a cavalry officer, was soon in conversation at the head of the table with the colonel about mutual experiences. Mr. Canady turned out to have friends who lived not too far from Tuny's sister Ivy, the Marchioness of Kendall. Belle's banter had even the usually taciturn Lord Ashforde smiling. Only Callie would have noticed that Fritz contributed little, staring at the food before him as if it held the secret to his future. A shame she could not ask what bothered him without someone overhearing the answer.

As the dessert course was being cleared, the reverend Mr. Broome stood up at the podium to gaze around at their guests with his impassioned grey eyes.

"As secretary of the society, I must thank you all for joining us," he said, his minister's voice carrying about the hall. "I think we can agree that our gracious hostesses, Lady Calantha, daughter of the Duke of Wey and affianced to Count Montalban of the Batavarian court, and Miss Petunia Bateman, sister to the Marchioness of Kendall and Sir Matthew Bateman, have given us much to be thankful for with this marvelous meal."

Applause rang out, and Callie shared Tuny's grin.

"We are also blessed with the beauty of these fine paintings," he continued when the guests had quieted again. "I know you will show your appreciation of them with your generous bidding."

He stepped aside, and the man they had hired to perform the auction took his place at the podium. He would not have been Callie's first choice, as he was short, slender, and unassuming, but she had to own Mr. Wyss had chosen well, for now the auctioneer's deep voice resonated around the room.

"Each painting will be brought up before the group," he explained. "I will read its title and artist and provide any other pertinent information, then suggest a starting point for the bidding. Raise your hand if you would like to bid."

"Remember that your donations go to fund the important work of the society," Mr. Broome put in, glancing around at them all, "specifically publishing tracts and sermons on the moral obligation to protect those who have no voice, the creatures of this earth, and hiring inspectors to ensure markets treat all animals humanely."

"And keeping those ponies out of the mines," Tuny whispered across the table to Callie, who nodded agreement.

The auctioneer waved his hand, and two footmen carried up the first piece and set it on another easel beside the polished podium.

"Evening at Grace-by-the-Sea," the auctioneer read from the sheet Tuny had prepared for him. "By

Mrs. Abigail Bennett, wife of the noted spa physician. Her work has frequently been featured in the Royal Academy's Summer Exhibition, below the line, where only the best pieces are shown. A good-sized piece in watercolor. Bidding starts at five pounds."

Callie glanced around the hall. A man at the back raised a hand.

"Five pounds," the auctioneer noted. "Who will give me ten?"

Another fellow near the far wall raised his hand.

"Ten. Do I hear fifteen?"

No one else moved.

"Ten, going once, going twice…"

Fritz raised his hand.

"Fifteen," the auctioneer noted, voice pleased. "Do I hear twenty? No? Fifteen going once, going twice… Sold, to Count Montalban of the Batavarian court."

Dozens of faces turned in their direction. Fritz smiled at Callie as if he hadn't noticed.

"Thank you," she murmured.

"We only begin," he promised.

The next few went for between ten and thirty pounds each, likely depending on the size of the piece and the fame of the artist.

Tuny looked to Callie, her friend's shoulders squeezed up in her spring green gown. "We're over one hundred pounds," she mouthed.

Callie grinned.

After a heated battle over the painting of David and Goliath by Lady Brentfield, which went for an astonishing one hundred and fifty pounds, a painting of horses galloping across the fields came up. Mr. Canady raised his hand on the opening bid, and Tuny beamed at him.

"It is for a good cause," he assured her, voice hinting of the green fields of Ireland.

"An excellent cause," Lord Ashforde put in, and he raised his hand to up the bid.

Mr. Canady narrowed his bright blue eyes at him, head cocked, as if measuring him up for size. Lord Ashforde ignored him, offering Tuny a confident smile instead.

Tuny frowned at him as if she wasn't sure what he was about.

"I have ten," the auctioneer called. "Who will make it fifteen?"

To Callie's surprise, Fritz raised his hand.

"Fifteen, who will… thank you, my lord."

Lord Ashforde's cool look belied the speed at which his hand had shot up.

The auctioneer hadn't even announced the next step before Mr. Canady raised his hand.

Tuny glanced between the two men, blinking. Then she looked askance to Callie, who shook her head in equal confusion.

Belle, however, was smiling a little half smile, as if she'd arranged the entire thing. Had she?

Fritz raised his hand at twenty-five, and both Lord Ashforde and Mr. Canady shot him a look.

Callie leaned closer to Fritz. "Do you want it so badly?" she murmured.

"No," he whispered back. "But they do, and I want to see you earn that money."

Mr. Canady raised his hand for thirty.

Lord Ashforde eyed him a moment, then raised his voice instead of his hand. "One hundred and fifty pounds."

Gasps rang out here and there, followed by a smattering of applause.

The auctioneer waved both hands for quiet. "I have a bid of one hundred and fifty pounds for Early Morning Charge. Do I hear two hundred?"

All eyes were on Mr. Canady. He regarded Lord Ashforde as if the baron were something Mr. Canady had found smearing the bottom of his boots. "Two hundred."

"Three hundred," Lord Ashforde countered before the auctioneer could respond.

The room went silent as the two men leaned forward and stared at each other around Tuny, who seemed to be shrinking in her seat.

"Four hundred," Mr. Canady said.

Lord Ashforde leaned back as if he had decided to let the matter go.

The auctioneer licked his lips. "I have a bid of four hundred pounds. Going once, going twice."

"One thousand pounds," Lord Ashforde said, as calmly as if he'd been asking for another bowl of strawberry trifle.

Mr. Canady turned white. Then he shook his head and settled back in his seat.

"One thousand pounds going once," the auctioneer said, sounding decidedly giddy, "going twice… Sold! To Lord Ashforde."

Callie looked to Tuny, stunned and overjoyed, but her friend did not look nearly so happy. She was gazing at Lord Ashforde, jaw set and eyes hard, and Callie knew there needed to be a meeting that night in Larissa's room.

He'd come for dinner and an auction and found combat instead. Fritz shook his head as the auctioneer went on to another piece and Belle praised Lord Ashforde for his generosity. Though the bids were fought with words, it was little different than engaging with swords. Thrust, parry, strike, first blood. Knowing when to lunge and when to back away.

Ashforde may have paid the highest price, but, by the end of the evening, Fritz had managed to acquire six of the pieces. Miss Bateman was sufficiently pleased by his performance that she offered to allow him to call her Tuny as the others did.

"Thank you again," Callie said as he and Leo were saying goodnight to her and her family at the door to the Athenian Rooms. "You helped make the night a success."

"*You* made the night a success," he countered. For him as well as her society. How could any man fail to admire the sparkle in her eyes, the flush of pink in her cheeks?

"More than two thousand pounds," Miss Bateman reminded them all, still looking a bit stunned. "And that doesn't count the price of admittance."

"Mr. Broome is very pleased," Callie agreed, glancing toward where the society's secretary was talking with the long-faced, white-haired Mr. Wilberforce.

"And you should be pleased too," Belle informed her before turning to Fritz with a bright smile. "I'm sure you'll want to congratulate your fiancée properly, Count Montalban."

Tuny and Larissa frowned at her, and Callie began to look alarmed, but her mother and father were nodding fondly. He knew what she feared. A kiss, here? It might be the undoing of them both.

He leaned closer. "You are safe," he murmured before pressing a kiss to her cheek.

It had been the merest of touches, the sort of kiss one might give a mother or a good friend. Yet it called to mind another kiss, one that had shaken him. Its echo rang through him now. He had to force himself to straighten away from her.

"Thank you," she murmured, and now her eyes rivaled the starry sky in their glow.

It was all he could do to make his farewells and follow Leo out to the coach.

"What are we going to do with all these?" his brother asked as the footmen were loading Fritz's purchases into the boot of the carriage.

"Start an exhibition," Fritz said. "Invite all of London to view them. If we charge a penny for entrance, we might recoup the cost eventually."

"And if we let everyone in free of charge," Leo countered, "we might continue to increase our goodwill."

Unfortunately, the morning proved that would be impossible.

CHAPTER FOURTEEN

"BATAVARIAN SAVAGE ATTEMPTS to Repair Reputation," Leo read from *The Times* to Fritz after they had sat down to breakfast in the family dining room of the palace the next morning. His brother lowered the paper with a shake of his head. "You would think the reporter would want to cover the amount raised by the society and its good aims."

"It is far more entertaining to skewer me," Fritz said, poking at the coddled eggs the footman had set before him. "The dastardly count, seducing English women, beating English servants, and stealing English art."

"Not stealing," Leo said, raising the paper again as if to study the account. "'Bought with a ferocity of his wild, impetuous nature, like a wolf rending its prey in two.' And you purchased a vicious beast to guard your treasure, while your staff cower in terror."

Fritz groaned, dropping his head to the table. "Bury me now."

From his place on the floor beside Fritz's chair, Dolph humphed his agreement.

"I would laugh," Leo offered, "but it isn't funny."

Fritz straightened. "No, it isn't. Did the fellow not notice Ashforde and Canady nearly coming to blows? Or the two young lords who battled over Lady Brentfield's work? My bidding was nothing compared to that."

"Someone wants to blacken your name," Leo said,

lowering the paper again, this time with enough force to crumple the words. "Have you made no progress in determining who?"

"No," Fritz snapped. "I've been entirely too busy trying to appear the perfect gentleman, much good that it did me. Perhaps I should visit the newspaper."

"No doubt the editor would refuse to allow you to approach the reporter," Leo cautioned him.

"Thinking I'd beat his man within an inch of his life," Fritz agreed with a sigh.

Leo leaned back in his chair. "Callie heard your quarry at the House of Commons once. She might hear him again."

"Possibly," Fritz allowed. "But she won't be able to identify him from the Women's Gallery. It is no more than an unkind joke, with little opportunity to actually view the goings on."

"A shame she cannot sit in the Stranger's Gallery with you," Leo said.

Fritz's fork fell. "You, Brother, are a genius!"

Leo grinned. "I cannot argue against that, but I see nothing in what I said that would aid you. The Stranger's Gallery, as you explained, is for men only."

It was. Or at least, it was for a person everyone assumed was male.

Most of his life, Fritz had been playing a role: the determined member of the guards and then their captain, the charming crown prince, the soldier who had returned from the war unscathed, the devoted fiancé. The role he had in mind now was perhaps the most outrageous of all.

If he could only convince Callie to play along.

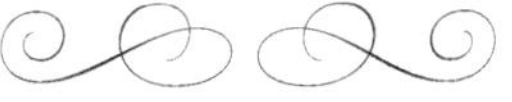

Belle had insisted on a meeting the night after the benefit. Callie could only agree. They all congregated in Larissa's room after they had changed into their nightgowns, piling up on her sister's large bed with its blue and white hangings.

"Lord Ashforde," Belle told Tuny, "likes you."

Tuny started, then made a show of leaning back on the bed. "Don't be daft."

"He does," Belle insisted. "He was clearly trying to impress you by buying that painting for such an exorbitant price. I didn't realize he'd shown such interest."

"He hasn't," Tuny said, glancing around at them all. "And he won't. Not ever. Not that one."

Tuny might protest, but Callie heard the note of despair in her voice. She edged closer and put a hand on Tuny's shoulder in support.

"Tuny," Larissa said with a frown, "is something wrong?"

Tuny threw up her hands, forcing Callie to release her. "No! It's been a long night. So if you're all done poking, I'd like to go to bed."

Lord Ashforde. Callie sorted through the few conversations in which someone had mentioned his name. Wealthy. Studious. Honorable. Some thought him arrogant. She thought he might merely be quiet, like her. Though he had certainly made his presence known tonight. And the tone in Tuny's voice the few times she'd spoken to him…

"You admire him," she said.

Tuny reared back. "What? No! I don't even like him."

Belle crossed her arms over her chest and let the silence lengthen.

Tuny slumped with a sigh. "Oh, very well. When I met him, our first Season, I fancied myself in love. I mean, look at him! Listen to him! But I quickly realized that's all it was, an unlikely dream. I see who he is now, more clearly tonight than ever before: a spoiled, rich lord who cannot accept defeat. I wish Mr. Canady had beaten him to that painting."

Belle dropped her arms and edged forward. "I think there may be hope for Mr. Canady. He seems to appreciate animals as much as you do. Let's invite him to the house party."

Larissa shook her head. "Mother hasn't agreed to host a house party."

"She will," Belle predicted, as always supremely confident in her own abilities. "Then Tuny and Mr. Canady can become better acquainted."

"I suppose I wouldn't mind," Tuny allowed. Then she pointed a finger at Belle. "But no Lord Ashforde. Promise me."

"I will do all in my power to see you have the best house party ever," Belle said.

Callie seemed to be the only one who noticed she hadn't agreed to Tuny's request.

And Fritz's request the next day was even more shocking.

Callie and her family had attended services at St. George's Hanover Square and returned home to a light luncheon. Belle had offered to entertain Thal and Peter so their parents could take a carriage ride through Hyde Park together. Callie, her sisters and brothers, and Tuny had been in a frenetic game of charades when Underhill announced Fritz. Of course, he brought his brother along, and Leo and Larissa soon sat, heads close together, in one corner.

Peter rolled his eyes. "She won't play anymore. Will you, Captain?"

"It's count now, Peter," Belle reminded him. "But yes, please join us, Count Montalban."

"Actually, I was hoping for a moment alone with your sister," Fritz told them both.

Callie rose on legs that wanted to wobble. "Of course.

Let's try the library."

Peter sighed. "You better not become betrothed, Belle, or there'll be no fun to be had at all."

Callie left Belle attempting to interest Peter in a game of whist instead, with Tuny partnering Thal.

As always, the library was cool and quiet, and it wasn't hard to settle on one of the upholstered chairs near the hearth.

"What did you want to talk about?" she asked, arranging her pink lustring skirts about her.

He paced to the hearth and back to the door, head down and hands fisted. Dread pressed her deeper into her seat.

"You decided to call it off early," she said, amazed her voice didn't crack on the words.

"What?" He stopped to stare at her. "No. I had an idea that seemed wise this morning, but after attending services, I find myself questioning it."

She frowned, straightening. "What idea?"

He perched on the chair closest to hers, knees tight and arms braced. "There might be a way to find Mr. Eager, if you could sit closer to the floor of the House of Commons."

"Really?" She offered him a smile. "Then we must try. You deserve every opportunity to catch your opponents."

He cocked his head. "Even if the opportunity presents some risks?"

Callie felt her smile fade. "What sort of risks?"

He raised his hands as if in surrender. "Hear me out. As you know, only men are allowed in the Stranger's Gallery, and many of the seats are taken up by reporters."

She nodded. "So my father told me."

"But any man is allowed to attend. Or anyone who appears to be a man."

Callie shot to her feet. "You want me to masquerade, as a man! Are you mad?"

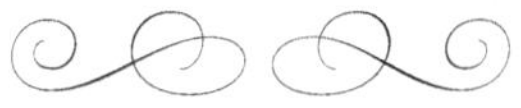

Perhaps he was mad, for anyone seeing her now—cheeks flushed, eyes flashing, chest heaving—would have no doubt she was female, even if she had been wearing male attire.

"Forgive me," he said. "It truly was mad."

She drew in a breath and returned to her seat in a flutter of pink. "Yes, yes it was. There must be some other way."

"I am open to suggestions," he said.

She screwed up her face as if thinking hard. "We know Mr. Eager is a member of the House of Commons, because I heard his voice on the floor, not in one of the galleries, and only members of the House are allowed to speak on the floor."

"True," he said.

"And we know he is not a lover of animals, or he would have been on the list to attend last night's benefit dinner," she reasoned.

He suspected a great many other people in the metropolis cared about animals, but she was right that a good number of Parliamentarians had been present. "We also know he has not attended any other event with you," he added.

"Except the drawing room at Carlton House for the king's birthday," she reminded him. "Which may associate him with the diplomatic corps."

"How many members of the House of Commons are associated with the diplomatic corps?" he asked.

She made a face. "Entirely too many. Lords arrange for second sons, cousins, and friends to win positions in the House, and they end up on various committees associated with foreign affairs." She drummed her fingers on the arm of the chair. "There must be some way to narrow down the field."

He waited, afraid to hope, determined not to push her.

Finally, she straightened. "I'll do it. It might be the only way to find Mr. Eager before something worse happens than a few rumors in the newspaper. But we must be careful."

Relief surged through him. "Thank you. I have frequently impersonated my brother, but this will be more difficult."

Her pale eyes twinkled. "Perhaps not as difficult as you think. Let me go borrow Thal."

Her brother returned with her a few moments later. About twelve years of age, he had a shock of dark brown hair and jade-colored eyes that reminded Fritz of the duke's. He could also effect that inscrutable look that made his father a power to be reckoned with.

"What intrigue are you planning now?" Thal asked, glancing between the two of them.

Callie pressed her back against the door as if making sure it was securely shut before venturing closer to her brother. "I intend to sneak into the House of Commons, dressed like a boy."

A grin split his face. "Outstanding. Please tell me I can come too."

Fritz did his best to look regretful. "I cannot in good conscience bring you as well. You would be recognized as the heir to the Duke of Wey, and someone might more easily guess the identity of the other young man at my side."

Thal sighed. "You're right. How can I help otherwise?"

"You and I are about the same height," Callie said. "I want to borrow your clothes: trousers, shirt, jacket, waistcoat, and cravat."

"And hat," Thal mused, glancing up at her head. "Though I don't like the chances of it staying in place.

I know how many times I've had to ride after a hat that fell off."

She blushed. Fritz could imagine all that platinum silk made it difficult to keep anything from slipping for long.

All that platinum silk.

He shook his head. "The plan is doomed. We cannot cover that hair."

Her hand shot to the pale tresses. "I suppose I could cut it."

"No," Fritz said. He must not have been the only one surprised by his vehemence, for Callie blinked and Thal's dark brows went up.

"You have sacrificed enough for me," Fritz told her. "I would not have any part of you harmed."

Her face softened. "Thank you."

Thal clapped his hands together. "I have it! The footmen sometimes wear wigs to serve at important functions. We can borrow one of them."

She grimaced. "But they're powdered white and years out of fashion."

"Leave that to me," Thal said. "Just promise me you'll give me every detail of your adventure. I know you'll remember."

She likely would. And Fritz thought he'd never forget.

He wasn't sure what to expect when he had their coachman drive him to Weyfarer House just before three on Monday. He had worn civilian dress—a Navy coat and trousers—in hopes of being less conspicuous. Callie was dressed in a high-necked wool gown that seemed a little too large for her slender frame and too warm for the summer day, and she handed him a large satchel as she met him in the entry hall.

"Those items I promised to donate to the cause," she said with a tilt of her head toward the watching butler.

Fritz took custody of the satchel. "Thank you. Ready for our outing?"

She straightened her spine. "Ready for our outing to the park."

"The park?" he murmured as he ushered her out to the waiting carriage. Their footman reached for the satchel to stow it, but Callie shook her head at him.

"In the coach, please," she instructed the footman. She didn't answer Fritz's question until they were safely ensconced in the carriage.

"I let everyone think we were going for a drive to the park. It's a short distance, and we would be surrounded by others, so there was no need for a chaperone."

"Then where do you intend to change?" he asked.

She closed the shutters on the window closest to her. "Here."

His heart skipped a beat. "Here?"

"Yes." She slid over and closed the shutters as well, plunging them into twilight.

The dim light, the tight space, and the warmth of the day pushed against him, as did the walls. He could not breathe. "Open the shutters."

She must have mistaken the strangled tone in his voice, for she squared her shoulders. "You asked me to do this for you, Fritz. I would not have expected you to balk now."

She was right. He fought off the memories. He was in England, in a coach. He wasn't alone or at anyone's mercy. "Forgive me," he gritted out. "What would you have me do?"

"Help me with my buttons." She turned her back on him, and he made himself focus on where a series of cloth-covered buttons secured the gown. And then it struck him.

"You want me to undress you?"

"It's all right," she assured him. "I borrowed the dress from Tuny. I have the trousers and shirt on underneath, but the waistcoat and coat were too bulky."

He drew in a breath and made short work of the buttons, then helped her ease the gown off her shoulders, the coach growing warmer by the second. Or perhaps the warmth came from inside him. What, was he blushing? He busied himself opening the satchel and handing her its contents.

She pulled on the paisley waistcoat, then the navy coat with silver buttons. She swapped her slippers for riding boots.

"Thal and I do not have the same size feet," she explained. "But I think these will do."

Finally, she began tucking her hair into a wig that appeared to be some shade of blond.

"That's a footman's wig?" Fritz asked.

She nodded as she shoved the last platinum strands inside. "Thal cropped off the worst of the curls. What do you think?"

Before him sat a young man with a head of unruly blond hair partially covered by a tweed cap. His features were still too fine, his carriage dainty.

"Sit taller," Fritz said, and she complied. "Broaden your shoulders. A man takes up more space than a woman."

She attempted to mimic his stance, raising her chin and squaring her shoulders.

"Better," he allowed. "Let me speak for both of us. If something happens and you are put in a position to speak, make sure to drop your voice to its lowest register."

She coughed. "Like this?"

The husky voice skipped along his nerves. "Yes. Fine."

She frowned. "Is something wrong, Fritz? Will I not pass?"

Perhaps with others, but every moment that went by he was more aware she was a woman. Those trousers clung to shapely legs. Though the coat and waistcoat obscured her bosom, he could not forget how she'd felt in his arms.

"Stay close to me," he advised.

The coachman let them down outside the Houses of Parliament. The fellow raised his brows, as if surprised to find two men exiting when a man and a woman had entered, but Fritz sent him a look, and he focused over the horses.

"Return for us in an hour," he told the fellow.

"Right you are, my lord." With a cluck to the horses, he drove on.

"An hour?" she whispered as they moved toward the building.

He had to stop himself from taking her arm. "If we have not found our culprit by then, I am ending this charade."

Before he betrayed himself further.

CHAPTER FIFTEEN

HOW STRANGE IT felt to wear trousers. The material rubbed against Callie's legs as she walked beside Fritz. Mindful of his instruction, she tried to copy him, lengthening her stride, keeping her head up and her gaze assessing.

But once again, her invisibility was her ally. Barristers in their black robes passed, gaze on the stone pavement. Members of the House of Lords strode along on either side. One or two glanced at Fritz as if measuring his character, but their gazes passed over her as if she were of no consequence. For once, she was glad of it.

He led her into the building and up a set of stairs into a balcony running along the side of the House of Commons. Below, a few gentlemen ranged on padded wood benches, facing each other across the table she'd seen from the Women's Gallery. A chair under the brass chandelier waited for the speaker.

"This is much better than the Women's Gallery," she whispered to Fritz as they were seated near the door and along the back wall.

He glanced at her and shook his head. Right. He'd told her not to speak. She swallowed and edged closer to him, then realized a gentleman hardly needed support in such instances. With a huff, she settled back on the bench.

"Fresh from the country, eh?" the man on the other side of Fritz said with a chuckle. "Boots and all."

Glancing down the row, she saw that most of the men were wearing shoes.

"I thought a little sophistication might rub off," Fritz told him.

Callie willed herself not to cringe.

Below, members continued filling the benches. A few she'd seen at social events, sons of lords appointed by their fathers to the position. She looked up into the other balconies around the room.

Directly across from them, her father sat with his arms crossed over his chest.

She pressed her lips tight to keep from gasping. What was he doing in the House of Commons? Did he know she was here? She glanced at Fritz and tipped her head in her father's direction. He stiffened.

The speaker banged his mace down on the table. "Order!"

Once more, voices quieted, bodies stilled. She chanced a glance at her father, but his gaze was fixed on the action below them.

All Callie could do was wait.

The speaker brought a bill to them for consideration, and the debates began. Some speeches were well-considered; she found herself nodding along. So did Fritz. The urge to touch his arm, take his hand, was nearly overpowering, but she made herself sit straight and tall.

It wasn't easy. As in the Women's Gallery, the men around her began losing interest. One was reading the newspaper. Another two had eyes closed and heads nodding as if they had fallen asleep. The scritch of the reporters as they wrote was loud.

"I must protest this unseemly divide."

Callie stiffened, then leaned forward. She could feel Fritz watching her as she scanned the group.

"The chair recognizes Mr. Wellmanton."

This time she did gasp, and heads in the gallery turned

her way. She brought her gaze back into the assembly below. The slender blond fellow whose mother and sisters were long-time acquaintances stood and looked around at his comrades.

"Are we not English?" he asked. "Are we not brothers in arms? How, then, can some say this bill shall not pass?"

She clutched Fritz's arm. "It's him. Mr. Eager is Lord Wellmanton's son, Robert."

Fire raced up Fritz, pushing him from his seat. Callie's hand on his arm pulled him back down.

"Not here," she whispered, and he became aware of the other members in the gallery staring at him. He must have made sufficient noise, because some below and across from them glanced his direction as well. Among them was the Duke of Wey, and his eyes narrowed.

"We will leave," Fritz said. "Now."

She did not argue.

Other men huffed or glared, but Fritz managed to get them out of the gallery, down the stairs, and out into the clean light of day.

"Wellmanton," he growled, pacing back and forth in front of her. "What do you know of him?"

"He fits the clues we had," she admitted, rubbing a hand along the arm of her borrowed coat. "His father has the ear of the king, Lord Wellmanton appointed Robert to the Commons to take a seat granted to his lands, and his family is connected with the diplomatic corps. When we were trying to determine who might be out to harm your father, the king, last month, Tuny's brother, Sir Matthew, related that Lord Wellmanton and his family have invested in silver mining in Württemberg."

"In Batavaria, you mean," Fritz fumed. "And Lord

Wellmanton was the one who arranged for our father to tour Kew Gardens the day our enemies thought they had kidnapped Leo and held him for ransom there."

Their enemies had had no idea they actually held Fritz, who had been masquerading as Leo at the time. It still galled him they had been able to capture him so easily as he had come out of a ball at the house of a London lord. Let them try now that he was on to them. He could imagine planting his fist in Robert Wellmanton's narrow face.

"Do you think the carriage will return soon?" she asked.

The plaintive tone cut through his frustration. She had shrunk in on herself, to the point that her cap and wig were beginning to slip. More than one man passing was glancing their way. He had to fight the urge to take her hand.

Instead, he schooled his face to pleasantry. "We have only a few minutes before he returns. Do you know where Robert Wellmanton lives?"

She nodded, and the hat slipped further on her freshly trimmed wig. He tapped his own hat, and she hastily righted hers.

"The entire family lives not far from Clarendon Square," she explained. "My sisters and Tuny and I have called on them on occasion. What will you do?"

Before he could answer, he heard his name being called. Turning, he nearly groaned. The Duke of Wey was striding toward them. His face was flushed, his hands fisted at his sides.

"Oh, dear," Callie murmured, as if she had seen him too.

Her father came to a stop in front of them, green eyes blazing. "Count Montalban. This is no time or place for this discussion, but I want your assurance that you will take your companion directly home and leave… him to his mother's care." He did not so much as glance at his daughter.

Callie hung her head.

Fritz straightened. "You have every reason to be proud of each of your children, Your Grace. They are willing to sacrifice much for those they love."

"And those who love them would be wise not to take advantage of their generosity," he countered. "You will wait for my return, and we will speak further then."

He pivoted on his heel and stalked back toward the building.

"I've disappointed him," she said, voice low and trembling.

He was never so thankful to see the green lacquered sides of the royal carriage come trundling through the press. Disguise be hanged. He put his hand on her arm and drew her to meet the coach.

Once inside, she slumped against the seat. The tears on her cheeks burned a hole in his chest.

"I'm so sorry, Callie," he said. "I should never have asked you to do this."

"I volunteered," she reminded him with a hiccough. "It was the right thing to do. We know who is plaguing you now."

"At least one of them," he allowed. "And through him, we will find the other. You may have saved my father and Leo's lives."

"Then it was worth it," she said, chin coming up.

It still trembled.

He twisted across the space to sit beside her and took her in his arms. "You are one of the bravest women I have ever met. Crowds trouble you, yet you endure them for your family and your beliefs. Dressing this way could have led to scandal, yet you did it for my family."

She lay her head on his shoulder. "You make me feel brave."

And she made him feel humble. His arms tightened. He only wanted to protect her, comfort her, prove to her that she was worthy of all praise.

He wasn't sure how long they sat like that. He was in no hurry to end the connection. But she pulled away and reached for the satchel. "Help me dress."

Her father already knew the worst of it. Her mother would shortly. Yet he could not gainsay her a moment of pride. He fought off the panic when the drawn shutters darkened the space and focused on her.

She drew off the coat and waistcoat, and he helped her don the dress over the top of the shirt and trousers. She was pulling on her slippers when the coach came to a stop in front of Weyfarer House.

"The wig," he cautioned, and she yanked it off and shoved it into the satchel with the rest of her disguise. Her coiffure had been crushed and tumbled from her pins, and her long tresses hung like sheets of silk on either side of her face.

His heart turned over in his chest.

"Here," he said. "Allow me."

She turned her back. Knowing he would never be able to deal with the fine strands with his gloves on, he pulled them off. Her tresses crackled with energy under his fingers, and he caught himself marveling at the sleek satin flowing against his skin as he began braiding it.

"Have you ever put up a woman's hair before?" she asked, beginning to hand him pins over her shoulder.

Another woman might have asked the question in jealousy, but he heard only curiosity, and perhaps the slightest bit of trepidation in the tone.

"No," he admitted, fixing the braided hair in place. "I have flirted and flattered where it seemed appropriate, but there was never time to court a woman properly or even for a serious dalliance. There."

She turned to face him and reached up to pat the

braid that wound around her head like the crown she so deserved. "Then how did you know what to do?"

Fritz shrugged. "I've watched stable hands braid horses' tails."

"Oh!" She seemed to be caught between indignation and laughter.

He leaned forward. "Your hair is far finer and softer than any horse's."

As flattery went, it was a poor description, but she flushed as if pleased. "We should go."

He opened the door and handed her out.

The duke had been explicit in his instructions, and Fritz hardly wanted to make matters worse for Callie, so he sent the carriage back to the palace with the intention of calling for a hired hack when it was time to return. In the meantime, he greeted Callie's family as if his doom wasn't approaching any moment. Callie excused herself to go change. Thal motioned to him.

"There's something I'd like you to see in the library, my lord."

Their mother eyed them as Fritz followed him out. Thal waited only until he had shut the library door behind him before rounding on Fritz. "Well? What happened?"

"Your sister is extremely talented," Fritz informed him, leaning a shoulder against the hearth. "She identified the culprit the moment he opened his mouth."

Thal rubbed his hands together. "Excellent! Then the disguise worked."

"For most," Fritz said. "Your father saw through it."

The boy paled, hands falling. "Father? What did you do?"

"Apologized, but it did little good. I am to wait here upon his pleasure, or displeasure, as it were."

"Does he know?" he asked, pausing to lick his thin lips. "About me, I mean?"

"You played absolutely no role in our masquerade,"

Fritz said. "You and I never so much as spoke about the matter."

Thal sagged. "Thank you, Count Montalban. I will not forget this."

Fritz inclined his head. "It is my honor, Lord Thalston. I appreciate how you look out for your sister's best interests."

"And I appreciate how you admire her," he said. "She needs that, you know. She too often compares herself to Larissa and Belle." He shook his head at the vagaries of sisters.

"And what makes Callie so different?" Fritz asked, intrigued by the boy's insight.

"Her heart," Thal readily answered. "Larissa is all cool logic. If you want to know the best way to approach a matter, you go to her. Belle is always up for a lark. You want to forget about something unpleasant, she's your best choice. But Callie? Callie will listen when you want to rail at the world. Not that I rail, mind you," he hurried to add.

He remembered Leo mentioning that Thal had been a sickly child and was even now hovered over by his parents. Fritz could imagine he did on occasion have reason to rail.

"And she will remember," Fritz said.

He nodded. "Everything. It can be tremendously helpful and rather embarrassing at times. One doesn't always want to remember every harsh thing one has said."

He certainly didn't. He had enough trouble remembering the past with equanimity. And he had a feeling Callie's father was about to add another memory he would not relish.

CHAPTER SIXTEEN

ONCE MORE IN the comfort of one of her pink gowns and enjoying the swish of the muslin skirts and petticoats about her legs, Callie came back downstairs. It had been a challenge enough brushing out and repining her locks without enlisting Anna's aid, and having to explain the reason, but Callie kept remembering the feeling of Fritz's fingers in her hair, gentle, soft. She had barely managed to compose herself before locating Thal and Fritz in the library, heads bent over the chess set that saw regular use from her mother and father. Her brother popped up as soon as he noticed her.

"Count Montalban informed me what happened," he explained, edging around her as if she had some dread disease. "I'll speak to you later, after Father." He hurried from the room.

"A wise man," Fritz said, starting to return the pieces to their original spots on the board.

"Stop," Callie said, going to sit in her brother's chair. "I'll take Thal's position."

Fritz raised a brow, but he pulled back his hands.

She surveyed the board. Her father had taught them all to play over the years, so she recognized the familiar opening gambit. A bit tame for a man like Fritz. She would have attacked first.

"I take it Thal was pleased with the outcome," she said, moving a bishop along its course.

He contemplated the board a moment before advancing his castle. "Very much so, until he learned about your father."

She fingered a pawn before moving it, the polished wood warming in her grip. "Well, no one argues with a duke."

"Or a prince," he agreed, adjusting a knight.

He would be one of the few who would understand such family dynamics. "What do you intend to tell my father?"

"I will apologize again and assure him I will never abuse your good grace." He studied the board.

"You didn't abuse my grace," she corrected him. "I wanted to help."

"I did not protest," he countered. "I should have." He slid a bishop into position to threaten her king. "Your brother says you compare yourself unfavorably with your sisters."

She started. "Thal said that? I hadn't realized he'd noticed." Or anyone else, for that matter.

His long fingers toyed with the other bishop. "You have no need, you know. You are beyond compare."

She simply couldn't understand why he persisted in complimenting her. It wasn't as if they were truly betrothed. And no one had been around in the carriage, or here, to hear him if he had been trying to build up the fiction of being besotted.

"I have my skills," she allowed, rescuing her king from check. "But I've heard the conversations at balls and soirees. It generally goes something like this." She raised her voice to a sharp, high pitch. "Lady Larissa is so elegant and refined, and Lady Abelona has such marvelous animation. A shame about Lady Calantha. She has neither."

He lay his hand over hers where it rested on the edge of the table. "What would you change, if you could?"

Oh, so many things. "My hair?" she suggested. "It won't hold a curl or stay in its pins. And my eyes are far too pale."

He cocked his head, and she steeled herself to hear him agree. "You should wear blue."

She blinked. "What?"

"You favor pale colors like pink," he said, pulling back his hand. "A clear blue or a golden yellow would look well on you. And as for your hair, let it hang in all its glory."

"Oh, I couldn't," she said. "It's simply not done."

He shrugged, moving his knight to challenge her queen. "I see no reason why, if it suits your hair and your looks better. Check."

She toppled the knight and repositioned her queen. "Check. Is this more advice from your observations of horses?"

"No," he said, moving his king out of harm's way. "It is from my observations of you."

The very thought that he had been observing her left her almost too warm to think. But she aligned her queen again. "Check and mate."

He stared at the board a moment, then tipped over his king. "I surrender." His gaze came up and met hers, and thought became entirely impossible. She was leaning closer, and he was on the way to meeting her.

"Thank you, Underhill," her father said as he came through the library doorway. "No need to announce me in my own home."

Fritz jerked away and surged to his feet to face her father, chin up and back straight. Callie stood as well and came around the table to align herself with Fritz.

Her father paused to eye them both. "Explanation?"

Fritz kept his gaze forward. Thal did the same when confessing some error in judgment. "Lady Calantha overheard two men plotting to harm my family," he told her father. "She was unable to catch sight of them at the time."

"Hiding behind the shrubbery again?" her father asked with a look to her.

Callie nodded, swallowing. At least her father didn't look particularly angry, brows flat and face calm.

"Since then," Fritz continued, "we have been attempting to identify them. She heard one of them again when we visited the House of Commons, but she was unable to see clearly."

"The Women's Gallery is atrocious, Father," Callie put in. "Someone really should look into improving it."

Her father held up his hand. "Thank you, Callie. Whose idea was it to smuggle you into the Stranger's Gallery instead?"

"Mine," Fritz said immediately. "She protested, but I won her over."

"Of course you would," her father said before she could respond. "I warned you about such behavior. It seems while my daughter hears everything, you hear little."

Fritz's gaze now seemed to be pointing over her father's shoulder. "I take full responsibility for my actions. No discredit should fall on Lady Calantha."

"And if I should order you from our home? Tell you the betrothal is over?" her father challenged.

Callie opened her mouth to protest, then shut it again. She had done her part and identified Robert Wellmanton. Fritz himself had pointed out it should not be difficult to locate his conspirator, especially since she had confirmed he was from Württemberg. Though it wasn't harvest yet, she would not have blamed Fritz for backing out of the betrothal.

"Such would be your right," Fritz acknowledged. "But I made your daughter a promise, and I will not break it."

Air filled her lungs. Joy lifted her head. She wanted to dance around the room, throw the desk into disarray, sing at the top of her lungs even if it set every dog in a five-mile radius to howling along with her. She settled for beaming at Fritz.

"There will be no more such stunts," her father warned, though his voice sounded less harsh. "You will comport yourself as a gentleman."

"I will," Fritz said. "And as a pledge, may I invite you and your family to dinner at the palace on Wednesday? I believe Parliament does not sit that night."

"Callie," her father said, "go ask your mother if Wednesday is free."

She disliked leaving the two of them alone, but she moved to the door and took a step out. Underhill scuttled away from the opening, eyes wide in alarm, likely at being caught eavesdropping.

"Will you tell Mother she's wanted in the library?" she murmured.

"At once, your ladyship." He trotted down the corridor for the withdrawing room and quickly followed her mother back.

"Everything all right?" her mother asked, gaze on Callie's face.

"I think so," Callie said, keeping the door mostly shut behind her. "But Father's in a taking."

Her mother raised a brow. "Does he have reason?"

Callie winced. "Perhaps. A little."

"Reason enough for me," her mother said, and she pushed past Callie to sail into the library.

Callie followed. Underhill hovered in the doorway.

"Count Montalban has invited us to dinner at the palace on Wednesday," her father told her mother. "This is in penance for a decided lack of judgment earlier today that might have jeopardized Callie's reputation."

Her mother clacked her tongue. "What are we to do with you, Fritz?"

Fritz bowed to her. "Allow me the opportunity to

show I can be redeemed."

She nodded slowly. "Dinner Wednesday is a start. Callie, I will have the whole story from you later. For now, bid his lordship good day."

The words did not want to come out of Callie's mouth. As if he knew it, Fritz advanced to her side, took her hand, and bowed over it. "I will call tomorrow."

"I look forward to it," she said.

Underhill hurried to see him out.

"Well," her mother said, putting an arm about her shoulders. "That was interesting. What were you two up to?"

Her father waited.

Callie swallowed. "You taught us we should do all we can to help those in need, Mother. That's what I did today."

Her mother looked to her father. "Can't argue with that, can we?"

He crossed his arms over his chest. "We can when it puts Callie at risk of censure."

"Oh, I imagine we can weather a little censure," her mother said.

Callie drew in a breath and turned to kiss her mother's cheek. "Thank you, Mother. Things will be better from here out. You'll see."

She could not know how wrong she was.

Fritz could not quite believe his reprieve. Dinner had been a spur-of-the-moment thought, but it appeared to have been a good one. He'd told Callie he would protect her from unwanted social obligations as much as he could until the Season ended. Even though he now knew the name of the English conspirator, he saw no reason to back out of their agreement.

He returned to find Dolph waiting in the entry hall on the private side of the palace. The plumed tail thumped against the parquet floor a moment before the *Sennenhund* rose to meet Fritz's outstretched hands.

"Not the most exciting place at the moment, is it?" Fritz commiserated, sinking his fingers into the soft coat. "We need to find you somewhere you can run."

Dolph trotted along beside him as Fritz started for the salon. Leo was at the desk, reading a letter. He looked up and nodded a greeting to Fritz. "It's from Father."

Their father, the king, had left England several weeks ago now, intent on facing the ultimate source of their troubles, the ruling party in Württemberg. Fritz went to accept the letter, while Dolph plunked down by the hearth.

King Wilhelm has agreed to see me, their father reported. *But there are many here who are troubled by my presence. We have heard rumors that someone in England is attempting to halt our efforts. He may be associated with the Envoy for Württemberg. Be on your guard.*

"So he confirms what Callie suspected," Fritz said, dropping the letter onto the desk in the salon in front of his brother. "And I know his conspirator. Callie identified him today: Robert Wellmanton, son of Lord Wellmanton."

Leo leaned back and narrowed his eyes. "Wellmanton may be the source of those rumors, then. I imagine the word of a member of the House of Commons would go far with a reporter."

Fritz snorted, and Dolph raised his head to eye him. "Farther than the word of a Batavarian count who seduces women and beats his staff."

"And buys artwork and takes in stray dogs to cover his evil tendencies," Leo agreed with a look to Dolph. He sighed. "A shame. Robert Wellmanton is well protected.

We cannot strike at him without proving his points to King George. But we may be able to work around his machinations, so long as your behavior remains above reproach…" He stopped, and too late Fritz tried to school his face.

"What have you done?" Leo demanded.

Dolph barked at the sharp tone. Fritz went to offer him a pat, using the time to think how he should respond to his brother. The dog dropped his head to his paws.

"I have done nothing that was noticed by anyone except the Duke of Wey," Fritz assured his twin, hands stroking the fur.

Leo glared at him. "Have you angered our future father-in-law?"

"Perhaps a little," Fritz admitted. "But I have already begun making amends. We will be hosting a dinner at the palace for the duke and his family on Wednesday."

Leo's smile reappeared. "Excellent. Speak to Lawrence about the arrangements."

"I would prefer that to be your role," Fritz said, straightening away from the dog. "He'll actually listen to what you tell him."

"He'd better listen to you as well," Leo said, voice turning harder again. "You are my brother, the son of the king. But, if you prefer, I'll direct the arrangements."

Fritz thanked him before realizing he should have agreed to see to the matter himself. Between their father's edicts and Leo's, there was little more he could do except remain watchful. And he had never been good at waiting.

At least he had the visit with Callie to look forward to on Tuesday. In the meantime, he took Dolph out onto the fields surrounding the palace. There were no animals to herd, and the unusual heat of the summer had turned the grass brown and brittle, but the *Sennenhund* enjoyed snuffing about. And Fritz couldn't deny it felt good to move.

He almost brought the dog with him on Tuesday, but he wasn't sure Callie's father would approve. As it was, the butler opened the door to his knock, but, to Fritz's surprise, he showed no sign of allowing Fritz inside.

"I believe Lady Calantha is indisposed at the moment," he said.

From beyond him came a whoop, and two bodies shot up the stairs. The butler drew the door a little tighter against his body, smile firm.

"She requested that I call," Fritz pointed out, mystified. "Is she unwell?"

"Not unwell," the butler hedged.

"You won't escape this time!"

Surely that was the duchess's voice. Feet thudded down the corridor.

"No! No!" That sounded like Belle.

Fritz pushed on the door. "Your family is in trouble, sir. Let me in. I can help."

"Run, Belle!" That was Callie. Nothing would stop him now. He rammed his shoulder against the panel and shoved the butler back just enough to allow Fritz inside. Chaos met his gaze.

Callie and her youngest sister were halfway up the stairs, skirts bunched. Larissa peered out of the withdrawing room for only a moment before diving back inside. Upstairs, feet thundered, and doors slammed. Then everything went silent.

The butler sighed.

The duchess came down the corridor, her elegant grey gown at odds with the wicked grin on her face. "I'll find you, you know. You will not escape." Her cackle echoed against the plastered walls. Then she nodded to him, and her voice turned far less threatening. "Good afternoon, Fritz. Would you like to join the game?"

"Game?" he asked.

"Hunter and hunted," the butler offered. "A time-honored tradition at Weyfarer House."

"Played ever since Belle was five," the duchess agreed. "The girls are generally too old for it now, of course, but Peter was feeling pent up, so we thought we'd entertain him." She cocked her head and glanced into the withdrawing room. "Far too easy, Larissa. I can see your slippers sticking out from under the draperies."

"Oh, bother!" Larissa came to join her, one hand smoothing her coiffure back into place. "Good afternoon, Fritz. I trust Leo is well?"

"Fine," Fritz said, trying to gather his wits. Hadn't Tuny mentioned the game in connection with the castle library? "So all this running about is a game?"

"A very fine game," the duchess informed him. "One person is the hunter." She bobbed a curtsey. "The rest find places to hide. If you manage to slip back down to the hunter's home, in this case, the library, without the hunter catching you, you are free. Otherwise…" She waggled her brows.

"She tickles," Larissa explained.

No wonder Belle had squealed. Fritz grinned. "Would you like help with hunting?"

The duchess clapped him on the shoulder. "Good man. I'll take the downstairs, you go up. Be sure to check the linen-room on the chamber story. Callie was always rather fond of it."

With a nod of apology to Underhill, Fritz climbed the stairs.

The chamber story was silent as he came out onto the landing. He walked on the toes of his boots down the center carpet, trying to give no indication he was coming. Most of the doors were closed, but he peered into several of the rooms—breakfast room, sewing room. He reached the end of the corridor and grasped the latch on the door there, then yanked it open.

Callie blinked at him. "Fritz?" She grabbed his jacket

and tugged him into the shelf-lined space. "Quick! She's coming!" She pulled the door shut behind him.

It was dark. Tight. Small. Breath fled. Memories swamped him, threatened to pull him under. He could hear the steps of the jailors, the jingle of keys a moment before they scraped in the lock. It wasn't the duchess but his enemies who were coming for him, and this time, they would not stop until he had dishonored his calling.

Or he was dead.

His hand fumbled, trying to find the latch. "Let me out."

"Sh!" Callie warned. "She'll hear you."

His lungs would not fill. His mind would not work. His fingers scrabbled at the wood.

"Fritz?" she asked, but he could not answer. He shoved open the door, fell through the opening, and sank onto the floor, head in his hands.

CHAPTER SEVENTEEN

"Fritz!" Callie clambered out of the linen-room and bent beside him. "Fritz! What is it?"

His gaze was unfocused, or at least she couldn't think of a reason he would be staring so blankly at the carpet. Sweat trickled down from his forehead.

Callie straightened. "I'll fetch Mother. She's very good with illnesses."

His hand shot out and gripped hers. "No, please. I cannot be alone."

Was that fear making his voice tremble? Surely not Fritz. She glanced up and down the corridor, but her brothers and Belle were hunkered in their hiding places, and she could hear her mother downstairs, threatening the usual dire consequences should they not appear.

Gathering her skirts, she crouched beside him and put a hand on his shoulder.

He flinched as if she had struck him. Her heart hurt. "Oh, Fritz," she murmured. "What can I do?"

He gulped in air as if he had just come up from a long time under the sea. "Stay with me. Talk to me."

"Very well." She put her back to the wall, sat, and arranged her skirts over her limbs. "I'm sure you were surprised to find us all dashing about like this. Peter was fretting. It's not easy being eight years old and in London for the Season. Everyone has been too busy to pay him much mind."

As conversation went, it wasn't original or even all that entertaining, but he drew in another deep breath. "You are kind to your brother." At least he sounded less desperate this time.

Noises below told her that her mother would be climbing the stairs shortly. She put her hand on his arm. He didn't pull away this time. "Why don't we sit in the breakfast room while Mother collects the others?"

He gathered his legs under him as if with an effort, but he managed to stand, and she rose and led him down the corridor to the cozy room. When he made no move to sit at the round table, she held out a chair for him.

That roused him a little. "I should hold the chair for you."

"Another time," she assured him, taking the seat beside him.

"Now, where could they be?" her mother demanded from the corridor. She glanced in the breakfast room. "You all are making this entirely too easy."

Fritz managed to bob his head. "My apologies, Your Grace. I will do better next time."

She eyed him a moment, and Callie shook her head. Her mother smiled. "See that you do. Now, to find the others." She stomped down the corridor.

"Why does she make so much noise?" he asked. "They will know she is coming."

"That's part of the fun," Callie said, glad to hear his voice returning to normal. "As a child, we would squeeze ourselves into the tightest corner and try not to giggle at the things she'd say. Belle always lost the battle first."

He chuckled. "And you always went for a place you knew. She said you would be in the linen-room."

She laughed. "Well, I am nothing if not predictable."

He sobered. "There is comfort in predictability. Safety too."

From down the corridor came a squeal from Belle,

who shot past the door on her way to the stairs. "You didn't touch me! I still have time to reach the library." She galloped down the stairs.

"Oh ho, my boys," their mother called. "You're all that's left to me, and I won't let you escape."

The words seemed to trouble him, for he closed his eyes and breathed through his nose.

"What is it?" Callie murmured. "What's wrong?"

He opened his eyes, and the weariness in them twisted around her heart like cold fingers. "It is not a tale for a lady."

She took his hand, held on tight. "Do not consider me a lady. Think of me as your friend. Let me help."

"You cannot help."

The despair was back, and it tore at her. "Yes, I can. I listen, remember? Tell me your story."

Once more he gulped the air, but he seemed to have no more will to protest. "Leo and I fought in the war against Napoleon. Because my brother was the crown prince, his efforts were confined mainly to the capital, patrolling for enemy soldiers who might have slipped through, plotting strategy, and the like. I led a group to where the Batavarian border runs along France's. It's mostly mountainous, except where the river exits the valley. That's where we were captured."

A shiver ran through her. "Captured? By the French?"

He nodded. "They took us to the nearest fortress, where they had a prison in the lowest part. My men told me the cells were three strides by three strides. I wouldn't know. I spent most of my time chained to the wall."

"Oh, Fritz." Her hand rose to his cheek, the skin cool and slack, as if all his energy had fled. "How horrid. But you escaped."

"After about a week. But in that time, I had been beaten and questioned so often I no longer remember most of the faces, the words. What I cannot forget is the dark, the damp, and the walls closing in. I never told Leo or our father. I did not give the French what they wanted, but I nearly did, and for that, I am ashamed."

Small wonder the linen-room had overset him. Even now, the vacant gaze, the pale skin proved he struggled to return to her. He relied on his skills and confidence, and they had failed him then. Used to protecting his father and brother, he was clearly ashamed of needing to protect himself instead.

Callie straightened in her seat. "Look at me."

He must have been surprised by her command, for his head snapped up. But his gaze brushed hers warily.

"You nearly gave your life for your country. There is no shame in that, only honor. You are here now, with me. The French are far away in their horrid little dungeon. They cannot harm you. I won't let them."

That won a smile from him. "Determined to fight them, are you?"

"Very," she assured him. "I won't let someone I care about be hurt, not if I can help it."

His smile softened. "And do you care about me then, Callie?"

Too much. Far too much. "Yes, Fritz," she said, and the words came out in a whisper.

He leaned closer and brushed his lips against hers. She was warming, melting, until he was as much a part of her as her skin. This, this was where she belonged.

"Ew!" Peter said.

Callie pulled away and opened her eyes to find her brother staring at them from the doorway.

"I have you now!" their mother threatened.

He dashed off with her on his heels.

In the quiet that followed, Callie heard Fritz take a breath.

"Thank you," he said. His face was still close enough that she could feel his warmth returning. "For listening, for caring, for understanding. You are good for me."

Looking into his eyes, she might think herself the most beautiful woman in England. It was enough for now. "And you are good for me," she said. "Now, let's catch Thal."

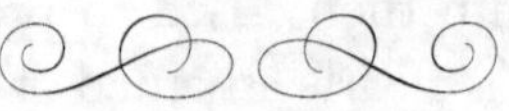

Such little things—a kind word, a compassionate glance, the touch of a hand, the brush of lips—yet he felt cleaner than he had in years. It was as if she had seen the tattered parts of him and sewn them back into a whole. He could only marvel as he gathered his feet under him and went to rejoin her family.

They played two more rounds of this interesting game, and both times Fritz hid with Callie. If a few more kisses were exchanged, he would not comment on it. But if he left with a fatuous grin on his face, he would not have been surprised.

Yet the coach hadn't even exited the confines of Clarendon Square before he was restive again. Callie had pushed back the memories of those dark days, but the feeling of helplessness remained, and he knew why. Leo was so certain they should do nothing while Robert Wellmanton and this staff member of the Württemberg Envoy planned their next move. Fritz had been waiting his entire life, standing silent along the wall while Leo and their father negotiated treaties and planned events. He'd been taught that waiting was merely a prelude to acting whenever danger reared its head. Danger was breathing in their faces. Why continue waiting?

He rapped on the roof, and their English coachman slid open the panel to peer down at him. "My lord?"

"Do you know where Lord Wellmanton lives?" he asked.

"Aye. Around the corner from Clarendon Square."

"Take me there."

"At once." The panel snicked shut.

The Wellmantons had one of a row of white houses squeezed together along a fashionable street. Fritz climbed to the red-lacquered door and knocked, possible strategies still tumbling through his mind.

"Count Montalban of Batavaria to see Mr. Robert Wellmanton," he told the white-haired butler, whose eyes widened a moment before he pulled his face into submission.

"I will inquire as to whether Master Robert is home," the butler said, swinging wide the door. "Won't you wait, my lord?"

Fritz stepped into an entry hall with a marble-tiled floor and pale green walls. From a room on the left, feminine voices chatted.

A few moments later, not the son but the father trotted down the corridor on the heels of his butler.

"Count Montalban, a pleasure," Lord Wellmanton greeted.

The voices in the other room stilled, as if all the ladies were listening.

"My lord," Fritz acknowledged. "I was hoping for a moment with your son."

"Robert takes his duties in the House seriously," Lord Wellmanton said, chest puffed with obvious pride. "He is not expected back before nightfall. But I'd be delighted to be of service." He stepped aside and waved Fritz down the corridor. "Join me in the library."

There was nothing overtly dangerous about the house or its occupants, yet Fritz hesitated. Even if Lord Wellmanton was more threatening than he appeared, Fritz was in better physical condition. And surely the viscount would do nothing with a bevy of belles just down the corridor. He nodded agreement and followed his host to a wood-paneled room. Unlike the library in Callie's house, only a few books were visible on one shelf, and he was not surprised to see dust peppering the tops.

Instead of sitting behind the massive desk at the back of the room, Wellmanton settled his girth into one of the green velvet upholstered chairs near the hearth and nodded Fritz into the other across from him. "How might my son and I be of assistance to Batavaria?"

He beamed with all goodwill, hands resting complacently across his striped waistcoat. Could Callie have mistaken Mr. Eager? Could this English lord and his family be innocent?

Approach decided. The best way to find out was to attack straight on.

"We have heard some in England are displeased by our intent to enlist your king's support to recover our lands," Fritz said. "Tell me who would be so bold."

Instead of taking umbrage at the command, Wellmanton stuck out his heavy lower lip. "There have been rumors, but nothing substantial, I fear."

"Perhaps those who are invested in the silver mines?" Fritz pressed.

Wellmanton smiled congenially. "The silver mines will surely continue their output whoever holds those lands. I cannot see that as any indication of support or lack thereof."

Callie had named his son Mr. Eager. It seemed the father was Lord Reticent.

"It is a matter that troubles me greatly," Fritz allowed. "My duty is to protect the crown prince and the king. I cannot do that if I do not know who I must fight."

"A dilemma for certain," his host commiserated. "I wish I could be of more assistance."

Fritz leaned closer. "When we last saw you, in Lord Belfort's offices, you mentioned speaking with Herr von Grub, the secretary to the Envoy for Württemberg. Have you had any further conversations with him?"

"Certainly," he said. "My position puts me in contact with the staff of most of the embassies of other nations."

So calm, so logical. The son must be the one behind the rumors. Fritz was about to give up when a drop of sweat trickled down from his lordship's grey hair.

Not so innocent after all.

"Someone is trying to harm my family," Fritz said, rising. "I will not allow it. I have been called brute and savage. You would not want me to put truth to those lies. You may tell that to your son and your contacts from Württemberg."

Wellmanton licked his lips, gazing up at him but not bothering to rise. "Rather dour message, but I will pass it along as you request. If I may also offer a word of advice?"

Fritz inclined his head.

"I have been told there will be a masquerade at the Athenian Rooms on Saturday. You will likely find those opposed to the return of your lands there. In my experience, people are more forthcoming when they think themselves anonymous."

And they didn't know the woman listening would remember every word.

His silence must have assured the viscount of his interest, for Lord Wellmanton nodded. "I can arrange for tickets to be delivered to the palace, if you like."

Fritz eyed him. "Forgive me, my lord, but I'm not entirely sure who to trust at the moment."

Wellmanton rose at last, his bulk blotting out the sight of the hearth. "As a loyal Englishman, I can only do so much to help those from other nations. Allow me this opportunity to prove to you where my devotions lie."

There would be risks, but perhaps Fritz could manage them. Anything to stop this infernal waiting. And there might be a way to confirm Lord Wellmanton's character.

"Very well," Fritz said. "Thank you for your trouble. I would be in your debt if you would deliver four tickets to Weyfarer House, the home of the Duke of Wey, Thursday morning."

Now he hesitated, and Fritz feared he'd overplayed his hand. Then the viscount nodded. "That should be possible. Of course you would want to include your brother, the crown prince, and one or two guardsmen. Besides, I have had little opportunity to call on the duke and duchess this Season. I would be happy for the excuse."

So would Fritz.

CHAPTER EIGHTEEN

MEREDITH HAD BEEN debating whether it was time to change for dinner when Fortune suddenly raised her head and stared at the withdrawing room doorway.

"Do we have a caller so late?" Meredith asked a moment before the door knocker sounded.

Fortune jumped to the carpet and scurried to the landing to peer through the balustrades at the entry hall below.

Meredith set aside the book she had been reading on the sofa and put on a pleasant smile. Likely it was one of her girls from down the street, or one of her former clients—now closer to family. She and Fortune had matched dozens of couples over the years. Lydia and Worth had returned from Cornwall a few days ago. She couldn't wait to hear what they planned to do next on advancing the science of ballooning. And Patience, Sir Harry, and their family were due in for their annual London shopping trip.

Mr. Cowls, her elderly butler, paused in the doorway, soft-skinned chin up, gaze off in the middle distance. "Count Montalban requests a moment of your time, Lady Belfort." His lips quirked just the slightest as he said the last two words with particular gusto. He was beyond delighted with Julian's—and, by extension Meredith's—elevation, and he did all he could to work their new titles into any conversation.

Meredith could not help her frown. "Only Count Montalban? Without Callie or Prince Otto Leopold?"

Now Mr. Cowls' lips curled just the slightest. "Only Count Montalban, Lady Belfort."

Interesting. "Very well. Please show him up."

"Very good, my lady." He went to do as she bid.

"Perhaps you should come here," Meredith told Fortune.

The cat strolled into the sunny yellow withdrawing room but paused just inside the doorway and began washing one delicate paw.

Meredith chuckled. "We're neither of us good at obeying, are we?"

A few moments later, the count appeared. He was dressed in civilian clothes today, but even the tailored navy coat couldn't hide his princely swagger as he came forward to offer her a bow. "Lady Belfort, Fortune, thank you for seeing me."

Fortune stopped her washing to eye him speculatively as well. He'd once called her "kitty." He'd never made that mistake again.

"Count," Meredith said. "To what do I owe this unexpected pleasure?"

Fortune strolled closer but kept herself well out of reach.

Count Montalban claimed the seat across from Meredith on one of the satin-striped chairs. She hadn't remembered those lines around his eyes. Was something troubling him?

"I would like to ask your help," he said.

"Has something happened to Callie?" Meredith asked, leaning forward.

"No," he acknowledged. "But your involvement could help protect her."

Meredith pressed a hand to the chest of her lavender walking dress. "You have me all agog."

"You will likely have read some recent reports of me in the newspaper," he said, voice hinting of his displeasure.

"Shameful," Meredith told him. "I put no stock in them whatsoever."

"Thank you," he said, inclining his head. "Callie has been helping me investigate who might be behind the rumors. We thought we had identified at least one of the culprits, but I begin to wonder. I have been given to understand that the person we seek might be attending a masquerade this Saturday. I want Callie to attend with me."

"People do have a tendency to spill their secrets around her," Meredith acknowledged.

A wry laugh rumbled out of him. "So I've noticed. But this masquerade could also be a trap intended to embarrass and discredit me further. I would not want Callie caught up in that. Would you and Lord Belfort be willing to accompany us?"

Meredith leaned back as Fortune prowled past her skirts. "Some masquerades are known for their salacious behavior. Neither Callie, nor my husband and I, should be associated with such."

"All I know is that this event is to be held at the Athenian Rooms, where Callie and Tuny staged the benefit dinner, and Lord Wellmanton and his son are involved."

Meredith cocked her head, thinking. "The Wellmantons are generally well regarded, and the Athenian Rooms are beyond reproach. I don't believe we have anything planned for Saturday. Let me speak with Julian and send you a confirmation."

"Thank you." The words were breathed out with a sigh of relief. He edged forward on the seat, and Fortune chose that moment to leap up onto his lap.

Diamond blue eyes met copper-colored ones. Neither body moved. Fortune had disdained him at first sight but had later changed her mind. Had he done something to lower himself in her esteem?

"I am honored," he said, and he tentatively raised a hand and ran it down the grey fur.

Fortune arched her back against the touch, then began kneading his trousers with her paws.

Meredith reached across and pulled the cat onto her lap with an apologetic smile to Callie's betrothed.

Count Montalban smiled back, gaze still on her pet, who was suffering Meredith's touch. "I have one other favor to ask. Would you and Fortune be willing to visit Weyfarer House Thursday morning? There's someone I'd like her to meet."

Once again, Callie stood staring into the depths of her wardrobe, thinking. It was only a dinner, one of many over the course of a Season. She had no one to impress. She wasn't really engaged to Fritz, and nearly everyone else at the dinner would be family. Yet, it felt so much more important.

She had begun to hope that Fritz would see fit to make their pretend betrothal real. For so long, she'd thought he wasn't the man for her. Now she could imagine a future together: her encouraging him, him encouraging her. He had the strength to act when she hesitated. She had the strength to comfort when he faltered. They were better together than apart.

How could she help him see that?

The bedchamber door opened, and Belle, Larissa, Tuny, and Anna all converged on her.

"We are here to help," Belle announced, moving in beside her at the wardrobe. "I'd advise the one with the rosebuds at the hem."

"And your hair crimped in curls," Larissa added.

"With pearls at your neck," Tuny put in.

Anna nodded, smiling.

Callie stepped back from the wardrobe. "Thank you, but I have another idea. Tuny, did you intend to wear your yellow silk tonight, the one with the puffy sleeves?"

Her friend frowned. "No."

"May I borrow it?"

"Anna will have to make some tucks, but of course," Tuny said with a look to the maid, whose smile was fading. "Not sure why you want to wear one of my castoffs, though. You have day dresses nicer."

Callie moved to the dressing table. "An experiment, if you will."

Belle put her hands on her hips. "You don't experiment."

Larissa nodded, moving closer with a swish of blue satin. "I was under the impression you found variety in matters of dress decidedly dangerous."

Callie grinned at them in the reflection of the dressing table mirror. "Perhaps I've discovered there's something to be said for a little danger now and again."

Belle dropped her hands and grinned. "Oh, this will be fun."

And it was. Once they understood Callie's purpose, her sisters and Tuny entered into the effort with glee. Anna sat on a chair tacking in portions of the gown while Larissa fetched her citrine necklace and Belle offered a pearl-handled fan. Tuny went to work on Callie's hair, fingers deft and sure to pile up her tresses and leave a few silken strands to trail. Watching the transformation in the mirror, Callie felt her stomach flutter, as if a herd of Belle's beloved unicorns were capering inside her.

The end result was perfection. Her head was high as she walked down the stairs to meet her parents so that they could travel out to the palace.

Thal had been invited to dinner as well, but he had decided to stay behind so Peter wouldn't be alone.

Another time, Callie might have stayed with them. Now, nothing would have kept her from Fritz's side.

It was a squeeze in the coach to fit the six of them, but everyone was in such a good mood no one mentioned the tight quarters as they headed for the palace. The massive house glittered like a gemstone in the night as the coach pulled up before the public entrance. Lanterns glowed among the foliage along the walk. The guardsmen standing on either side of the lacquered doors looked neither left nor right as Callie's father and mother entered.

Callie nodded to each of them. "Mr. Huber, Mr. Roth."

Their looks never wavered, but they clapped their fists to the chests of their black uniforms in salute.

Callie couldn't help her grin as she sailed past.

Fritz, Leo, and their Lord Chamberlain Lawrence were waiting in the gold-medallion-lined gallery that led to the reception hall. Both Fritz and his brother were in scarlet coats tonight, their hair swept back and their bearing regal. Leo's gaze was all for Larissa, but Callie felt the weight of Fritz's stare. Was he actually gaping? Her cheeks heated.

A bellow of a bark echoed down the gallery, and Dolph galloped toward her. As he slid to a stop on the marble floor, Callie rubbed his head.

"My apologies," the Lord Chamberlain fussed, bald spot turning pink. "I thought this creature was confined."

"I don't mind," Callie said as a footman came puffing up to take custody of Fritz's pet. "Dolph and I are old friends."

"And Dolph obviously knows to appreciate beauty when he sees it," Fritz said as the hound surrendered to the footman's lead. Fritz took her hand and bowed over it. "Yellow becomes you."

"As you surmised," she reminded him.

He straightened, but he did not release her hand.

Indeed, the longer he held it, the warmer she felt.

She glanced around quickly. Her mother and father were now talking with the Lord Chamberlain, and Tuny and Belle were chatting with Leo and Larissa.

"No one will notice if you release me," she whispered.

"Ah, but if I release your hand, I will be too tempted to run my fingers through your hair," he murmured back. "And that, I promise you, others will notice."

Admiration set his silvery blue gaze to gleaming. Was admiration enough to make him rethink their pretend engagement? He'd shown her kindness, interest. Weren't some marriages built on less?

"Perhaps we should go in to dinner," he suggested with a smile, and she realized the others were all heading in that direction. She nodded, and he tucked her arm in his before leading her through the grand reception hall to the dining room beyond.

From previous events at the palace, she knew the long table could seat more than forty. Tonight, leaves must have been removed to allow it to be set for nine. Leo sat at the head, with Larissa on his right and Fritz on his left. Callie sat next to Fritz, with the Lord Chamberlain on her other side and her mother and father opposite. Tuny sat next to Callie's mother, and Belle was beyond the Lord Chamberlain. Her youngest sister did not appear amused, but Callie thought Belle stood a better chance at engaging the older gentleman in conversation than Tuny would.

"Your Grace," Leo said to Callie's father, "would you lead us in prayer?"

"It would be my pleasure," her father said. Callie bowed her head and clasped her hands. He went on to say the grace over the food and the company. As soon as she raised her head, she felt a touch on her arm.

"Thank you for coming," Fritz murmured. "I thought this was one crowd you would enjoy."

She smiled at him. "My family isn't a crowd. And neither is yours."

His answering smile was pleased.

It turned out to be a merry meal. Leo, Larissa, and Callie's father carried on a lively conversation about Catholic emancipation. Her mother and Tuny called questions to Belle and the Lord Chamberlain, who rose to the occasion well. All Callie had to do was talk to Fritz, and that was never a hardship.

"Dare I ask how the search goes for the other man?" she murmured at one point as he was toying with his salmon in dill sauce.

His face was devoid of emotion. "I have an opportunity to perhaps unmask him. May I call on you tomorrow to explain further?"

"Of course." Of all people, she could understand why he might not want to talk of it where he could be overheard. But she had to own her curiosity.

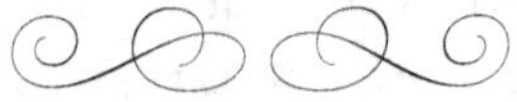

How lovely she was. Her sweet smile, the way she dipped her chin, the candlelight reflecting in her shimmering hair. He wanted to entwine her fingers with his, draw her closer. A shame he hadn't thought to tell Lawrence to hire a quartet so he could hold Callie in his arms at least in the dance.

It was the British custom for gentlemen to linger over drink while ladies waited in another room. Fritz saw no need to abide by the stricture. When the duchess rose, signaling the time for the ladies to withdraw, he went with them, leaving Leo, the duke, and Lawrence little choice but to follow as well.

Unfortunately, cozy chambers were hard to come by on the public side of the palace, where everything was so gilded and velvet-flocked it was sometimes difficult to determine function, and spaces were meant to entertain hundreds, not less than a dozen.

"Perhaps here, Your Grace," Fritz suggested to Callie's mother, indicating a corner of the gallery, where a crimson velvet sofa was surrounded by matching chairs. As they all settled into place, Fritz went to stand in the center of the space.

"I have seen how your family likes to play games," he told the duke and duchess, who sat side-by-side on the sofa. "Leo and I were not afforded the opportunity when we were young, but there is one favored by the Batavarian court: Mountain-Valley."

Leo grinned. "I haven't thought about that in years. You were good."

Fritz nodded as their guests looked up eagerly. "I hope I still am. Here's how it's played. I will be the Guide. I will point to one of you. The first person must think of something associated with a mountain. The second with a valley. Everyone else claps. If you cannot think of something before we reach five claps, you are out. Once one person is out, we decrease the claps to four, then three, then two, then one. And you cannot repeat a word."

"Challenging," the duchess said, edging forward on her seat. "I'm in."

They all nodded agreement.

"Very well, then." Fritz pointed to the duke. "Mountain." He clapped his hands.

"Snow," His Grace said before the second clap sounded.

Fritz whirled and pointed to Belle. "Valley."

Everyone had clapped three times before Belle said, "Grass!"

"Mountain," Fritz called, pointing at the duchess.

"Rocks," she said immediately.

"Valley," Fritz said to Tuny.

"I'm not a farmer," she said, glancing around as the

clapping began.

"Baaa," Belle said, waving her fingers beside her head.

"Sheep!" Tuny cried just as they reached the fourth clap. She collapsed back against her chair.

Fritz wasn't surprised when she was the first person out.

"I'll do better next time," she promised.

Lawrence was the next to miss a mountain word. Larissa missed a valley word by a single clap. Leo sent her a commiserating look before losing on a mountain word. Belle accidentally repeated a word and was out. The duke lost on the next valley word.

That left Callie and her mother. They faced off across the space, with Fritz in the middle. The duchess's eyes were narrowed and determined. Callie's eyes were wide, and she watched him, waiting for the second his directive left his lips.

"You will take the mountain words, Your Grace," Fritz told her. "Callie, you have the valley. Ready?"

"Ready," the duchess said.

Callie nodded, as if afraid to waste her breath on an unimportant word.

"Mountain," Fritz said to Callie's mother.

"Clouds," she snapped before the clap echoed.

"Fields," Callie shot back.

"Frost," her mother returned.

"Fen."

"Frozen."

"Pond," Callie said doggedly.

"Waterfall."

"Ants."

Her mother raised a brow, and the clap sounded. "Antlers!" she cried.

The duke looked to Fritz.

"I will allow it," Fritz said. "Callie, to you."

"Daisies," she said, fingers curling over the arms of the

velvet upholstered chair.

"Caves," her mother responded.

"Hares," Callie countered.

"Huts."

"Homes."

"This could go on all night," Lawrence murmured to Leo.

"*Sennenhunds*," her mother challenged.

"Beagles," Callie returned.

"Eagles."

"Unicorns!"

Her mother blinked, and the clap echoed. Then she started laughing. "Oh, well done, Callie!"

The others joined in her applause. Callie grinned at Fritz, flushing with pleasure.

"What does she win?" Belle asked as the sound faded.

"Our admiration," her father said, with a warning look around before anyone could suggest a kiss.

Callie certainly had Fritz's admiration.

But he managed a kiss when it was time to escort their guests to the door. As footmen helped her mother and father into the carriage, Fritz took Callie's hand and brought it to his lips. "You are magnificent."

"It's the company I keep," she murmured, cheeks once more rosy.

He stood with Leo and watched as the carriage trundled down the drive.

"I see it now," Leo said as they turned for the palace doors. "The two of you. She will make you a fine wife."

Fritz nodded. Words crowded his tongue, but the only person he wanted to share them with was driving off with her family.

"Have you thought about where you will live?" Leo asked as they came through the doors. Lawrence had already retired for the night, and footmen were putting out the lamps behind Leo and Fritz as they moved toward the private side of the palace.

He had never thought of living anywhere but with his father and brother, captaining the guard, working for the restoration of the kingdom. The thought of laying the burdens down, even for a moment, was unthinkable.

Until he thought of it.

"A house in the country," he said. "Where we can have dogs and sheep."

Leo raised his brows as they passed the portrait of their father along the corridor between the two sides of the palace. "After acquiring Dolph, I see the attraction of dogs. But sheep?"

"The dogs need something to herd," Fritz reasoned.

Leo laughed. "Sheep it is, then. A fine, quiet life, though not one I would have thought you'd enjoy."

"Perhaps you do not know me as well as you thought, then, Brother," Fritz replied.

Leo eyed him. "Perhaps I don't. But I look forward to learning more."

So did Fritz. First, however, he had to stop these men intent on ruining his name. Callie deserved a husband who came to her without the pall of scandal.

CHAPTER NINETEEN

CALLIE WASN'T SURPRISED when Larissa and Tuny showed up in her and Belle's bedchamber for a meeting that night after everyone else was abed. They all piled on her bed, eyes shining.

"You have made a conquest," Belle declared.

"I don't think this is going to be a pretend engagement much longer," Larissa agreed.

"Neither do I," Callie said with a smile. "He promised to call tomorrow."

"And we will be ready," Belle promised. "I'll keep Father busy."

"I'll take Mother," Larissa offered.

"Count on me to keep Thal and Peter entertained," Tuny said. "All you have to worry about is bringing him up to scratch."

Callie's smile faltered. Fritz had shown every sign of a man besotted, but what if he had simply been acting a part for her family? He'd played the role of his twin brother so well that few had ever caught on. How could she be sure of him now?

In any case, she planned to be available early the next morning, in case Fritz should call then, but she had no sooner come down to breakfast than Belle shoved the latest edition of *The Times* at her.

"What rot!" her sister said, nose up. "I have a mind to tell Father to cancel his subscription."

Callie glanced down at the story her sister had folded to the top. *Batavarian Count Attacks British Citizens in Kew Gardens*, the headline read.

What!

Callie sank onto the seat and pored over the paper. The report was a garbled account of the incident in Kew Gardens, when Fritz had been kidnapped. Larissa and Thal had been there, looking for Leo, and had been pulled unwittingly into the escapade. But Fritz hadn't attacked anyone. Thal had told Callie the entire story. Hands tied behind him, Fritz had shoved into their captor to prevent the man from harming Larissa, at a danger to his own life. He was the hero, not the villain.

"The piece says the incident was kept quiet, as if to cover something shameful," Belle complained, flouncing to take her own seat across the table from Callie. "It was kept quiet to protect those who were innocent. If that reporter had interviewed Leo or Larissa, they could have told him the truth."

"Whoever told him the story made him think *they* knew the truth," Callie said, lowering the paper. And, if he'd sought a second opinion, he might have gone to Lord Wellmanton, whose son would have been happy to fill his head with lies.

Across from her, Belle raised her head. "Was that a knock at the door?" She grinned. "He *is* eager!"

During the Season, it wasn't uncommon for callers to be knocking at the door of Weyfarer House, but generally in the afternoons. Young ladies came to compare notes with Larissa on the latest styles. Young men came to importune Belle for a ride. Members of the Society for the Prevention of Cruelty to Animals might call on Callie and Tuny, and all four of them had friends they could count on to stop by and share triumphs. Mr. Canady had been a more frequent caller of late.

But in general, the *ton* did not rise before ten, some

not before noon. Was Fritz really calling on her at half past nine?

Boots sounded in the corridor a moment before Underhill appeared in the doorway of the breakfast room, Fritz just behind.

"Count Montalban, my ladies," the butler said. "I will alert your mother."

As the butler took himself off, Fritz bowed to them both, dapper in his bottle green coat and fawn trousers. "Callie, Belle. Forgive the early morning call." He held out a cloth-covered basket. "I bring pastries from our cook by way of apology."

Belle rose and motioned to the table. "Good morning, Fritz. Set them down, if you will. I'll just go see what's keeping Mother." She wiggled her brows at Callie before disappearing out the door.

Callie offered Fritz a smile. He returned it, but his gaze was already going after her sister. "No other callers yet this morning?"

"No," Callie told him. "I wouldn't have expected them."

That he was expecting them was evident over the next little while. Belle must not have been able to keep the other members of the family busy, for, one by one, they trickled into the room. At least everyone was dressed for the day, except her father, who wore riding clothes. Fritz answered their questions as readily as always, even her father's questions about the story in the newspaper, but his gaze kept drifting to the door.

Who did he think was coming?

Fritz kept his conversation light, but his thoughts turned faster than the wheels on the royal carriage when his coachman had driven him into London. The story in the newspaper was fresh proof that their enemy was still active. How could Fritz involve Callie further, possibly risk her reputation if not her life?

Yet, how much easier to unmask the enemy with her beside him? Lord and Lady Belfort would be there to assist him in keeping her safe. Surely others had been invited to this masquerade. But would having additional guests around them be sufficient to safeguard her?

"Fritz," the duchess called from the other side of the table in the breakfast room. "I think you're just the man to solve my problem."

Fritz smiled at her, bringing his thoughts back to the moment. "How might I be of assistance?"

"We're looking for places to take Peter before he and Thal must return for Michaelmas term," Callie's mother explained.

"We've been to the Horse Armory and the other Tower attractions," Tuny offered, "as well as the British Museum and Mr. Soane's."

"We also tried the menagerie at the Exchange," Thal reminded them. "Though Callie refused to come."

Of course not. Like him, she did not like seeing creatures in cages. He felt their plight too keenly. He looked to her, and she smiled. Her hair was back up today, and he had to own he missed the falling tendrils she had effected at dinner last night. All he'd wanted to do was bury his fingers in them.

He forced himself to look at her youngest brother, seated next to her mother. Like his father, he had a longer face, but his green eyes looked more wary than thoughtful.

"What do you enjoy, Lord Peter?" he asked.

Peter gazed back at him with a slight frown. "Soldiers. Battles."

Callie reached out to take Fritz's hand. "Battles aren't always pleasant, Peter."

Her touch banished the dark thoughts that threatened to swoop closer. "Indeed, no," Fritz agreed. "However, I can give you soldiers. How would you and Lord Thalston like to come to the palace and train with the Imperial Guard?"

Peter's face lit. "We would like it above half!"

Thal, on the other side of the duchess, tempered his grin. "That is, it is very kind of you to suggest such an outing, my lord. When would be convenient for you?"

"Friday I was planning on saber drills at eleven. And I know Dolph would enjoy a good romp." He glanced at Callie, who nodded.

"Friday it is," the duchess said. "And thank you, Fritz."

He inclined his head. Still the knocker hadn't sounded. It seemed he'd misjudged the English customs again. Or had Lord Wellmanton decided not to call?

All the more reason to talk to Callie about this masquerade.

"Would you allow me to borrow Lady Calantha for a few moments, Your Grace?" he asked.

Her mother's smile was amused. "I don't see why not. A turn about the park might be good. Peter and Thal can accompany you."

Wise woman. It would be hard for any suitor to take advantage of the situation with two boys along. And he already knew what Callie's youngest brother thought about kisses.

Peter and Thal were keen to accompany them, so, a short while later, the four of them crossed the street and entered the park in the center of the square. He'd become accustomed to the London parks, bits of greenery among all the stone and brick, but they still seemed an odd convention. In Batavaria, greenery had been everywhere.

At least he could keep an eye on the house as they walked, to see when Lady Belfort, Fortune, and Lord Wellmanton arrived. Now, for a moment of privacy with

Callie.

"A good soldier must be able to move quickly and silently," he told Peter, who was scampering along beside them. "Lord Thalston, would you by chance have a pocket watch?"

"Of course." Thal pulled out a silver case and popped it open.

"I suggest you time your brother from here to that bench, and then he can time you."

"Excellent." Thal nodded, and Peter sprinted off. The older boy focused on the face of the watch.

Fritz drew Callie back a little ways. "When we were at dinner last night, you asked about my investigation. I visited the Wellmanton house."

She pressed her hand to her lips a moment. "Was Robert there? What did he say? What did he do?"

"Robert was absent," Fritz admitted. "But his father was remarkably composed as I questioned him instead. He would not admit to helping any specific person from Württemberg. But, when I pressed him, he urged me to attend a masquerade this Saturday evening."

Ahead of them, Peter had come pelting back and now held the watch for Thal, who sprinted off.

"Why a masquerade?" Callie asked.

"I gather the other gentleman you overheard will be there."

She made a face. "But masked! How will you find him?"

Fritz rubbed the toe of his boot on the path. "I had considered inviting you along, but it's likely to be very crowded."

"I'd be willing to come," she said.

Relief was as loud as Peter's crow.

"A quarter of a minute! I did it in ten seconds. I won."

Thal was panting, and Fritz couldn't like the way his breath wheezed out.

"It's entirely too warm," the older boy protested, pausing to cough. "I'll do better when it cools."

"Of course you will," Callie readily assured him. "Though ten seconds is very good time, Peter. Do you think you can beat it?"

"Right now!" He dashed off.

Thal sat on the closest bench, shoulders slumped, and he did not consult the watch. Fritz thought he knew what was going through the lad's mind. He went to sit beside him.

"Leo is the older brother in my family," he told Callie's brother.

Thal frowned. "But you're twins. You were born at the same time."

"Not the same time," Fritz clarified with a nod to the watch in the lad's hands. "Leo was born a quarter hour earlier. And I beat *him* at a foot race too. But he's still crown prince. He will be king one day. It is his job to see to the wellbeing of our family, our people, and our kingdom."

Thal visibly swallowed. "Does he find it a difficult burden?"

"Sometimes," Fritz admitted. "But he was born to it, trained for it. Just as you are being trained to take your father's place one day."

Peter came thundering back and dropped onto the last few inches of the bench, face red. "Well?"

"Nine seconds," Thal said though he hadn't consulted the watch. He managed a smile. "An improvement."

Peter beamed.

"Perhaps enough of an improvement for today," Fritz said, rising before the boy could offer to dash away again. "Your brother is right. It is rather warm. We should return to the house."

Peter slid a glance between him and Callie. "But you haven't kissed her yet."

"Peter," Thal scolded even as Callie turned pink.

"I can remedy that on the way back," Fritz promised.

Peter shuddered and took off toward the gate, Thal not far behind.

"You don't have to kiss me to please my brothers," Callie said, falling into step beside Fritz.

"I don't kiss you to please anyone but myself," he replied. "And, I hope, you?"

"As a lady, I should not answer that," she said primly, but her color was deepening.

Fritz put out a hand to stop her. "You said I should not consider you a lady but my friend."

"I remember," she murmured.

He lay his hand against her cheek, watching as her eyes widened. "I am having difficulty thinking of you as a friend." Bending, he brushed her lips with his. Her sigh of pleasure was his reward.

She broke the kiss and stepped back, drawing a breath as shaky as her brother's. "If you continue to kiss me, you will raise expectations."

"Expectations I am willing to meet," he assured her.

Her gaze searched his, then her lips curled up. "I am delighted to hear it."

From the street came the sound of her brothers arguing. She sighed, a far less enticing sound this time.

"We should go," she said. "Perhaps we should talk about costumes for this masquerade. I don't want to appear too ostentatious or too remarkable. What will you wear?"

The words were as quick and sure as her steps as they headed after her brothers. As much as their duty might frustrate him, he knew she was right. Now was not the time to tell her he was falling in love with her. But soon, he promised himself.

"My guard uniform," he answered, pacing her.

She shot him a look. "Oh, Fritz, really? But that's no different from what you usually wear. Everyone will know it's you."

"Precisely," he agreed, smile lifting. "I am who I am. It's time the English realized that."

Every time Fritz kissed her, Callie's hopes soared. In England, a gentleman did not dispense kisses, or appear to enjoy them so much, if he was not intent on marriage. Most of the times he'd kissed her, there had been no one to see, so he had not been playing a role. And he had said he was willing to meet expectations. Perhaps, perhaps, she had captured his heart.

She had nearly forgotten his obsession with the door that morning until they returned to find that Aunt Meredith and Fortune had arrived. Although he had long overstayed the length of a typical call, Fritz sat in the withdrawing room with her mother and aunt while Tuny and Larissa took charge of Thal and Peter.

And still Fritz watched the door.

Callie couldn't understand why until Underhill announced Lord Wellmanton. She tensed at the sight of him, but the heavy-set viscount bowed to her mother and asked after her father as politely as any caller.

"Have you met Lady Belfort and Count Montalban?" her mother asked after she'd answered his queries.

"I know Count Montalban," he said, "but I have not had the pleasure of meeting Lady Belfort." He bowed in her direction.

Aunt Meredith inclined her head. "Lord Wellmanton."

"And there is someone else I'd like you to meet," Fritz said. He nodded to Aunt Meredith, who promptly set Fortune on the floor in front of her. Suddenly, Callie knew what he'd been waiting for.

Lord Wellmanton, however, missed his cue. Instead of

noticing the cat, he glanced at Callie. "You look familiar."

"You remember my daughter, Lady Calantha," her mother told him, voice crisp, before Callie could respond. "She's called on your wife and daughters often enough."

His brow cleared. "Yes, of course. My apologies, Lady Calantha."

Callie hoped her answering smile didn't look strained. Then she turned her attention on the cat.

Fortune had an uncanny ability to know a person's worth. She might curl around their skirts in approval or stalk off in high dudgeon.

This time, she took one look at Lord Wellmanton, barred her teeth and hissed. Then she turned her back and disappeared behind the sofa.

"Well," Aunt Meredith said, even as Fritz crossed his arms over his chest.

Callie's mother rose. "It was very kind of you to call, Lord Wellmanton. Do give our regards to your lovely wife and daughters."

Lord Wellmanton, who had yet to so much as take a seat, blinked at her.

Fritz dropped his arms. "I will walk you out, my lord."

Lord Wellmanton recovered. "Yes, thank you. Good day, Duchess, Lady Belfort, Lady Calantha." He followed Fritz out the door.

Aunt Meredith went to find Fortune, where she had slunk behind the draperies. "Not a promising introduction."

"I've never seen such a reaction," Callie said, gaze going after the viscount.

"Rarely," her mother said as Aunt Meredith returned with Fortune up in her arms, one hand running along the cat's back. Fortune's eyes were still narrowed, and a low rumble came from her throat that did not sound like her usual contented purr.

"What do you know of this, Callie?" her mother asked.

It wasn't her story to tell. She was just glad that Fritz returned then, tucking an envelope into the breast of his uniform.

"Allow me to explain, Duchess," he said. "I asked Lady Belfort and Fortune here today because I suspect Lord Wellmanton of conspiring with his son to harm my family."

Her mother nodded. "Callie mentioned she'd overheard two men plotting. I've seen the stories in the newspaper since. You think Lord Wellmanton provided the fodder?"

"I think he may have done more than that," Fritz admitted. "He may be supporting someone on the staff of the Württemberg Envoy to stop us from convincing King George to help us retake our country. However, he claims all innocence."

Aunt Meredith glanced down at Fortune, who had finally begun to relax in her arms. "Fortune thinks otherwise."

"So it would seem," Fritz said. He turned to Callie's mother. "And I am reminded that I have been remiss in protecting Lady Calantha's reputation. I would like to rectify that."

"You'd like to keep from hearing another lecture from His Grace," she said with a smile.

Fritz inclined his head. "That as well."

Callie was fairly sure what Fritz intended. "Lord Wellmanton invited Fritz to a masquerade, Mother. He would like me to accompany him."

Her mother frowned. "We've just established he's a ne'er-do-well, and you want to join him at a masquerade?"

"I have been led to believe our enemies will be attending," Fritz told her. "Callie could be invaluable to helping me identify them once and for all, regardless of whether they are wearing masks."

"Count Montalban asked Julian and me to attend as well," Aunt Meredith put in. "Like you, Jane, I want to see his enemies vanquished. It does neither Larissa nor Callie, not to mention the Batavarian court, any good for people to think Count Montalban a villain."

Callie held her breath as her mother glanced around at them all.

"Very well," her mother said. "You have my permission to attend." She leaned forward. "Now, to the important question: what are you going to wear?"

Callie let out her breath. "Thank you, Mother. I have an idea for a costume, but I'll need help."

"Help," her mother said, "should not be a problem."

CHAPTER TWENTY

INDEED, BELLE, LARISSA, and Tuny were delighted to help, offering any number of suggestions as to what she could wear. But since Fritz was going to come in his uniform, Callie wanted her costume to align with his, which meant she needed to dress like a Batavarian lady. Though she had seen sketches of the ladies who worked on the Batavarian alpine ranches at various art exhibits, she searched her father's library for other information as well. Then she made a list of what she would require to play the part and consulted with the others in the library that afternoon after Fritz had returned to the palace.

"My sister Ivy has a red shawl," Tuny reported. "I'm sure she'd loan it to you."

"Perfect," Callie said.

"You can use my wide-brimmed, flat straw hat," Belle offered, "though we'll have to change the trim. No peacocks in the Alps, I fear."

Callie peered down at her list. "We'll need a band of ribbon and some flowers instead."

"I'll pick up the flowers from Covent Garden the day of the masquerade," Tuny volunteered.

"And you may have one of my ribbons," Larissa said.

Callie tapped her chin with her pencil. "My muslin day dress should do for the base, and Mrs. Hurley, the cook, said I could borrow one of her aprons. That leaves the mask."

Belle squeezed up her shoulders. "Leave that to me."

Callie was almost afraid what her sister would devise, but she nodded agreement.

Larissa leaned closer from her chair. "Has Fritz said anything about prolonging this engagement of yours?"

Callie dropped her gaze to the list, but instead of the closely written words, she saw Fritz's handsome face. "It's not as simple as that."

"I don't see why not," Belle said. "You admire him. He clearly admires you. That's all that matters."

"Perhaps a little more than that," Larissa interjected.

"Such as?" Belle demanded.

Callie looked up at her sister. Belle's face was set in militant lines, and her curls positively bounced with her emotions.

"If it's that easy," Callie challenged, "why haven't you found your own suitor?"

Belle colored. "I will only say that I haven't found a young man I can admire *enough*. But I have hopes. Mother's about ready to send the invitations to our house party."

Callie groaned. "Oh, no! You managed to convince her!"

Belle frowned. "Was there any doubt?"

"Who's coming?" Tuny asked, head cocked.

"All of us, of course," Belle said, "and your brother, Sir Matthew, and his wife and daughters. Aunt Meredith and Uncle Julian and Fortune. Leo and Fritz. And the appropriate gentlemen."

"The appropriate gentlemen," Tuny repeated, gaze narrowing. "Which gentlemen?"

Belle waved a hand. "Ones guaranteed to be congenial. I made sure of that. You need have no worries."

"And when she says that, I *only* worry," Tuny said with a look to Larissa.

"I'll ask Mother," Larissa promised. "She'll have the full

list. We can head off any concerning fellows."

Tuny appeared satisfied with that, but Belle merely smiled.

Friday, Callie rode out to the palace with her mother, Larissa, Thal, and Peter. Belle and Tuny stayed at Weyfarer House, and Aunt Meredith and Fortune came to join them while they entertained callers. They had high hopes that Mr. Canady might put in another appearance.

Peter had a difficult time remaining in his seat. He'd traveled between Surrey and London often enough that the change from city to countryside no longer amused him. Now he was too excited about meeting the Imperial Guards to sit still.

"Father said they fought Napoleon," he told them all as the coach rumbled out of Mayfair.

Callie did not want Fritz to be reminded of those days. "You wanted to see them in action, Peter," she said. "Sometimes it's better to watch quietly."

"Why?" Peter asked with a frown.

"Because," their mother said, slipping an arm about his shoulders where he sat beside her, "if you're always talking, you might miss what others are saying. God gave us two ears and one mouth for a reason."

"So we can listen twice as much as we speak," Thal said with a long-suffering sigh.

Whether it was that discussion in the coach or her brothers' awe of Leo and Fritz, Callie wasn't sure, but Thal and Peter paid close attention as Mr. Wyss explained the various drills in the courtyard. Larissa and Leo wandered off, with Callie's mother ambling not far behind, so Callie stayed with her brothers, and Fritz.

"I thought you were going to introduce them to

Dolph," she murmured as Thal made a credible thrust with a dulled practice saber.

Fritz smiled. He was dressed in looser clothes today, a rough black jacket without the usual braid and wide-legged trousers. The outfit made him look like the pictures of pirates in her father's books.

"Dolph is a bit eager to help us practice," he told her. "I cannot risk he might be hit or knock down one of my guards." He raised his voice. "Higher, Huber! You want to catch him in the arm, not the hip."

"Though it was an impressive strike!" Callie called.

Mr. Huber bowed to her, and Mr. Wyss smacked him on the rump with the flat of his sword to call him back to attention.

"They crave your good opinion," Fritz said, gaze on his men. "I understand. I feel the same way."

Callie blinked. "Why, Fritz, surely you know I admire you above all men."

His hands slipped down and captured hers. "Then I am a fortunate man indeed." He pulled her hand to his lips and pressed a kiss against her knuckles.

"There they go again!" Peter complained.

"Attend to your mission, Corporal Lord Peter," Mr. Wyss ordered, but his grin spoiled the command.

Callie didn't see Fritz again after they left the palace until he came for her Saturday evening for the masquerade. That didn't stop her from reliving their conversations, their kisses. Though he too was the offspring of wealth and power, his world was, in some ways, very different from hers. In any given day, her duties were minimal and more of her own choosing, while he carried the responsibility of safeguarding his father and brother. She was used to quiet introspection. He was a man of action. Could she truly bridge the gulf to make a good marriage?

At least her costume was ready. As Belle had promised, she had produced a lovely mask of white satin edged with silver sequins, which covered Callie's cheeks, nose, and forehead. It paired very well with the red and white satin ribbon Larissa had donated for the straw hat. Anna fixed Callie's hair simply in a knot at her nape. Another woman looked back at her from the pier glass mirror.

But she would never mistake the gentleman waiting for her at the bottom of the stairs. Fritz wore the black and gold uniform of an Imperial Guardsman. The braiding across his broad chest sparkled in the candlelight. The black satin mask obscured the top portion of his face, leaving only his lips and chin clearly visible. Just the sight of him raised delicious gooseflesh along her arms.

"You look charming," he said with a bow. "I thought perhaps these might complement your costume."

She glanced down at the posey of violets in his hand, tied with a satin ribbon. Callie stretched out her arm, and Fritz secured the flowers to her wrist.

"Stay no longer than the unmasking," her father ordered from the doorway to the withdrawing room, where he stood beside her mother. "Tell Julian I expect you and Callie home by one at the latest."

Fritz inclined his head. "Of course, Your Grace."

With a shaky smile, Callie nodded.

"They worry for you," Fritz said as he escorted her out to the royal carriage, where Lord and Lady Belfort waited. "I promise, no harm will befall you."

"They may worry," Callie said as he handed her in. "But I don't. Not when I'm with you."

Uncle Julian was on the rear-facing seat, so Callie took the spot next to her aunt. Aunt Meredith wore the fitted, silver-embroidered bodice and wide velvet skirts of an earlier period, with a white silk wimple covering her dark hair. A gold band encircled her head above a satin mask of vibrant blue.

"How lovely!" Callie exclaimed.

"Always my queen," Uncle Julian agreed. He wore a green velvet doublet with puffy sleeves tied in ribbons and fawn hose running down to pointed-toe shoes. The gold mask complemented his red-gold hair, mustache, and beard.

Fritz's coachman was able to maneuver them close to the entrance to the Athenian Rooms. From other coaches, all sorts of characters alighted, from harlequins with bells on their caps to fanciful creatures with glittering scales. She had to glance in every direction to take them all in as Fritz ushered her inside. Once through the doors, however, and she found herself clinging to his arm.

The room had seemed polished and elegant when she and Tuny had chosen it for the benefit dinner. Now it teemed with so many people she could not see to the back wall. They milled about, laughing, peppering each other with questions about their costumes, trying to guess the identity of the person under the mask, some of which completely covered their faces. The chorus of voices reached fever pitch.

"I'm not sure I can do much good here," she told Fritz, raising her voice above the din.

He squeezed her arm. "Just do the best you can. If you hear nothing in the next hour or two, we'll go."

As it turned out, she heard entirely too much as Fritz led her through the throng, Uncle Julian and Aunt Meredith close behind. The conversations generally started innocuously enough.

"Are you a cat or a bear?" one lady in a diaphanous gown asked a fellow dressed all in fur.

"Is that Lady Helen under all those draperies?" he countered.

Perhaps it was the way her aunt and uncle carried

themselves with confidence and elegance, perhaps it was Fritz's authoritarian stride, but few guests questioned them. Those that did suggested Aunt Meredith and Uncle Julian might be related to the royal family. Callie could only smile at that.

Gentlemen seemed more determined to ask her about her outfit, suggesting she was a Dresden shepherdess or a Swiss farmgirl. A few connected her costume with Fritz's.

"A Batavarian couple, I see," a man in a black domino guessed, voice amused.

"No," his companion said from the drapes of her silver domino. "He's dressed like that Batavarian heathen who's been in *The Times.*"

Callie took Fritz's arm and steered him away. Aunt Meredith and Uncle Julian followed.

But, as the time wore on, and more of the guests carried goblets brimming with amber liquid, steps became unsteady and comments suggestive.

"Climb up my balcony and rescue me," a woman with a long, braided wig begged Fritz.

Callie was so determined to draw him away from her that she lost sight of her aunt and uncle.

Fritz must have realized it too, for he stopped in the press of crowd and glanced around. The harlequin she'd seen earlier tumbled into him, separating Fritz from her. Others pushed in to take Fritz's pace, and suddenly, she was alone in a sea of masks, riding a wave that carried her farther from shore. Callie looked this way and that, panic building.

Then a guardsman appeared at her side, and she reached out to anchor herself to him, relief surging. "I almost lost you for a moment there."

"Never would I stray far from such rosy lips."

Callie recoiled. "You're not Fritz."

He attempted to retake possession of her arm. "I will be Fritz, Ralph, or Paul. Whatever pleases you."

Callie pulled away from him. "It pleases me for you to go away."

He bowed. "As you wish. Plenty of fish in this sea." He disappeared among the crowd.

She drew in a breath and turned, only to find three more Imperial Guardsmen bearing down on her. One held out a hand.

Callie arced away from him. "Please. Leave me alone."

"Callie, what is it?"

She sagged at the sound of Fritz's voice, then buried her head in his shoulder. "I didn't know what to do. You're everywhere!"

His arms came about her, steadying her. She glanced up to find him looking around. Then he stiffened, and she saw them too. One, two, four, six. She counted at least that many Imperial Guardsmen weaving their way through the crowd. One slapped a lady on the behind, and she gasped. Another was guzzling a tankard of something, and she didn't think it was punch. Still another ran past, a sash streaming out behind him, as if he'd snatched it off someone else's costume.

"Oh, Fritz!" Callie cried, clutching his arm. "Everyone will think those are you!"

He growled. "Our enemy strikes at my name, and his aim remains true."

Callie straightened. "Not true enough. Anyone here knows Lady Calantha is engaged to the real Count Montalban. And I know how to prove that." She wrenched off her mask, then grasped the braid on his uniform and pulled him down for a kiss.

One moment, Fritz was standing in the crowd, dismayed and frustrated, and the next he was kissing Callie. The noise, the movement, faded against the sweet pressure of her lips. His hands stole around her waist, pulling her closer even as he drank her in. She was his, the woman he loved.

The thought robbed him of breath, and he pulled back to stare at her. She stood there beaming besottedly at him, hat askew, and eyes glowing. Anyone looking at her would see a woman in love.

With him.

"Care to share?" someone called.

She flamed, and Fritz drew her closer once more.

"She does not," he said, and some of what he was feeling must have sounded in his voice, for the fellow who had been so brazen hurriedly backed away.

"This is no place for you," Fritz told her. "I should not have asked you to come. Let's find Lord and Lady Belfort and get you home."

She nodded, remaining close to him as they turned and threaded their way through the crowd.

A Roman warrior, scrawny calves showing below his scarlet tunic, planted his staff and his feet in front of them. "Leaving so soon?"

Callie's head came up. "Mr. Wellmanton."

"What?" he asked, obviously surprised she would recognize him in the armor and mask. "No, no. I am the Centurion Maximus. And you are a sweet milkmaid from Batavaria, I think."

"Step aside, sir," Fritz said. "This is no place for a lady."

"Indeed not. I'm sure many here will be surprised to learn the daughter of the Duke of Wey was willing to play our games. Not quite the innocent she claims, eh?"

Callie sucked in a breath, and Fritz's fists curled. "Get out of my way. I will not ask again."

"And I will not give way. The view is too fine." He leered down at Callie, as if he could see through the shawl crossed over her chest.

Fritz's fist flew. It caught the Parliamentarian under his chin, and he staggered. Fritz pulled Callie past.

"I demand satisfaction!"

Wellmanton's cry stopped all conversation and movement in their immediate vicinity. Lord and Lady Belfort squeezed through to join them before others hemmed them in. Putting Callie protectively behind him, Fritz turned to meet the fellow's gaze. He had expected to see outrage. Instead, he saw triumph.

"Name your second," Wellmanton insisted.

"I will not duel you," Fritz said.

"Indeed, gentlemen, this is unseemly," Lord Belfort put in, his solicitor's voice soothing. "I'm sure we can settle this matter amicably, tomorrow."

"I demand satisfaction," Wellmanton repeated. "If you call yourself a gentleman, you must meet me or be forevermore known as a coward, and your bride as a cheap…"

Fritz struck him across the mouth with the back of his hand, raising cries all around. "Mr. Wyss of the Imperial Guard is my second. You challenged, which gives me the choice of weapons. I choose saber. Where and when?"

"Primrose Hill," Wellmanton said. "At dawn."

Fritz did not so much as incline his head in acknowledgment. He gathered Callie close and shouldered his way toward the door, Lord and Lady Belfort right behind. No one tried to stop them.

Which was only to the good, for if one more person threatened Callie tonight, he would not answer for his response.

CHAPTER TWENTY-ONE

CALLIE SHIVERED AS they came out of the building, for all the night was still warm. Fritz showed every sign of walking until he located the royal carriage in the line of coaches waiting, but Uncle Julian stepped in front of him.

"Take her home. I'll do my best to talk sense into Wellmanton."

Fritz nodded, jaw so set Callie wasn't sure he could speak.

Aunt Meredith gave her a hug. "All will be well. I'll check on you in the morning."

Uncle Julian must have raised a hand, for a hack pulled in beside them, and Fritz opened the door to help her up. He climbed in and sat opposite her, but the carriage lamp must not have been kind, for one look at her face, and he shifted across to take her in his arms.

"Don't be afraid," he murmured. "I promised no harm would come to you."

She pulled back to look at his face. In the dim light, it seemed that the confidence she was so used to seeing had slipped just the slightest. He'd removed the mask, and lines marred his brow.

"I'm not worried about me," she told him. "I'm worried about you. You can't fight a duel, Fritz. It's against the law."

His jaw hardened again. "I have been left with little

choice."

"But you do have a choice. Send a note of apology."

"Why?" he asked, straightening away from her. "I did nothing wrong. All these rumors, those so-called Batavarian guardsmen, they have nothing to do with me. And I will not allow anyone to treat you that way."

A sob was building in her throat. "And you think I want him to harm you? I could never live with myself if those ridiculous comments led to you being injured."

"Do you really think Wellmanton could best me?" His incredulity showed on his face and sounded in his voice. "Did I misjudge him? Is he some wizard with a sword?"

"I have no idea," Callie admitted. "But I suppose all gentlemen have some training." She reached out and clasped his hand. "Please, Fritz. Find another way. Don't risk yourself for me."

His face softened, and he reached up his free hand to stroke the hair at her temple. "I have come to realize I would risk anything for you."

Callie stared at him, and he bent toward her and kissed her. She clung to him, trembling for him and for the realizations that wrapped around her as strongly as his arms.

She loved him, and he cared enough to fight for her honor. How could she sit and do nothing?

She gave herself over to his kiss, and his arms tightened even as the kiss became more urgent. She could not get enough of him. This night might be all they had.

She yanked back. "No. I refuse to believe this is the last time I'll see you. You will return to me."

"I promise," he said, so solemnly she could not doubt it.

"I will hold you to that vow," she said.

The carriage was slowing. He took her hand and turned it up. Then he pressed a kiss into her palm and closed her fingers around it. "Keep that for me until I return for it."

She nodded, the words stuck in her throat.

The carriage came to a stop. The footman opened the door, and Fritz jumped down and handed her out.

"Tomorrow morning," Fritz said, leading her toward the door, and she nodded again before Underhill opened it to her.

"Good evening, Lady Calantha." He blinked and peered closer. "Are you all right?"

"Take care of her," Fritz said before bowing to them both. He remained on the step, as if craving the sight of her as much as she craved the sight of him, until the butler slowly closed the door.

Underhill looked at her askance, but Callie schooled her face. If her father or mother learned what had happened tonight, they might well go to the authorities, and Fritz would be arrested. She could only hope Uncle Julian could convince Robert Wellmanton to withdraw his challenge.

She took a deep breath. "Thank you, Underhill. I'm fine. Just tired. Please let my family know I returned home safely and went straight to bed."

"Of course, your ladyship."

As she started past, he cleared his throat. She glanced back at him.

"If I may be so bold, your ladyship, I do believe Count Montalban is a good man. If he has given offense, I'm sure you can bring him to apologize."

Her voice caught in a sob. "No, Underhill. I can't. But if, no, *when* he arrives tomorrow, no matter how early, please let me know at once."

"Of course."

She hurried up the stairs.

She should have known her sisters and Tuny would not be content to leave things be. She made it through Anna's work to prepare her for bed, answering the maid's questions about the success of her costume and her enjoyment of the evening with as few words as possible.

But she hadn't even turned out the lamp for what she was certain would be a sleepless night before Larissa, Belle, and Tuny arrived. They had been out at a soiree with her mother and father.

"Was it so much fun that you were worn out and had to go straight to bed?" Belle asked hopefully.

"Or did it go so badly you had to escape us?" Tuny countered.

Callie sighed, pulling up her legs under the covers so they could all perch on her bed. "Both. My costume was a success. Fritz thought I looked very fetching."

"Which you did," Belle agreed, snuggling next to Larissa.

"But there were those lying in wait for him, including at least a half-dozen other men dressed like Batavarian guards."

Tuny rolled her eyes. "Unoriginal."

"Worse than that," Callie said. "It would have been impossible for anyone who did not hear their voices to tell one from the other. They behaved badly—insulting women, guzzling alcohol, disrupting conversations. He will be blamed for it."

Larissa shook her head. "We will make sure others know it wasn't him."

"Perhaps," Callie said, gaze dropping to her fingers, which were wrapped so tightly around the edge of the blanket she wasn't sure she could detangle them. "But Robert Wellmanton was there, and he showed his true colors. He insulted me, and, when Fritz reacted, he challenged him to a duel."

Belle jerked upright. "But that's against the law!"

"So I told Fritz," Callie said. "I'm sure Robert Wellmanton is aware of the fact. Neither was willing to back down regardless. Unless Uncle Julian can make Robert Wellmanton see reason, the two will meet at dawn on Primrose Hill."

Larissa pushed off the bed. "I'll write to the palace and have Davis take the note straightaway. Leo will put a stop to this."

Callie straightened. "Don't! Fritz is already beset on all sides. He doesn't need to have to fight Leo too."

Her sister hesitated.

"Swords or pistols?" Tuny asked.

Callie blinked. "What?"

"Which weapon will they be using?" her friend clarified.

"Swords," Callie said. "Why?"

"Harder to kill with a sword," Tuny reasoned. "A pistol ball could go astray or right to the heart. I daresay Fritz will be able to control the fight."

"Very likely," Larissa said, venturing back to the bed. "But someone could still be hurt."

Belle shifted closer to Callie and put an arm about her shoulder. "What can we do?"

"Pray," Callie said. "For his safety and Robert Wellmanton's. That they can somehow come to see reason."

Belle held out her free hand to Tuny, who took it and offered her other to Larissa. Larissa clasped her hand and lay the other on Callie's shoulder. They all bowed their heads.

No one spoke for some time, at least, not in words. She knew they loved her. They were trying to comfort her. And there was One who could comfort her most of all.

At the moment, she was finding it hard to allow that comfort to flow through her. All her thoughts were on Fritz and what would happen at dawn.

She cared about him. If Fritz had had any doubt, her fears tonight, her tender kisses, had proven to him that he and Callie stood a chance at a real engagement, a lasting love. But first, he had to remove the dangers that crowded his steps. Only then could she be safe.

As soon as he returned to the palace, he went straight to Wyss's chamber. As Fritz's second in command, the veteran had his own room, while most of the other guards shared one of the massive bedchambers close to the king and Leo.

Fritz rapped on the portal. The answer was immediate. "*Komm herein.*"

He pushed open the door even as Wyss sat up in bed and lit the lamp beside it. He frowned at Fritz. "Report?"

"I was challenged to a duel, and I accepted," Fritz said. "Will you serve as my second?"

Wyss eyed him. "This duel is necessary to protect the king or crown prince?"

Fritz's duty mocked him. "No," he admitted. "So I will understand if you refuse. One of the men who has been blackening our names threatened Lady Calantha."

Wyss swung his long legs out from under the covers. "When do we fight?"

Fritz drew a breath. "At dawn. With sabers. At a place called Primrose Hill. The coachman knows the way. We have three hours to prepare."

Wyss stretched his broad shoulders. "And your opponent?"

"Robert Wellmanton, the skinny son of a lord, with more bravado than sense," Fritz returned. "I do not know why he challenged me."

"Drink?" Wyss asked, going for his uniform.

"Not enough to warrant his behavior. This duel discredits him as much as it does me."

Wyss nodded. "He will seek to enrage you, then put in a lucky blow. He wants to show you up."

"He won't," Fritz predicted.

"Don't be so sure," Wyss warned, pulling up his trousers. "You have been slow lately. Your mind is not on where you are. You must put away thoughts of your lady."

Fritz snorted. "Impossible."

"Then you could die at dawn, and I will be left to avenge you."

The thought sobered him. "For her sake, I will keep my focus. I do not want her wearing black before she wears white as my bride."

Wyss nodded as he cinched his belt close. "We have time to practice."

"Meet me in the courtyard in a quarter hour," Fritz said, turning for the door. "There is another I must speak with. Say nothing to anyone else, especially the crown prince."

"As my captain wills."

Lawrence was harder to wake. Fritz had to rap at the door three times before the Lord Chamberlain opened the door and peered out.

"We must speak," Fritz said, shoving past him into the room.

Lawrence eyed the pale face of the porcelain clock on the mantle. "Now?"

"I am fighting a duel at dawn. If I do not return alive, you must know what to do."

Lawrence trotted to meet him as Fritz lit the lamp on the table by the hearth. "A duel? What is this?"

"A plot of our enemy," Fritz assured him. "I am confident in my ability to meet the threat, but if I am wrong, I need your help."

"We should tell the crown prince," Lawrence warbled, pacing with his nightshirt flapping about his knobby knees. "Write to your father."

The Lord Chamberlain had paper and ink on his table. Fritz sat and pulled a piece of parchment to him.

"No time. If something should happen to me, you will deliver a note to Lady Calantha and one to Leo. They will explain everything. Promote Wyss to captain of the guard. He will see that you all are protected. And see that Dolph is cared for."

Lawrence kept pacing, shooting questions and squeaks of complaint at him, but Fritz bent to the letters. The one to his brother was easy. He reiterated all he knew about their enemies and wished him a good life with his bride. The one to Callie was harder, but in the end he wrote what was on his heart. He sanded the two notes, folded and sealed them, then handed them to Lawrence.

"There must be another way," the chamberlain protested, hair hanging limply around his face.

"None that I know of," Fritz said. "Do I have your promise to do as I've asked?"

Lawrence stood taller. "Yes, my lord. Of course. Please, be careful."

"I will do all I can," Fritz said, heading for the door. "I intend to survive this duel and bring our enemies to their knees."

He and Wyss practiced for a couple hours in the dim light of the courtyard. Thoughts of Callie kept intruding, but he forced them ruthlessly away. He could only return to her if he survived. Therefore, he must survive.

"I'll get you there right and tight, my lord," his coachman promised. The man could only have had a couple-hour nap since returning and dealing with the horses, but his round face was as jolly as ever. "And I wish you the best of luck."

"Luck," Wyss said as he opened the door, "is for fools."

The coachman's sobering face was the last thing Fritz saw before he climbed into the carriage.

Dawn was a thin pink line as the coach drew up to a rise north of Mayfair. Trees dotted the grassy sward, their limbs black against the fleeing night. As the footman opened the door, a blast of cool, clean air entered, as if determined to push through the gloom.

Wyss climbed down first, casting about as if checking for dangers. Fritz followed him. They removed their swords from the cases and strode out onto the field.

The sun leaped into the sky, sending shadows scurrying across the grass.

Wyss grinned. "He was afraid of you."

Fritz wasn't so sure. Something was moving among the trees to their right. Truncheon in hand, a man in a red waistcoat strode toward them. At his side was another man, this one carrying a short staff. Wyss raised his sword.

"Put up your weapons, in the name of the king," the one with the staff barked.

"What king?" Wyss demanded. "I know no king save Frederick."

Fritz put a hand on his arm. "Put down your weapon. These are not our enemies."

Wyss frowned but complied as the men reached them. The one with the red waistcoat was slender and wiry, but the light in his eyes told Fritz he would give no quarter in a fight. His older companion was more seasoned, with a scar along his right cheek, attesting to at least one battle hard fought. Fritz put up his sword as well.

"Frederick, Count Montalban?" the older man asked, grey eyes narrowed on him.

Fritz nodded. "Who are you?"

"John Chancey of Bow Street," he said, extending his staff. "And you are under arrest for threatening violence against a British subject."

CHAPTER TWENTY-TWO

FRITZ DID NOT come for her Sunday morning. Callie was up to watch the sun rise over the rooftops of Mayfair. Uncle Julian must not have been able to convince Robert Wellmanton to retract his challenge. She imagined Fritz standing tall and proud on the grass of the hill. Perhaps Robert would grovel. Certainly one look at Fritz, and he would be rethinking his brash words. Fritz could be quite intimidating.

Not to her. Not anymore. He had been kind, gentle. He had been understanding. And he had won her love as surely as if he had penned her poetry and sang her serenades outside her window. So, he would return to her. The only question was when.

How long did a duel take?

She watched the hands move far too slowly on the clock on her dressing table. Across the room, Belle murmured in her sleep. He would come any moment. Callie should be ready.

She took out a proper dress for church and laid it on the bed. She picked apart her night braid, letting her hair fall around her shoulders. She'd always thought it too pale, so thin it defied the curly styles that had been in fashion for much of her life.

Fritz liked her hair. The way he touched it, the way he gazed at it, he found it marvelous.

No one else had ever found anything about her

marvelous. She could quite accustom herself to the feeling of being admired.

When Anna tiptoed in to light the fire around six, Callie stood to meet her. By seven, she was dressed and downstairs. Food was impossible, so she sat, hands clasped in her lap, in the withdrawing room.

Waiting.

Belle and the others found her there around nine.

"He hasn't come," she said.

Belle went to take her in her arms. "He will. I know it."

Callie clutched hope as tightly as she clutched her sister.

The knocker sounded.

Callie yanked away from Belle and jumped up to run for the entry hall even as Tuny said, "About time."

She skidded to a stop as Underhill let Leo and the Lord Chamberlain into the house. She had never seen Leo look so solemn. Her heart, which had been beating a rapid tattoo, seemed to seize up.

Belle must have followed her out of the withdrawing room, for Callie heard her voice behind her. "I'll get Mother and Father." Her footsteps clattered on the stairs.

"Fritz?" Callie asked, nearly cringing at the whine in her voice, as Larissa and Tuny joined them.

"My brother has been imprisoned for attempting to harm a British citizen," Leo said in a strangled tone, nothing like his usual confident voice. "Lord Belfort is working for his release. Your uncle will speak to the magistrate tomorrow."

"Tomorrow!" Callie cried, clasping her hands in front of her to keep them from shaking. "He can't be in prison for a whole day. He won't survive."

Leo frowned. "What do you know that I do not? Does someone wait for him in the prison?"

Callie swallowed. Fritz had said he'd never confessed his previous imprisonment to his brother and father from a sense of shame. How could she explain to Leo that Fritz must be dying in that cell? She shuddered just thinking about his torment.

"No one is waiting that I know of," she managed. "Please believe me. We must remove him, immediately."

"I would like nothing better," Leo told her. "But Lord Belfort assures me that no magistrate is going to trouble himself on a Sunday."

Just then, her mother and father came down the stairs, and Leo was forced to explain the situation to them. The Lord Chamberlain approached Callie.

"May I offer my condolences, your ladyship?" he murmured, bending his tall frame closer.

"No," Callie said. "He isn't dead, and I won't let him be harmed."

His smile was kind. "You are very brave." He held out a note to her. "He told me to give this to you should anything happen to him. I believe he meant in case he was killed in the duel, but perhaps the note will provide some comfort now."

She accepted the parchment with trembling fingers and broke the seal.

My beloved Calantha, for that is who you are. Please know that my last thoughts were of you. I had hoped to offer you a true proposal, all that I am and all that I ever will be, for only when I am with you am I capable of being my best self. But if you are reading this, you have a different future before you. Remember that you are beautiful, wise, and the most caring person I have ever met. Let no one put you in the shade again. I see who you are, and I marvel. All my love, Fritz.

He saw her. He saw her, and he thought she was beautiful and clever and caring. He saw her soul.

Callie raised her chin. "I will speak to the magistrate."

Around her, conversations continued. Her mother was telling Leo about how he might bring food to Fritz at the Bow Street holding cells. Her father and the chamberlain were debating what legal arguments might be put forward to convince the magistrate to release him. Belle, Tuny, and Larissa were discussing how they could support her. She was invisible again.

She could not be invisible if she was to save Fritz.

Callie took a step forward and raised her voice. "I will speak to the magistrate. Today."

They all stuttered to a stop and stared at her.

"But Lord Belfort said…" Leo started.

"Tell Uncle Julian he must do better," Callie interrupted. "He is known for solving problems for those in high places. Surely one of those people can get a magistrate to the bench on a Sunday."

"Calantha," her father said.

She lifted her chin and met his green gaze. "I will not be gainsaid in this. Fritz must be released from prison immediately. Every second counts. Now, will you send for Uncle Julian, or shall I?"

His cell at the back of the Bow Street Magistrates Court was three paces by three paces. Fritz knew, because this time he wasn't chained to the wall.

Still, the light was as dim, coming only from a high, narrow window, and the same scent of despair clung to the brick walls. He had little doubt that his enemies intended to see him hanged. After all, the British hanged its own citizens for the least offense. How much harsher would they treat a foreigner they considered a savage barbarian?

They cannot harm you. I won't let them.

Callie's voice rang in his mind, and the walls faded away, to be replaced by her shy smile, the shine of her pale hair. All his life, he had been commanded to be strong. The one time he had failed had haunted him. She knew all, and she still admired him. If the worst should happen again, she would be at his side. There was no shame in leaning on her strength. He'd told her he'd return for her. He could not break that promise. He would not break, because of her.

And so he focused on walking and breathing and thinking of their future together, when he would gown her in gold and surround her with those who would appreciate and admire her. He could imagine children—a boy with her blue eyes, perhaps a little girl with his curls. For the first time in his life, peace sounded marvelous.

He wasn't sure how long he'd been in the cell—hours? Days?—before Chancey, the older man who had arrested him, returned with keys, a burly fellow with a truncheon at his side. The man from Bow Street unlocked the door, then advanced on Fritz to remove the shackles on his wrists.

"Where are you taking me?" Fritz demanded.

"The magistrate would like a word," he said. "Be grateful he was willing to come in on a Sunday, and mind your mouth."

"Royalty swings as well as the next bloke," the other man reminded him, smacking the truncheon against his palm.

Chancey sent the fellow a look, and he dropped his gaze.

They marched Fritz down a corridor and through some doors until they came out into a courtroom. The high desk was separated from the rest of the room by a wooden fence that reached to mid-thigh. He nearly sagged with relief when he saw Lord Belfort standing near it. Callie's uncle offered an encouraging smile and tipped his head just the slightest to indicate the gallery along one wall. Closest at hand, a thin man was hunched over a notepad. A reporter, perhaps? Next to him, a slender blond gentleman sat with eyes narrowed, as if he watched Fritz's every move. But beyond him…

Callie.

He only vaguely registered Leo, Lawrence, her parents, and Lady Belfort around her. His gaze drank her in as if she were the water he had been denied since arriving here. Dressed in blue today, with a dark-crowned hat wrapped in netting, she sent him a brave smile.

"Count Montalban," the magistrate said, and Fritz snapped his attention back to the high bench at the front of the court. The man in a black coat and simply tied cravat had hair as curly as his own, though darker, and a look as critical as when Fritz considered the battlefield.

"Make your answer to Sir Richard," Chancey warned Fritz before backing away.

Fritz inclined his head. "Sir Richard."

"Do you know why you have been called before me on a Sunday afternoon?" the magistrate asked, leaning forward over the polished desk.

"My enemies seek to blacken my name," Fritz said. "So that King George refuses to help us take back our kingdom."

Sir Richard glanced down at the papers in front of him. "Yes, I see that you are brother to the crown prince of Batavaria. That does not make you exempt from obeying our laws."

"Certainly not," Lord Belfort put in. "But I think you will find, sir, that Count Montalban is innocent of the charges of attempting violence on a British citizen."

The magistrate sighed. "I have come in at the specific request of His Grace, the Duke of Wey, on a Sunday, sir, to determine whether to remand this fellow over to trial. Do not make these proceedings any harder than they should be."

"I have no intention of making things difficult, your honor," the solicitor assured him. "But his lordship is innocent of this scurrilous charge. He would very much like to know who had the temerity to bring it against him."

The magistrate peered down at the papers before him. "A Mr. Gruber von Grub, secretary to the Envoy for Württemberg."

Something or someone squeaked behind him, and Fritz glanced back to find the reporter staring at the gentleman beside him. Leo was glowering in the man's direction as well. Slender, with sleek blond hair, he wore an impeccable coat and a thin smile that was entirely too smug. Here, at last, was the true enemy. von Grub must have used the excuse of the duel with Wellmanton to stab another knife into Fritz's reputation. Fritz shot a look to Callie, but she was focused on the magistrate as if she could see into his mind.

Listening? Why?

"And has Mr. von Grub supplied Your Honor with information to substantiate his claim?" Lord Belfort asked as if inquiring about the weather.

Fritz turned his face forward as the magistrate shuffled through his papers. "He has. I have here signed affidavits from Mr. Robert Wellmanton and a half dozen others who witnessed the altercation at the Athenian Rooms at which Count Montalban issued a challenge."

"I did not issue it," Fritz said.

The magistrate's head bobbed up. "What's this?"

"I did not issue the challenge," Fritz repeated. "Mr. Wellmanton issued the challenge. I accepted."

The magistrate's brows dipped down over his nose. "Then you admit to seeking to harm Mr. Wellmanton."

"I admit to accepting his challenge," Fritz said. "He insulted a lady. A gentleman could have responded in no other way."

A frown was forming on Lord Belfort's face, but Fritz would not lie to the magistrate. Nor did he intend to volunteer Callie's name. It was bad enough her parents had brought her to this place.

For all her presence made him breathe easier. If only he knew a way to discredit von Grub!

"As a native of Batavaria, Count Montalban is not well versed in our laws," Lord Belfort offered.

"Ignorance of the law is no excuse," the magistrate said. "Count Montalban may not be well versed in our laws, Lord Belfort, but you should be. If you are so worried for him, I would have expected you to hire a barrister instead of standing to defend him yourself."

The solicitor inclined his red-gold head. "Forgive me for my presumption. I am well acquainted with the Batavarian court, having served as King Frederick's representative to England, and it is, as you observed, a Sunday. I merely wished to point out that Count Montalban's intention was not to break a law or to harm any British citizen. That is surely to his favor."

"Perhaps," the magistrate allowed. He returned to studying the papers stacked before him. "What is it you want from me today, Lord Belfort?"

"I ask that you release Count Montalban on his own recognizance and fix a swift day for his hearing in court, at which time he will prove his innocence."

"Denied," the magistrate said. "He has proven himself a danger to our nation. I have before me accounts of the many incivilities he has perpetrated. Beating his British staff, attacking men in Kew Gardens, seducing innocents."

"Lies!"

The word echoed in the courtroom, and Fritz was only surprised it had not come from his mouth. Every gaze turned to stare at Callie, who had risen from her seat in the gallery.

The magistrate frowned at her. "Have you something to add to this discussion, miss?"

"Certainly not," Lord Belfort put in. "I beg the court to forgive her interruption."

"And I beg the court's indulgence to speak," she said. Even from here, Fritz could see her trembling. The fetching fringe on her gown fairly danced with the movement of her body. "I can bring witnesses that will refute those accusations. And I myself was witness to the altercation that led to him being imprisoned today."

"Your Honor, I must protest," Lord Belfort started.

"Please don't, Uncle Julian," Callie said. "Let me speak."

"Do as she says," Fritz told the solicitor. "She has been silenced for far too long."

The bang of the gavel made every gaze return to the magistrate. "Silence! This is my court. I will decide who speaks." He looked to Callie as if weighing her, judging her.

She did not wilt or attempt to hide behind her mother and father. She met the magistrate's cool gaze unflinchingly. She was magnificent.

"You may enter the dock and speak," he said. "But do not waste this court's time with flowery frippery, or I will see you in prison yourself."

CHAPTER TWENTY-THREE

CALLIE CLUNG TO the railing as she moved away from her seat, afraid she'd fall otherwise. Her father was frowning, and her mother looked uncharacteristically worried. The man next to the reporter, the loathsome Mr. von Grub, Leo had whispered to them, kept his cool gaze on Fritz, as if nothing she could say would matter. And the reporter was so busy scrawling on his pad of paper that he barely glanced at her.

Callie would not quail. Too much depended on her making her case.

She followed the gallery to the end and went down the short flight of stairs to the floor of the chamber, then to the enclosed cage of the dock. The little wooden gate shut behind her. She drew in a breath.

"State your name," said Sir Richard Birnie, one of the two Bow Street magistrates, her father had informed her as they'd taken their places in the gallery.

"Lady Calantha Dryden," she said.

The magistrate's brows rose just the slightest. "And your relation to the House of Dryden?"

"I am the Duke of Wey's daughter," she said.

He looked to her father as if for validation. Callie glanced back in time to see her father nod.

"Didn't know he had more than two," the magistrate muttered before making a show of straightening his papers. "What have you to say to this case, Lady Calantha?"

"I was with Count Montalban at the masquerade last evening," she said. "Lord Wellmanton, father of the man who challenged the count, provided us with tickets and told us it would be a private affair. My parents would not have allowed me to attend otherwise, even with our chaperones. A few moments there, however, and Count Montalban and I discovered it was not a suitable place for polite company. He was attempting to extricate us when Mr. Wellmanton approached."

He nodded his dark head thoughtfully. "You are acquainted with Mr. Wellmanton?"

"I am. His mother and sisters are acquaintances. I have visited them frequently."

He glanced down at his papers. "It was a masquerade, I believe. How did you know him through his mask?"

"I recognized his voice."

He cocked his head. "Among dozens of others."

"Yes, Your Honor. I am rather good at listening."

A smile pulled at his mouth. "Are you?"

"I am. Would you like to know what you've said since Count Montalban entered? You asked him if he knew why he'd been called before you on a Sunday afternoon. You noted that he was the brother of the crown prince of Batavaria and was not exempt from obeying our laws. You then mentioned that you had come in at my father's specific request on a Sunday and told Lord Belfort not to make these proceedings any harder than they should be. When he asked who brought the charges, you volunteered that it was Mr. von Grub, secretary to the Envoy for Württemberg, who had provided signed affidavits from Mr. Wellmanton and a half dozen others who witnessed the altercation at the Athenian Rooms. But you didn't need those affidavits. You knew what happened in the Athenian Rooms. You were there."

He stiffened. "What? How could you know that?"

"Because I recognize your voice too. You were the one

who realized that Count Montalban and I were dressed as a Batavarian couple, and your companion said he was dressed like that Batavarian heathen who had been mentioned in *The Times*."

His face was reddening. "Be that as it may, Count Montalban enacted any number of pranks at the event."

"He did not," Callie said. "He was standing guard next to me. There were at least six men dressed like him, acting outrageously. I suspect someone was trying to further damage his reputation, building on the ridiculous rumors printed in the newspapers."

"Indeed," Uncle Julian put in. "We are prepared to prove Mr. Wellmanton hired those charlatans for that very purpose."

The magistrate eyed her. Her father had said he was known as something of a wit, often making sport of those brought before him. Her story did not seem to amuse.

"You have made your point," he said. "You have an exceptional faculty for hearing and remembering. That doesn't change the fact that Count Montalban attempted violence on a British citizen."

"What British citizen?" Callie asked, spreading her hands. "Do you mean Mr. Wellmanton? Why isn't he here bringing the charges? He issued the challenge after Count Montalban protested over an insult the fellow made to me. If Count Montalban is guilty of anything, it is of protecting me and himself from further violence."

He regarded her a moment longer. "May I ask, Lady Calantha, what your relationship is to Count Montalban?"

Callie raised her chin. "We have been pretending to be engaged so that he could use my listening skills to find the persons responsible for these terrible rumors. I suppose you could say we have succeeded."

A noise behind her made her glance into the gallery. Her father was on his feet and glaring down at Fritz. But Fritz's gaze was all for her.

"She's wrong," he said, voice ringing. "We may have started by pretending, but I fell in love. I fully intend to make her my wife, if she will have me."

Joy raced up her, and she nodded so swiftly she nearly lost her balance.

With a thump, her father fell back into his seat.

The magistrate brought down the gavel with another bang that made Callie jump. She turned to face him once more.

"It appears to me," he said, "that this case has no bearing. Indeed, the person bringing the charges could well be held up on counts of barratry by spreading false rumors and prosecuting malicious lawsuits. I suggest you consider pursuing the matter, Count Montalban."

"Your Honor," he said, inclining his head. "I would be only too happy to pursue it immediately." He swiveled and pointed to the gallery. "There is your villain, Mr. Gruber von Grub."

The reporter dropped his pencil and clutched his pad to his chest as if he thought they would seize it. Mr. von Grub leaned back in his seat, brow raised in challenge.

"Mr. Chancey," the magistrate said. "Arrest that man, and have Count Montalban swear out a proper complaint. I will see to Herr von Grub's charges tomorrow. Perhaps a night in the cells will help him consider his plea. For now…" He banged his gavel one last time. "Case dismissed. The rest of you may go."

As Mr. Chancey headed for the gallery, Callie flipped open the gate of the dock and all but ran toward Fritz. He met her halfway. She threw herself into his arms, and he held her close.

"Once again, you are magnificent," he murmured against her hair.

"I was scared out of my wits," she said. "But I could not see you in prison another moment." She pulled back to study his face. He looked little the worse for wear, for all golden stubble specked his chin. "Are you all right?"

"I am now," he assured her, tucking her closer once more. "You promised you would let nothing harm me, and you kept that promise, at the risk of your own reputation."

"I had to," she said, cuddling against him. "I love you, Fritz. I have since the moment you walked into our withdrawing room pretending to be Leo. I simply never thought you'd notice me."

He bent his head closer. "I was a fool not to notice you sooner. But I will not waste another moment."

"Good," she said, love making her bold. "Because you left something with me, and I have yet to return it." She stood on tiptoe and kissed him.

Fritz savored Callie's kiss, even sweeter now that he knew she returned his love. A humph beside him made him break off.

The Duke of Wey had come down from the gallery and was standing beside them, regarding Fritz solemnly. "My daughter has made it plain she is courting you, Count Montalban. I take this demonstration to mean you *really* intend to marry her now."

Fritz smiled as he gazed down at Callie's pinking cheeks. "I do."

"And I couldn't be happier about it," Callie added.

Her father nodded. "Very well. I believe a few changes are in order."

Fritz stiffened, but the duke was turning to the magistrate, who had approached him.

"I will speak to Canning, the Foreign Secretary," His Grace told their judge. "If you have trouble keeping von Grub in prison, I will insist that he be dismissed and leave

England."

"Agreed," the magistrate said. "And you should be able to pressure young Wellmanton and his father into retiring from diplomatic associations, at a minimum. Their ladies will not thank them for ruining the family name."

"Mr. von Grub said he had a superior," Callie told them both. "We have yet to determine who that is. It's possible the Envoy was in on the plot as well."

"Then I have two people to bring to Canning's attention," her father said.

"Thank you, Your Grace," Leo said, joining them with Lawrence and Callie's mother, even as Uncle Julian drew closer as well. "It appears, then, that the danger is past for the moment. Now we need only convince your king that our cause is worth supporting. Perhaps, when the truth is known about Fritz, von Grub, and Wellmanton, King George will find it in himself to agree with us."

"I will do all I can toward that end," the duke promised.

"What does that mean?" Callie asked, glancing between Fritz and his brother.

"It means," Leo said, "that we have work ahead of us. But not, alas, until after harvest. I have been informed that your king is retiring to his country estate as soon as Parliament ends."

"But we will be ready to argue our case when he returns," Uncle Julian assured him.

Fritz's duty loomed. Once it would have been all he considered. Now, he knew how much more he had to fight for. "Then we are staying in London?" he asked.

"No," Leo said with a smile. "We will be joining the duke and duchess at their house party."

A very diplomatic response, typical of his brother, but Fritz could not allow the future to remain nebulous, not when he knew he'd won Callie's love. "And after that?"

"Lord Belfort and I will continue the fight," Leo said. "You have sacrificed enough for the kingdom, Brother.

I give you control of your own future. Wyss will be the Captain of the Imperial Guards. Lawrence and I have talked, and the treasury is sufficient to set you up that estate in the country you spoke of, if that is what you truly want."

The Lord Chamberlain nodded with a smile.

Once again, Fritz felt the odd sensation of shackles coming free. He smiled down at Callie, looking up at him with hope and love shining from her eyes. "What I truly want is to marry the woman I love and live happily ever after."

And there, in front of her parents, his brother, the Lord Chamberlain, and the Bow Street Magistrate, he kissed her to prove it.

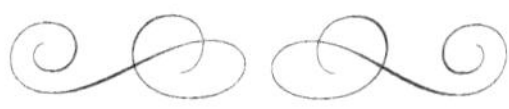

"And so we will have two weddings to celebrate," Meredith said as she and Julian were taking a walk with Fortune in the park at Clarendon Square the next morning. Her cat enjoyed being out of the house, for all she loathed the jeweled collar and leash Meredith insisted on using to keep her safe.

"We very nearly had one wedding and a trial," Julian cautioned, opening the wrought-iron gate to allow them into the greenery. "But Callie moved from Observer to Speaker, and few could argue against her. You should have seen the look on Sir Richard's face when she pointed out he had been at that masquerade."

"I would have liked to have seen that," Meredith said with a smile. Fortune brushed past her skirts to stalk along the shrubbery as if determined to unearth its secrets. "And now a house party, it seems."

"We needn't stay, if you'd prefer," Julian said, tucking her arm in his. "Our estate at Rose Hill is within easy riding distance. We can retire there earlier than usual for the year and go over to Wey Castle for particular activities."

"I may need to keep Fortune closer," Meredith said as the cat scampered back to them to wind her way around her skirts. "I expect Belle will have a gentleman that we should meet."

Fortune mewed, and Meredith bent to lift her up. The cat regarded her accusingly.

"Or is it time for Tuny?" Meredith asked.

Fortune turned her gaze out into the park as if she couldn't make up her mind.

"Well," Julian said. "This should be an entertaining house party."

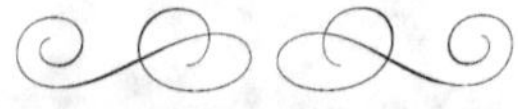

THANK YOU FOR choosing Callie and Fritz's story. They each had a need for someone to understand them. Don't we all!

If you missed the earlier books featuring Meredith and Fortune, I suggest starting with *Never Doubt a Duke*, which tells the story of how the duke and duchess fell in love.

Be sure to sign up for my newsletter at my website, *www.reginascott.com,* so you'll be the first to know when a new book is out or on sale. I offer my subscribers exclusive, free short stories and behind-the-scenes glimpses. Don't miss out.

Keep reading for a sneak peek of the next story in the Wedding Vow series, *Never Romance a Rogue*, in which Belle's attempts to find a match for Tuny surpass everyone's expectations, including her own.

SNEAK PEEK:

BOOK
THREE
THE WEDDING VOW

REGINA SCOTT

CHAPTER ONE

Wey Castle, Surrey, England
Late July 1825

LADY ABELONA DRYDEN, youngest daughter of the Duke of Wey, had never heard the word no.

Oh, it had been uttered occasionally in her presence, but her sunny disposition, winning smile, and engaging approach generally banished it fairly quickly. If those didn't work, a few blinks of her jade-colored eyes and a toss of her golden curls usually did the trick. So it was peculiar that she was having such a difficult time convincing her dearest friend, Petunia Bateman, to settle on a gentleman to marry.

It wasn't as if Tuny had no choices. Several gentlemen had shown interest this Season, but, one by one, seeing no encouragement from Belle's friend, they had succumbed to the blandishments of other ladies. Belle had held out hope for the shy Lord Ashforde, even though Tuny insisted they were incompatible in spirit. And then Owen Canady had joined their circle.

Mr. Canady appeared to have untold depths of possibilities behind his sparkling blue eyes. Tuny found him charming. Truth be told, most everyone Belle knew found him charming. She herself was not immune to the tousled raven hair, that endearing smile, and the lilt of an Irish accent. But Tuny had been on the *ton* for three

Seasons to Belle's one. It was only fair that she should become betrothed first. Belle had plenty of time to find her own true love.

She paused in the act of placing the last lily in the arrangement on the ebony credenza in the withdrawing room overlooking the drive. How many times had she imagined meeting THE ONE? She knew exactly what would happen. Her pulse would stutter, then hammer against her chest as he gazed deeply into her eyes. He'd ride brilliantly, dance divinely, and be able to converse on any number of subjects with ease. Fortune, her aunt's cat, who had matched every lady in the family since Belle's mother and father, would approve of him with a purr. He would be, all in all, perfection.

Just the thought put a smile on her face as she slipped the lily into place. Within hours, they would all be here, the guests she had so carefully selected to attend a house party at her family's country estate, Wey Castle. The games, activities, and outings she planned were designed to bring Tuny and Mr. Canady together. Frequently. Surely, under such congenial circumstances, love would blossom.

It had already blossomed for her two older sisters. Larissa and Callie were engaged to twin brothers, Prince Otto Leopold and Count Montalban of Batavaria. And it was because Belle had convinced them and Tuny to agree to a vow: all four of them would be happily wed by harvest. Once she had Tuny betrothed, it would be Belle's turn. Surely, the perfect gentleman was only days away.

"That's a contented sigh," her mother mused as she came to join her by the window. "Ready for this party to begin?"

"Very," Belle assured her. "Thank you for agreeing to host it, Mother."

Her mother's face widened in a grin. Some said to this day that she did not resemble a proper duchess, having first been governess to Belle and her sisters. Rubbish. Anyone looking at that thick, dark hair wound in a coronet braid around her head, the warmth in those brown eyes, and the confident way she held her sturdy figure would know they were meeting quality.

"It was my pleasure," her mother said. "Though I was a bit surprised by your guest list. There seems to be more married or engaged couples than bachelors and ladies."

Belle wiggled her eyebrows. "Which leaves the bachelors with little to do but find the proper lady."

Her mother chuckled. "Clever girl. And which bachelor holds your interest?"

Mr. Canady's face came to mind, all firm lines and planes, look challenging. "None. This party is for Tuny."

Her mother slipped an arm about her waist as they headed toward the door. "Good for you for helping a friend. So, which bachelor is for Tuny?"

"All of them," Belle said merrily. "But I have the highest hopes for Mr. Canady."

From downstairs came the sound of carriage wheels on the courtyard outside. Belle broke away from her mother to give her hand a squeeze. "They're here!"

Her mother laughed as Belle picked up her green plaid skirts and dashed to the landing. She clung to the polished wood railing and leaned over to gaze down at the entry hall below.

Mrs. Winters, their white-haired housekeeper, was already at the door, with footmen flanking her.

"Sir Matthew, Lady Bateman, welcome back to Wey Castle," she said as Tuny's brother and sister-in-law came through the wide doorway. Sir Matthew nodded his thanks, his broad shoulders taking up considerable space. He bent his dark head closer to his wife's flame-colored hair and murmured something. Charlotte smiled up at him.

Tuny came through the door next, one hand clutching

that of her older niece, Rose, and the other her younger, Daphne. Rose had the same red hair as her mother, while Daphne favored their father's sable hair. Both were squirming in their cape-fronted pelisses.

"That's our cue," Belle's mother said to her, and the two of them sailed down the stairs to greet their guests. From other parts of the castle, Belle's sisters Larissa and Callie, her younger brothers Thalston and Peter, and their father came to join them, until the elegant entry hall was quite crowded indeed.

"I'm so glad you came," Belle told her friend as the nursemaid they'd hired for the party took charge of Rose and Daphne.

Tuny waved to her nieces before turning her attention to Belle. Her friend's blond hair was sleeked up under a feathered hat, and her warm brown eyes glowed with excitement. "Is he here yet?"

"*He?*" Belle teased. "There were so many presentable gentlemen on the guest list."

"Only one that I saw when Larissa and I looked," Tuny said. "Leastwise, only one who wasn't married."

She hadn't seen the name Belle had added later. "Mr. Canady has yet to arrive, but I promise you I will be watching and will bring him to you at first opportunity. I want to see you happy."

Tuny's smile blossomed. "How can I not be happy surrounded by my good friends? Now, don't go to any trouble for me, Belle. I've survived three Seasons. I can survive another if need be."

Not if Belle could help it. Because Tuny and her family came from trade, there were those who looked down on her, and that, in Belle's mind, was simply unacceptable.

Mrs. Winters had barely sorted everyone—the children up to the schoolroom with Peter and Sir Matthew, Charlotte, and Tuny to change from their trip out from London—when the next guests arrived.

The green and gold of the royal carriage gleamed as it stopped before the door. Larissa and Callie remained in the doorway just long enough for their loves to step down before going to greet them. Because of the attempts made previously on the prince and count's lives and reputation, three of the Imperial Guards had come with them to protect them. Callie introduced them as Mr. Huber, Mr. Keller, and Mr. Tanner.

"And what of Mr. Canady?" her mother asked Belle as Mrs. Winters led the royal delegation to their rooms, and Belle's father and Thal departed for more interesting pursuits. "He's the last on the list except for Meredith, Julian, and Fortune, and they'll only be coming over for some of our activities."

Her aunt and uncle planned to stay at Rose Hill, their estate farther along the Thames.

"I had hoped he'd be here by now," Belle said, craning her neck to see through the front door to the wide gate. Castle Wey was built around a central courtyard, with a wide archway leading to the drive down to the island proper. While they had a small stables on one side of the courtyard, the main stables lay at the base of the hill, away from the house. Surely Mr. Canady hadn't stopped there. She had been very specific in her instructions.

"You told me Lord Ashforde might be a few days yet," her mother said.

Belle turned to put her finger to her lips. "Sh! Tuny doesn't know he's coming."

Her mother raised eloquent brows.

"She has convinced herself he isn't the man for her, but I'm not so sure," Belle explained. "However, if Mr. Canady is half the man I suspect, he and Tuny will be betrothed before Lord Ashforde arrives, and it will serve his lordship right for waiting."

Her mother patted her shoulder before turning for the door. "Wait for him if you like, then, but don't stay out too long. It's perishing hot."

Not as warm as it had been in London, but Belle felt it too. An almost ominous heat lingered in the air, as if something was drawing closer. With the moisture off the Thames, which flowed past on either side of the island on which the castle sat, even her clothes felt tight against her body.

If only Mr. Canady would arrive!

She had been cultivating his friendship by standing up with him at balls, chatting at soirees, receiving him when he called, and looking for him in Hyde Park ever since they had met in London a few weeks ago. He had distinguished himself by attempting to out-bid Lord Ashforde over a painting at a benefit auction Tuny and Callie had arranged to support the Society for the Prevention of Cruelty to Animals. The two men had clearly been trying to impress Tuny. Surely her friend would find one of them suitable.

As if summoned by her thoughts, Mr. Canady rode through the gate, moving easily with his mount, carriage upright and noble and smile pleased. As he drew up before the stables, her pulse stuttered then hammered against her chest as if desperate to reach him.

Belle blinked. She wasn't supposed to be having such a reaction. If he was THE ONE, he was the one for Tuny. She didn't even know a great deal about him as yet. Surely her breathless anticipation had everything to do with her plans for this party, and Tuny's future, not him.

Owen Canady considered himself a gentleman by birth, a pauper by circumstance, and a cozener by necessity. When all one had was a horse and a desire for more, one did what one must. He had been carefully cultivating a friendship with the Duke of Wey's family since first meeting their good friend, Miss Bateman, at a ball during the Season. Like him, Miss Bateman must look to her own future, for she had neither family connections nor fortune to recommend her. His family connections were distant, his fortune nonexistent. But that had never stopped him from making his way. All he needed was the entre.

Normally, Jasper was his voucher to social circles above him. A Thoroughbred through and through, the stallion did not appear to be much, being of average build and so pale a grey as to be almost white, but he could outrun any other horse alive. So long as Owen kept to the smaller meets and moved from one part of England to the other, so no one could sing Jasper's praises, he could take part in friendly races and walk away with a tidy sum each time. If he was careful and frugal, one day he might even be able to afford a small estate of his own. He'd been well on the way toward building his fortune when his entire world had been shaken to its foundations.

Now, he must steal the duke's secrets or lose the only being who had ever cared about him.

He patted the horse as he drew up before the stables on one side of the courtyard.

"It won't come to that," he murmured against the closest upright ear. "I won't let them take you."

Jasper tossed his head as if Owen's loyalty had never been in doubt.

The stable hand pulled up short as Owen dismounted. A younger man with sandy hair and the beginnings of a beard, he eyed Jasper as if he had never seen a horse of his sort before. Likely he hadn't. White horses had fallen out of favor some years ago now. No gentleman rode one.

No gentleman had ever been blessed with a horse like Jasper either.

He patted the Thoroughbred again before offering the

reins to the stable hand. "What is your name?"

"Walters, sir," he said, bobbing his head respectfully.

"Walters," Owen said, "this is Jasper. He's rather particular about his care. He prefers to graze rather than be fed hay, so be sure to take him out at least three times a day onto pasture, and check that there's no ragwort about. Treat him with a carrot, but no apples. They give him gas. Allow no one to ride him except me. He won't tolerate it, and I would hate for anyone to be thrown or trampled on his account."

The stable hand's head had kept bobbing throughout Owen's instructions, but his eyes were widening.

"Did you get all that?" Owen asked. "I can repeat it or put it in writing."

He knuckled his forehead. "I'll remember, sir. I promise."

Owen took a step back, hand on Jasper's warm withers. "See that you keep that promise. I'll be out to check on him regularly."

Once more the lad's head was bobbing.

Owen leaned closer to the horse. "Be a good fellow for Mr. Walters, Jasper. I'm sure he'll do his best."

Jasper snorted as if he highly doubted that.

Holding the reins gingerly, the young stable hand led the horse into the stables.

Owen nearly called the fellow back. Jasper was all he had in the world, his only true friend, his only opportunity to make something of himself. Letting the horse out of his sight was never easy.

Surely the duke's stables were as fine as everything else His Grace had owned in London, which had been very fine indeed. No one would harm Jasper. Not if Owen did as he had sworn and uncovered the duke's secrets.

"Mr. Canady."

He turned at the sweet voice and put on his best smile. The lady standing at the edge of the stable yard was the nicest part of this bargain. Golden curls offset a pleasing face above a figure with plenty of curves, and all wrapped up in a charming personality guaranteed to draw a man closer.

"Lady Belle." He swept her a bow. "Thank you for inviting me."

"You are very welcome," she said. "Everyone else has already arrived. Mother will be happy to welcome you too. And so will Miss Bateman."

She was careful to stress the last name. That had been a given since he'd become acquainted with the duke's family. It was perfectly acceptable for him to court the lovely Miss Bateman, but the duke's daughters were beyond his reach.

"I am honored," he said. He thought about offering her his arm, but his coat was a bit the worse for wear after the ride from London. Jasper took a perverse delight in stamping in every mud puddle, like a child let out of the schoolroom on a rainy day. After the hot weather they'd been having this summer, there had been relatively few puddles, but Owen's coat was dusty, nonetheless.

She had no such concerns. She latched onto his arm and steered him across the courtyard toward the double doors of the house. Castle, they called it. Stone walls encircled the courtyard, with windows looking down like narrowed eyes, suspicious of his every movement.

He could only hope the occupants were less observant.

"I hope you had a pleasant ride," she said.

"Not nearly as pleasant as my welcome at the end," he assured her.

She beamed. That was something about Lady Belle. When she smiled, her entire face lit. It was impossible not to smile along with her. The entire day seemed brighter.

He shook off the feeling. He wasn't here to bask in the warmth of her smile. He had a mission, and growing attached to her or any other lady would jeopardize it. No one before or after his horse had come into his life seven years ago had ever looked out for him the way Jasper did. Nothing Belle did would change that. Owen would play the game and trade her family's secrets for Jasper's safety, then be gone on the wind.

Without leaving a trace on her heart, Miss Bateman's, or his own.

Learn more at
www.reginascott.com/neverromancearogue.html

OTHER BOOKS BY REGINA SCOTT

Fortune's Brides Series
Never Doubt a Duke
Never Borrow a Baronet
Never Envy an Earl
Never Vie for a Viscount
Never Kneel to a Knight
Never Marry a Marquess
Always Kiss at Christmas
Never Pursue a Prince (The Wedding Vow, Book 1)

Grace-by-the-Sea Series
The Matchmaker's Rogue
The Heiress's Convenient Husband
The Artist's Healer
The Governess's Earl
The Lady's Second-Chance Suitor
The Siren's Captain

Uncommon Courtships Series
The Unflappable Miss Fairchild
The Incomparable Miss Compton
The Irredeemable Miss Renfield
The Unwilling Miss Watkin
An Uncommon Christmas

Lady Emily Capers
Secrets and Sensibilities
Art and Artifice
Ballrooms and Blackmail
Eloquence and Espionage
Love and Larceny

Marvelous Munroes Series
My True Love Gave to Me
The Rogue Next Door
The Marquis' Kiss
A Match for Mother

Spy Matchmaker Series
The Husband Mission
The June Bride Conspiracy
The Heiress Objective

And other books for Revell,
Love Inspired Historical, and Timeless
Regency collections.

ABOUT THE AUTHOR

REGINA SCOTT STARTED writing novels in the third grade. Thankfully for literature as we know it, she didn't sell her first novel until she learned a bit more about writing. Since her first book was published in 1998, her stories have traveled the globe, with translations in many languages including Dutch, German, Italian, and Portuguese. She now has more than fifty published works of warm, witty romance.

Alas, she cannot have a cat of her own, as her husband is allergic to them. Fortune the cat belongs to her critique partner and dear friend Kristy J. Manhattan, who supports pet rescue groups and spoils her four-footed family members. If Fortune resembles any cat you know, credit Kristy.

Regina Scott and her husband of 30 years reside in the Puget Sound area of Washington State. She has dressed as a Regency dandy, driven four-in-hand, learned to fence, and sailed on a tall ship, all in the name of research, of course. Learn more about her at *www.reginascott.com*.